ABOUT THE AUTHOR

Maggie Anderson writes paranormal romance, urban fantasy, and supernatural crime thrillers. She is currently working on the fifth and final book in this series followed by a stand-alone urban fantasy book and a cozy mystery series. Maggie resides in Brisbane, Queensland, Australia with her mischief rescue cat, Bella. You can find out more about her books on her website: www.m-anderson.com.au

Romance titles
by Maggie Anderson
Driving Me Crazy
Love's Twist of Fate
A Night of Passion
A Night of Passion CR Edition
Christmas, Mistletoe and You

Moon Grove
Paranormal Romance Series
Wolf Blood
Wolf Curse
Wolf Lover
Wolf Bonds
Wolf Haven (coming 2022)

Dark Legacy
Urban Fantasy Series
(Writing as M. A. Anderson)
Reece: Prequel
Dark Legacy
Once Bitten
Soul Chaser
Evil Nature
Most Deadly

Collections
Dark Musings

Non-fiction Titles
Write Your First Book

BOOK FOUR

WOLF BONDS

A MOON GROVE PARANORMAL ROMANCE THRILLER

MAGGIE ANDERSON

Bella Luna Books
Australia

First Edition
Bella Luna Books, Australia

Front and back cover photos from
canstockphoto.com and pixabay.com
Cover design by Maggie Anderson
and Amy Elizabeth Photography

ISBN-13-9780648483632

Published by Bella Luna Books
AUSTRALIA

ONE

Paige's shrill scream woke Eli with a jolt. He threw back the covers, flew from the bed, his sleepy gaze searching their room for an assailant, before he realized she'd had another nightmare. He came around her side of the bed, sat down, and pulled her into his arms. "Are you all right, sweetheart?" he said, frowning into her welling eyes.

She pressed her fist to her mouth, shaking her head, her body trembling, the tears spilling now.

Eli flicked on the bedside lamp, plucked a tissue from the box sitting in front of it, and wiped Paige's tears. "You've been having these dreams since you told me you were pregnant. Maybe it has something to do with the Lycan genes."

Paige didn't want to be analyzed. She needed to be held and comforted. "I don't care what's causing them. I just want them to stop. I can't imagine what my anxiety is doing to the baby." Another tear slipped down her cheek.

Eli brushed it away with his thumb. "Why don't we get away from Moon Grove for a while? Go on vacation somewhere tropical? Lay on a beach in the warm sunshine?"

"I wish I could, but I don't have anyone to take over my patients while I'm away. My appointment schedule is choc-o-block." She let out a heavy sigh.

Eli pulled her into his arms again and stroked her hair. "Do you have any idea why you're having these dreams? Apart from the obvious, that is."

"I have no idea."

"Maybe talking about it will help." He slid his index finger under her chin and raised her face up to meet his gaze. "I'm here for you, you know that."

"I know." She frowned. "The strange thing is, once I'm awake I can't seem to remember what it was about. I only know it's the same dream every time. And it terrifies me."

"You could always make an appointment with the shrink in Bellehurst. Perhaps he can help."

She shrugged. "I don't know. Maybe you're right, maybe it's hormones or something."

"Paige, if you need to see someone then go see them."

"I don't. I'll be fine." She gave him a thin reassuring smile to mask the anxiety she felt.

He kissed her forehead. "Want some warm milk? Maybe that'll help you sleep better." Eli headed for the bedroom door.

"Thank you. It might." She gave him another smile and watched him walk along the hallway to the stairs. *Why am I dreaming about Stephanie? It's been almost two years since she ended our friendship. And why is the dream so frightening? I wish I could remember it.*

Eli had gone to the station early, leaving Paige alone at the house. She busied herself with some light housework before heading upstairs to the nursery they were preparing for their new arrival. They had decided to keep the color neutral because they hadn't learned the gender of the baby... it would be a surprise for them all. As Paige folded white baby clothes and placed them carefully in the drawer a knock echoed into the downstairs hallway. Paige's frowning gaze moved to the open nursery door. *I wonder who that could be.*

Walking out into the hallway on her way to the staircase, another knock sounded. Paige let out an exasperated huff. "I'm coming, just a minute." She made her way down the carpeted stairs over to the front door and opened it. A gasp left her lips and her eyes widened. "Stephanie!"

TWO

E li sat behind his desk in his office, nick-named 'the fishbowl' and gazed around the faces of his deputies. Things had been quiet for quite some time and Cooper, Taylor, and Rick had very little to keep them occupied. They went out on their normal patrols, but with nothing going on in their sleepy little township there was never anything to report. A distinct difference to when Remus ruled their town. Alistair had kept to his word of governing their rural community fairly, without violence and it seemed to be working for the good of everyone.

While out on patrol, Rick and Taylor had been checking out their theories. They both felt something wasn't right with Moon Grove and, after the encounter with the animal that had bounded across the road in front of their car that night, their suspicions had only increased. Rick had thought at the time that it had been a large dog. Now he believed it was a wolf, although wolves didn't roam the area. So what had it been? Something they'd continue to look into while out on patrol.

"I think we're going to have to divide the patrolling of Moon Grove with more desk time. Right now, there isn't enough going on to have you all out on the road at the same time."

Taylor folded her arms. "But…" She knew if they were restricted to their desks, she and Ryan wouldn't be able to continue their personal investigation.

Eli raised his hand. "I'm sorry. I'll work on a new patrol roster and you'll be informed once it's done." He liked that the town was quiet. It was a far cry from what they had experienced the past couple of years. It felt good not to have to look over his shoulder every time he left the station, wondering what supernatural creature would arrive to wreak havoc on their town, or him personally.

Rick raised his hand. Eli gave him a nod. "I think it's important to keep a police presence in the town. Just because it's quiet now doesn't mean it will stay that way if we're not out there doing our job."

"I understand what you're saying, Rick, but no one has broken the law in Moon Grove for the past few months."

"Yeah, I know. But that's because we're out there."

"Maybe." Eli's frowning gaze moved to the open doorway. Rosemarie stood in it with a tray of coffee and a plate of cookies. "Come in, Rosy."

With Paige working less hours now while waiting for the arrival of her and Eli's baby, Rosemarie had gone back to the station on a part time basis.

The receptionist crossed the office and set the tray down on Eli's desk. "I have to agree with Rick, Eli. If we remove police presence from the town people will think they can do whatever they want. And we can't have that, now, can we?"

Eli gave a heavy sigh. He didn't want to jinx the good fortune they'd been having over the past few months.

Maybe Rick and Rosemarie were right. "Leave it with me. I'll let you all know what I decide when I've come to a decision." He picked up a mug of steaming coffee and took a cautious sip, then reached for a choc chip cookie, home made by Rosemarie. "Help yourselves," he said to his deputies.

Rick and Taylor gave each other a conspiratorial grin. Maybe they would be able to continue their quest to find out the secret of Moon Grove after all.

"What are you doing here?" Paige asked, unable to believe her ex-friend was standing on her front door mat after two years, especially with the bad dreams she'd been having and knowing Stephanie had been in each one. There was something different about her. Something that made Paige's solar plexus tighten and sent a chill down her spine. Had her dream been some kind of premonition?

"Now, is that any way to greet an old friend?" Stephanie gave Paige a peculiar smile, her eyes dark and ominous.

"You ended our friendship even though what happened at the Christmas fair wasn't my fault. Eli's father thought you were me but I didn't cause what happened to you. You wouldn't even give me a second chance. You just walked away."

"Part of that was my parents' doing. They didn't want me to stay friends with you after I was attacked for fear it could happen again."

"Don't lay blame on your parents, Stephanie. The choice was yours. You're a grown woman, you know."

Paige folded her arms over her loose robe. It stretched tight across her stomach. "I'll ask you again, why are you here?"

Stephanie's eyes widened when she noticed Paige's protruding belly. "You're pregnant?"

"Not that it's any of your business. What are you doing in Moon Grove and why are you here on my doorstep?"

At that moment, Clarissa came across the street and up the path to the front porch. She had sensed something was wrong. She climbed the three steps, passed Stephanie, stepped into the entry hall and stood beside Paige. "Everything all right here?"

Paige's gaze moved from Stephanie to Clarissa. "Yes, Stephanie was just leaving." Her eyes returned to her ex-friend. "Weren't you?"

Stephanie's right eyebrow arched. "We'll do this another time."

"Will we?"

Stephanie turned on her heel and walked down the path to the rental car parked on the street. Before climbing in, she glanced over her shoulder at Paige and Clarissa. "You take care now," she called.

Was that some kind of warning?

Once the car pulled away from the curb, Clarissa wrapped her arms around Paige and gave her a tight hug. "What was that all about? I had a feeling something was wrong over here."

Paige eased out of the older woman's embrace and looked into her concerned face. "To be honest, I have no idea. She didn't tell me why she's in Moon Grove. But I have a terrible feeling I'm going to find out."

11

THREE

Stephanie stepped into her room at the Moon Grove Inn, shrugged out of her knee length, chocolate brown jacket and tossed it onto the bed with a frustrated huff. Her visit to see Paige had not gone at all as she'd expected – and now she discovered her ex-friend was pregnant. That threw a spanner into the works of her plan. She wasn't the same person Paige had known and loved, a lot had changed in her life since then. Too much.

She walked across to the window, folded her arms, and gazed outside. Eli's grandmother would pose a problem, especially if she kept sticking her nose where it didn't belong. How could she remedy that? *Food for thought.* A smile spread across her face. *Yes, food for thought.*

A knock on the door pulled her back to the present and Stephanie crossed the carpeted, Victorian-style room to open it, her left eyebrow arching when she discovered Clarissa Baker, the offending grandmother of Eli Blackwood standing at the threshold.

"What can I do for you, Ms. Baker?"

"I want you to leave my granddaughter alone. I know you're here to make trouble for her but let me assure you

I'll be keeping a close eye on you." Paige was her granddaughter by marriage.

"Why would you think I'm here to cause trouble? Couldn't I be here to rekindle our friendship?" It wasn't the reason but the old woman didn't need to know that.

"You may think I'm old and stupid, but it couldn't be further from the truth. I've seen your visit in the cards and nothing about it is good."

"Why don't you come in so we can discuss this in a more private setting?" Stephanie motioned for Clarissa to step into the room.

Clarissa chuckled. "As I said, I'm not stupid. You'd do well to pack your belongings and leave Moon Grove before…"

"Before what?" Stephanie folded her arms.

"Never you mind." Clarissa turned and headed along the hallway, stopped, turned around. "If you stay you'll find out."

"Is that a threat or an invitation?"

"You work it out." Clarissa continued to the stairs.

Stephanie closed the door, a smug smile crossing her lips. She loved a good challenge.

When Eli walked through the front door, hanging up his jacket and Stetson on the coat rack beside it, he heard Paige upstairs. He climbed the stairs two at a time and headed to the place he knew she would be. The nursery. "Hey, sweetheart, how was your day?"

"Very strange." Paige pulled herself from the rocking

chair, stood on tiptoes and planted a kiss on her husband's lips.

Eli frowned into her eyes. "Oh, how so?"

"Stephanie's in town."

"Your old friend?"

"The very same."

"Did she come to mend your friendship?"

Paige crossed the room to the open doorway. "I don't believe so. She didn't exactly give me a reason for her visit."

"Why not?"

"Clary knew something was wrong and came across the street to be here for my protection. So, I'm assuming Stephanie isn't here to rekindle our lost friendship."

"I hope she's not holding a grudge for what happened to her. It certainly wasn't your fault my father tried to kill her by mistake." He crossed the room and followed Paige back to the stairs. "Do you want me to go speak to her? Let her know I'm watching her?"

Paige headed downstairs, Eli in tow. "No. Whatever the reason, I'm sure she'll make it known eventually."

"That's what troubles me. What if she's here to exact revenge of some kind?" He followed Paige into the kitchen. Dinner smelt great and he was hungry. "I don't want you and our baby in any kind of danger."

"What can she do? It's not as though she's a supernatural creature with any kind of abilities."

"That hasn't stopped people before. I should know."

Paige sat two plates on the kitchen counter and proceeded to dish up dinner.

Eli came over to her. "Here," he said, taking the spoon from her hand, "let me."

"Why thank you kind sir." Paige kissed his cheek, walked over to the table and sat down.

After a moment, Eli set a plate in front of her then took his seat opposite. "I've had a feeling something was coming. I'd hoped it was my imagination, but now I'm sure it isn't."

FOUR

Rick and Taylor were still on patrol, at this point, and as night set in the pair cruised the streets with their eyes wide open. None of the townsfolk offered any insight into their quest for answers to what they had seen that night, and Eli had made it perfectly clear they were not to ask questions around town anymore. If they wanted answers they were to go directly to him. Would he provide the answers they were seeking? Or would he vet those answers to keep the truth from them?

Moon Grove was quiet. No one on the streets. It seemed odd to Rick and Taylor that people were staying indoors after dark. With no crime in the town, it didn't make a whole lot of sense. When they'd first arrived, nights were quiet but still had people going about their business, either to the movie house or cafes open late. But not now. Did they know something the deputies didn't?

The four wheel drive turned the corner and headed to the steep narrow road to the church. With Eli mentioning there had been vandalism up there, Rick thought they should swing by and do a check of the building and surrounding area, just to be sure. When they reached the top of the drive, the pair could see a fire building inside the spired white church hall.

Taylor got on the radio to get the fire brigade from Bellehurst out there ASAP.

"We'd better let Eli know," Rick told her, throwing open the door to the patrol and racing up to the building.

Taylor radioed their boss. "Eli, come in, there's a fire at the church. I've called the fire brigade and they're on their way."

Eli responded. "I'll be there in ten. Stay clear of the building, I don't want you two putting yourselves in danger."

"Copy that," Taylor said and replaced the handset. Climbing out of the patrol she called to Rick. "Hey, Eli said to stay clear of the building. It's too dangerous."

Her companion strutted over to her. "He was right about vandals. Lucky we came up here or there would've been nothing left of the church tomorrow." He stood with hands on hips watching the flames rising higher as they licked the white wooden walls.

Eli screeched the Jeep to a halt beside the patrol, threw open the door and jumped out. Rushing up to the pair he said, "Thanks for getting on it so quickly."

Rick gave Eli a sideward glance. "No problem. Hopefully there'll be something to save out of it." The church looked vintage, like it had been part of the town since its inception. What a waste if it burned to the ground.

A siren screamed its shrill warning in the distance. Help was on its way.

The trio turned around.

The bright red glow of flashing lights lit up the night sky as the fire truck roared up the steep drive and pulled up close to the building. The firemen pulled the huge hose from the side of the truck and water gushed out onto the flames.

Eli hoped not too much damage was done to the interior of the church and it could be quickly repaired.

One of the firemen came over to him. "There's a bit of damage, but nothing that can't be fixed. I think it looks worse than it actually is."

Eli extended his hand. The fireman shook it. "Thanks for getting here so fast. It's appreciated."

Once the fire was contained and out, the firemen loaded up the hose, climbed onboard and headed out.

"Why would someone want to set a church on fire?" Rick asked Eli.

"Vandals do what's exciting for them. Whoever did this was probably hiding somewhere to watch the commotion."

Rick's gaze moved to the surrounding trees. "Should we check it out?"

Eli shook his head. "No point. Once the fire was out there wasn't a reason for them to stick around. They'd be long gone." He headed back to his vehicle. "Go home. Nothing more can be done here until daylight."

Taylor and Rick nodded and waved as Eli spun the Jeep around and drove down the drive.

"What are you thinking?" Taylor asked, giving Rick a curious frown.

"I'm not sure. I just don't get why someone would want to burn down a church. Do you?" He folded his arms, his eyes scrutinizing the building.

"Like Eli said… vandals…"

His gaze moved back to her. "You really believe that BS?"

"Don't you?"

He shook his head. "We're onto something. I can feel it. Maybe that's why Eli wants us in the office. So we don't find out what that something is."

"You don't trust him, do you?" Taylor and Rick walked back to the car.

"I feel like he's keeping things from us. Important things."

"Maybe he'll share them once he knows he can trust us." Taylor opened the passenger door and climbed in.

"We've been here for several months now. How long will it take for that to happen?" He closed the door for Taylor, walked around the hood and climbed into the patrol.

Taylor shrugged. "These things take time, and if we continue to go against what he's asked us not to do it'll take longer."

"There's definitely something about this town that doesn't add up. You know it. I know it."

"Then let's keep our investigation on the down low, otherwise we'll be confined to the office indefinitely and we won't learn anything." Taylor clipped in her seatbelt.

Rick started the engine. "Yeah, I guess you're right."

FIVE

P aige and Clarissa were waiting at the front door when Eli pulled into the drive. He'd called to let them know the fire was out and he'd inspect the building in the morning. No point doing it in the dark. Paige stepped out onto the porch as he climbed the steps. "Is there much damage?" she asked.

"The fireman I spoke to said it looked worse than it was, so hopefully not."

Paige wrapped her arm around his and they walked into the house together.

"Do you think it was just a random act of vandalism?" Clarissa asked, a concerned frown on her wrinkled face.

"It had to be." Eli sighed and shrugged out of his jacket.

"I – I wonder." Clarissa raised her hand to her mouth, her frown deepening.

"What?" Eli crossed the entry hall to her.

"Well…" Her eyes moved to Paige then back to Eli. "Paige's friend arrived in town today and this happens. Coincidence?"

Paige gave the older woman a curious frown. "You think Stephanie did this?"

"Don't you think it's strange the two incidences happened today?"

Eli folded his arms. "What do you know, Gran?" Clarissa hated him calling her that. He'd always used her name – well not always. When he wanted to make a point he called her Gran.

"What do you think I know?"

"If you know something you need to tell me so I can nip it in the bud before it gets out of control."

"The cards told me Stephanie's visit isn't... she's here to cause trouble."

Eli frowned into his grandmother's eyes. "What kind of trouble?"

"I don't know yet. They wouldn't elaborate."

Paige stepped up to her. "Is she here to cause me harm?"

"As I said, I don't know yet. But I will find out. In the meantime, please keep away from her. There's a dark aura surrounding her. Something I've been unable to penetrate."

"You've seen her again?" Paige frowned.

"I went to warn her off. I told her to leave Moon Grove, but I'm sure she won't. She's here with a purpose in mind."

"So you do think she wants to hurt Paige?"

"Nothing is clear at the moment. I'll revisit the cards in the morning and see what I can learn from them." Clarissa gave them both a tight hug then walked over to the front door. "I'll let you know what I find out." She opened the door and stepped out onto the porch. "Keep safe. Be alert."

Paige and Eli watched Clarissa cross the street and enter her house before closing the door.

"I had a feeling about Stephanie this morning when I found her on our doorstep. I knew she hadn't come here to mend our relationship."

"We need to find out what she is here for. If Clary's right we need to be prepared for what's coming."

"The house is protected. That's something."

Eli pulled her into his arms. "Not from humans. Only supernatural creatures."

Paige's stomach went hollow and a cold sensation rolled through her solar plexus. "Maybe Clary can fix that."

"We'll ask her tomorrow. But for now, we need to get some sleep. You go up. I'll set the alarm and be up in a minute." He kissed Paige's forehead and watched her climb the stairs. Whatever was coming, he'd be ready for.

Paige's shrill scream woke Eli and he sprang up in bed, his eyes roaming the room. No one. He turned toward Paige's side of the bed only to find her missing. *Where could she be?*

Eli threw back the covers, pulled on his jeans and wandered down the hallway to the nursery. Not there. He walked back and opened the other doors along the hall. Not there either. "Paige?" he called.

No answer.

Rushing back to their bedroom, he slid open the bedside table drawer to retrieve his weapon, checked the clip, then headed for the stairs. "Paige?" he called again. Still no answer. He'd heard a scream. He knew he had. So where was Paige and why wasn't she answering? His gut did an anxious flip flop above the waistband of his jeans as he continued down the staircase with caution.

Had someone gotten into the house? But how? He'd set the alarm.

"Paige?" He continued through the living room to the kitchen. No one. *Where is she?*

He noticed the back door standing ajar. *Why would she go outside at this time of night?* He eased the door back and stepped barefoot onto the patio, his Lycan eyes roaming the yard. There!

Paige stood in the center of the back yard, her soft pink nightdress billowing in the chill wind.

"Paige?" Eli moved closer.

As he reached her, he could see a pair of glowing eyes in the bushes not far ahead of them. A wolf? He stepped around Paige, raised his weapon and fired off a shot. The glowing eyes vanished.

When he turned back to look at Paige she was gone...

Eli sprang up in bed, his heart hammering against his ribs. *What did that dream mean?* Was there a new threat in town? Another wolf? But who and where?

At the breakfast table the next morning, Eli's concerned gaze sat on his beautiful, pregnant wife, remnants of his disturbing dream lingering in his consciousness. *What did it mean?*

Paige glanced across at him. "Everything all right?" She gave him an uncertain smile.

Eli reached across and rested his hand on hers. "Yeah, everything's fine."

"You'd tell me if they weren't... wouldn't you?"

He patted her hand. "Of course I would." He had to speak to his grandmother. "Mind if I go across to Clary's for a moment? I won't be long."

"If you wait I'll come with you. I want to find out if she's discovered anything else about Stephanie being here and ask her about the protection spell on our home."

"You haven't finished your breakfast and you'd need to go get changed. It'll only take me a few minutes and I'll be back."

Paige got the distinct feeling he had something on his mind that he wanted to discuss with his grandmother without her being there. She let the thought go. "Ok, if you need to do it right this minute."

Eli stood up, came around the table and kissed Paige on the top of her head. "Thanks, sweetheart. Won't be long." He walked through the kitchen door, out into the entry hall, and Paige heard the front door click shut.

I wonder what that was all about. Paige finished her breakfast, sat the plate in the dishwasher and headed upstairs to dress.

SIX

Clarissa opened the front door before Eli reached the porch. "Come in, come in." She waved her grandson into the house and closed the door. "I haven't consulted the cards yet. Do you need something?"

"Yeah, I do. I had a strange dream last night. Have you sensed any new supernatural creatures in town?"

His grandmother's eyes widened. "No, I haven't. But I've been busy with other things so I may have missed them. Tell me about your dream." She ushered him into the kitchen.

Eli sat down at the wooden table while his grandmother poured coffee. "In the dream I heard Paige scream, but when I turned over she wasn't in bed. I got up and checked the house to find it empty. When I went into the kitchen the back door was open and I found Paige standing in the middle of the yard transfixed on something I couldn't see at first. As I got closer, I saw a pair of glowing eyes in the bushes ahead of her. I fired off a shot and they vanished. I turned around to check on Paige but she wasn't there and that's when I woke up."

Clarissa set a mug of coffee down in front of Eli then took her seat opposite him. "It could've been just a dream. Perhaps it doesn't mean anything at all."

Eli gave his grandmother an incredulous frown. "Come on, Clary, you know better than that. What about the continuous dream Paige has been having and the fact that Stephanie has shown up here?"

The older woman shrugged. "I don't know. Not everything is related to the supernatural. People can have nightmares without there being a reason for them."

"I know you don't believe that." Eli took a cautious sip of his steaming coffee.

Clarissa gave a heavy sigh. "You're right. I don't believe it. Paige's friend is here to make trouble, that's a given. What kind I can't say. I will do my best to find out today and I'll let you know as soon as I have anything to offer. We have to keep your wife and baby safe at all costs."

"Agreed. The town has been too quiet. I knew it was only a matter of time before trouble came calling again. I had hoped we'd get through the birth first, though."

Clarissa reached across and patted her grandson's hand. "I will do everything in my power to keep them safe, but I'll need your help. Maybe Archer's and Cooper's too."

"Whatever you need. I know they'll want to help."

"Ok. I'll call you once I find out more."

Eli stood up. "Gran, please promise me you won't go and confront Stephanie again. I can't be worrying about you too."

The older woman let out a sigh. "I promise."

"Good." Eli headed for the door. "I have to go. I told Paige I wouldn't be long. Besides, I need to head into work soon."

"Have a good day, darling. I'll be in touch." She waved as Eli crossed the street. Closing the door and stepping into the living room, Clarissa said to the cards, "All right, tell me what I need to know. *Now.*" She had the foreboding feeling the situation had become a matter of life and death. Paige's.

Eli pulled the Jeep into the parking lot of the station, turned off the engine, and sat for a moment. He hoped Clary would get in touch with him before the day was out because he needed to take some measures to protect his wife and baby from whatever was going to happen. Why had Stephanie waited two years to return? What did she want? Revenge? Had she been involved in the fire at the church last night? Eli wanted answers. He knew where she was staying. The Moon Grove Inn. Should he pay her a visit? What if she was the wolf in his dream? Ridiculous notion. She hadn't been bitten or scratched. She'd been stabbed by his father as far as the medical team who attended could tell. But what if she *had* been scratched? What if his father's intended victim was *her* not Paige? Eli turned the key and backed out of the parking space. He needed to find out the truth.

Eli pulled into the curb outside the Moon Grove Inn, tugged the key from the ignition, and turned his gaze to the white double-story building. What would he find out from

Paige's ex-friend? Would she give anything away? He would know if his suspicions were correct. If his father had inflicted a wound with his claw, making it look like a knife slash, and Stephanie was now a werewolf, he would be able to tell immediately.

He climbed out of the Jeep and headed along the path to the glass and wood front door, pulled it open and stepped into the foyer, his eyes roaming the quiet café and living room. Breakfast was done and staff was preparing the tables for the lunchtime rush. He walked over to the reception desk and dinged the brass domed bell, the shrill, metallic high-pitched sound echoing around the walls of the quiet building.

Betty Rogers came out of a doorway behind the staircase wiping her hands on her white apron, and smiled when she saw Eli standing at the desk. "Hi'ya. Want some breakfast? I can make you something."

"Hi. Uh, no thanks, I'm good. I came here to speak to one of your guests."

"Oh, who?" Betty stepped up to the laptop, her fingers poised above the keyboard ready to check the room number.

"Stephanie Harris." Eli drummed his fingers on the wooden counter top.

Betty typed in the name. "Here it is. Room 12."

"Do you know if she's in?"

Betty shook her head. "Sorry, Eli, I don't keep track of my guests. You can go on up and check for yourself, though."

Eli tipped his Stetson. "Thanks, Betty, much obliged." He headed for the stairs.

SEVEN

When Paige stepped into her office, Rosemarie was already working behind the reception desk. It had been a difficult decision to reduce her hours but Paige had needed the time to prepare for the arrival of her and Eli's baby. Rosemarie was a definite asset. She was efficient, professional, and everyone who came to the office loved her, clients telling Paige so. Even so, it had been a plus for Eli, who was grateful for having Rosemarie back on a part time basis. She had been missed at the station.

"Good morning, Rosy," Paige greeted as she closed the door and crossed the office.

"Mornin', darlin'," Rosemarie offered with a cheery smile. "How's that beautiful baby doing?"

"The baby is doing great. Not long now and he or she will be here." Paige headed along the short hallway to her office, set her purse down and hung her jacket on the coat rail. Rosemarie followed.

"Your ten o'clock appointment canceled. He's got some bug or something. He's rescheduled for next

Monday, same time." Rosemarie's gaze moved from the iPad in her hand to Paige.

"Oh, ok. Well, then, that leaves me with a little free time. When's the next appointment?"

Rosemarie checked the tablet. "Uh, eleven thirty."

"Good. Why don't we go over to the inn and have some morning tea? Betty said we could anytime we felt like it. And right now, I'm craving pancakes."

"Sounds good to me. Let me just go and lock the computer, grab my purse, and we can head over." Rosemarie disappeared back along the hallway to the outer office.

Paige's cell vibrated on her desk and she picked it up. She didn't recognize the number but that didn't mean anything. She pressed the button. "Hello…"

"Paige, it's Stephanie. We need to talk face to face."

"I have nothing more to say to you. I really don't understand why you're here."

"You will when you meet me."

That sounded ominous.

Paige waited a moment before answering. "When? And where? It needs to be somewhere public."

Stephanie gave a huffy chuckle. "Good choice. You're wary of me… and you should be."

Paige's blood ran cold and an icy shiver traveled down her spine. What did that mean? "Is that a threat? Because if it is I'll be bringing Eli with me."

"I don't threaten, Paige. Is that diner… what was its name?... Dot's Diner. Is that still down the road near the Realtor?"

"Yes."

"Then we can meet there. Is that good enough for you?"

Paige contemplated her options. *Should I meet Stephanie or simply refuse? What's the point? What could she possibly have to say to me after all this time?* Her curiosity got the better of her. "When did you want to meet?"

"How about now?"

"I'm busy now. What about this afternoon? Say twelve forty?"

Silence.

"Stephanie? Are you there?"

"Yes, I'm here." She had wanted to meet Paige right away, but now she would have to change her plans. "All right, twelve forty it is." She rang off.

Paige pulled the phone from her ear and frowned at the blank screen, a feeling of foreboding washing over her.

Rosemarie came back into the office and noticed the odd expression on Paige's face. "Is everything ok? You're not in labor are you?"

"No, I'm not in labor, Rosy."

"Then what?"

"Remember my friend Stephanie?"

Rosemarie nodded.

"She's here in town and wants to see me."

"Oh? Maybe she wants to mend the friendship." The receptionist smiled.

"No, she doesn't. She's here for another reason. Clary said she's here to make trouble."

"So why do you look anxious?"

"I got a call from her just now. She wants to meet me."

"And you're worried she'll... what?"

Paige shrugged. "I don't know. She said I should be wary of her. What does that say to you?"

Rosemarie frowned. "Do you want me to use my magic and…?"

Paige raised a hand. "No. No, I don't want you to do anything, Rosy. I wouldn't ask and it's not necessary. Eli and I will handle it."

"If she's here to hurt you in any way she'll have me to deal with. That's a promise."

Paige came around her desk and rested a hand on Rosemarie's arm. "I appreciate your concern but it'll be fine. Clary's looking into it and Eli – well I know I can count on him to protect me."

Rosemarie pulled Paige into a hug. "I'm here for you, too, Paige. Don't forget that. If you need my help you only have to ask."

"Thank you. That means a lot to me." She shrugged off the uncomfortable feeling, her craving for pancakes with butter and maple syrup overriding everything else. "Let's go get that morning tea."

When Paige and Rosemarie stepped into the Moon Grove Inn Eli was coming down the stairs. *What's he doing here?* "Eli?" Paige called to him.

He crossed the foyer. "Hey, Paige, what are you doing here?"

"I could ask you the same thing." Her gaze moved up the staircase. "Did you come here to speak to Stephanie?"

"I did, but she's not in her room."

Paige's gaze moved to Rosemarie then back to Eli. "We came across for some morning tea. I'm craving pancakes with lashings of butter and maple syrup. Do you have time?"

"I want to go speak to Archer. But you enjoy your morning tea." He kissed Paige on the forehead, touched Rosemarie's arm, giving her a smile, then headed out of the inn.

Rosemarie watched him walk down the path through the glass front door. "You're right. He's on it."

The pair entered the quiet café and sat down at a table near one of the multi-paned windows. Betty Rogers spotted them from the serving counter and came out to them. "Morning, ladies, what can I get for you?"

Paige gave the older woman a grimace. "Would it be too much trouble to get a pancake stack for me and…" She glanced over at Rosemarie.

"The same for me," the receptionist said. "Oh, and a mug of coffee too, please."

"Sure. No problem." Betty glanced at Paige's rotund belly. "How's it all going? Can't be much longer now."

"Things are going well. I can't wait to meet our little human." Paige smiled up at Betty. "It could be any day now."

"I'm so excited for you and Eli," Betty said. "I'll go get those pancakes on the move for you."

"Thank you." Paige turned her gaze to the street outside. The day was warmer than usual, blue sky dotted with fluffy white clouds. It almost looked like spring had arrived in Moon Grove already. But that was a few weeks away yet. The snow had let up and Paige was grateful. She loved the white freeze at Christmastime but it could get pretty cold and she had felt it more since she got pregnant.

Rosemarie wanted to reassure Paige about the Stephanie situation. "Paige, you shouldn't worry too much about your friend. It's not as though she's a supernatural being or anything. She's human. There isn't a lot she can do, especially with Eli on the case."

Paige wondered about that. She'd had the distinct feeling Stephanie was different somehow. Her ex-friend had even mentioned it when she turned up on their doorstep. And what about the ominous comment she'd made? Paige should be wary of her. What did that mean?

EIGHT

During their morning tea, Rosemarie excused herself and headed to the ladies room. She was concerned about Paige meeting up with her ex-friend and made the difficult decision to call Eli. She slipped into a cubicle, tugged her cell from out of her bra, where she'd hidden it, and pressed speed dial. She couldn't have Paige walking into a situation that could potentially turn out to be dangerous.

"Hey, Rosy, what's up?" Eli said.

"I – I'm concerned about Paige. She got a call from Stephanie at the office and they plan to meet this afternoon."

Eli sprang out of his office chair. "What?"

"I hate to betray her trust, but I'm worried."

"No, Rosy, you haven't done anything wrong. Where are they meeting and what time?"

"Dot's Diner. Twelve thirty."

"I appreciate you calling me. You've done the right thing. I have my reservations about Stephanie Harris and I don't want Paige alone with her under any circumstances."

A cold feeling twisted its way through the receptionist. "What kind of reservations?"

"I'd prefer not to say right now. Just trust me on this, ok?"

Rosemarie nodded, even though Eli couldn't see it. "I do. One hundred and fifty percent."

"Leave it with me. Go enjoy your meal and I'll take care of it."

"Ok. Thank you." She rang off and stuffed her phone back into her bra cup, flushed the toilet, even though she hadn't used it, and stepped out of the cubicle to wash her hands. As she gazed at her reflection in the mirror above the sink, her cheeks flushed pink. Had she done the right thing as Eli had said, or was she betraying Paige by telling him?

Eli borrowed Taylor's car and parked in the street opposite the diner to wait. He wasn't about to let Paige walk into a situation without some kind of back up. He'd made the decision to wait for at least ten minutes after both women entered Dot's then go in. Stephanie arrived first, parking her rental outside the diner and going straight inside. Paige arrived several minutes later, closer to twelve thirty, parked behind her ex-friend's car, climbed out and stood for a moment before entering. Eli could see she was anxious. What had transpired between them during that phone call earlier?

An uneasy sensation crawled through his gut as he watched the dashboard clock. What could happen in a populated café? Just about anything, he realized. He wished he'd been able to suss Stephanie out before this meeting to find out if his suspicions about her were correct. When ten minutes elapsed, he tugged the key from the ignition, stepped out of Taylor's car and crossed the road.

Entering the diner, he spotted the women sitting in a booth close to the back of the café and strutted down to them. "Ladies."

Paige's head swung around. "Eli? What are you doing here? How did you know…?" She realized Rosemarie had contacted him. "Rosy."

"I saw you come in here."

"You've been waiting outside?" Paige's eyebrows rose.

"Yes. I wanted to make sure things went smoothly with this so-called meeting."

Paige didn't know whether to be mad or glad. She chose the latter because she knew Rosemarie and Eli were looking out for her and their baby.

Stephanie gave Eli a stern stare. "Why are you here, Sheriff? We're just catching up."

Eli stood with arms folded. "I doubt that very much." His gaze roamed her face, eyes. He wasn't getting anything from her. Perhaps he'd been wrong. "Why don't you tell us why you're here and we can work something out." He doubted that too. What he could sense was the hostility oozing from every pore of the woman.

"Why I'm here concerns Paige, not you. We need to talk in private."

"Well, I'm not going anywhere so you may as well get on with it." Eli scooted Paige over and sat down next to her. "So?" He gave Stephanie a curious stare.

She huffed out a frustrated breath. "As I said, it's between me and Paige." She stood up. "I'll be in touch." With that said, she walked through the diner, pulled open the door and left.

Paige gave Eli an irritated frown. "How am I supposed to find out what she wants if you won't let us talk? I know you're trying to protect me, but nothing would happen here. There are other people around."

Even though Eli hadn't been able to suss out if his assumptions about Stephanie were correct or not, he wasn't taking any chances. "Look, I have concerns about your ex-friend. I think there's more to her than what we're aware of and until I know for sure I'd appreciate it if you didn't meet with her alone."

Paige's frown softened. "What kind of concerns?"

Eli didn't want to worry Paige. "It's nothing you need to be worried about right now. When I know more I'll tell you. Just promise me you won't do this again."

Paige let out a soft sigh. "Ok. I promise." She could see the concern on Eli's face.

"If she asks to meet up again tell her to come to the house. I'll make sure I'm there, even if I'm upstairs out of the way."

"All right." She nodded.

After watching Paige drive down the main street heading for the house, Eli climbed into Taylor's car and drove into town to the Tribune office. He'd gone there earlier in the day but it had been closed and he wondered where Archer was. He wanted to talk to him about the Stephanie situation and tell him that Clary would need his help. He pulled the car into the curb not far from the corner and got out. The open sign was hanging in the window.

Archer Hamilton opened the door as Eli approached. "Hey, how's Paige doing? Not too long now." He smiled.

"She and the baby are doing great. Yes, I know. I'm nervous and excited at the same time."

"But that's not why you're here."

Eli stepped into the office and Archer closed the door.

"Is there something I can help you with?" He motioned for Eli to take a seat at his desk before rounding it and sitting down.

"You weren't living in Moon Grove when Paige's friend Stephanie was attacked by my deranged father. She almost died and it ruined her and Paige's friendship."

Archer steepled his fingers in front of him. "You did mention it. I remember you saying how upset Paige was that her friend didn't want anything to do with her afterward."

"Yes, her parents prevented her from seeing Paige and although she was old enough to make her own decisions, she agreed."

Archer frowned. "And the reason you're telling me this?"

"Stephanie has arrived in town. She has an agenda and I think it's to hurt Paige."

Archer straightened in his seat. "What?"

"She turned up on our doorstep a couple days ago but didn't give Paige a reason. Clary's cards told her she's here to make trouble. She's not sure yet what kind of trouble but I could tell she was worried."

Archer leaned on his desk. "What do you need me to do?"

"Clary said she'll need your and Cooper's help with whatever she's planning."

"Count me in." Archer frowned into Eli's eyes. "What else?"

"I think my father scratched her."

Archer shot up out of his seat. "So you think she's a wolf? Have you seen her? Have you sussed her out?"

"I have, but I couldn't pick up any Lycan vibes. That's not to say she is one and hides it well. She seems shrewd. Nothing like the Stephanie I met a couple of years ago. There is definitely something different about her."

"You know vamps and wolves don't hit it off. Want me to approach her and see what kind of reaction I get?"

Eli gave the question some thought. "That would put you in danger. A bite or scratch from a wolf would kill you."

"Not if I do it in a public place. If she is a wolf she would make it known only to me."

Eli inhaled a deep breath through his nostrils and blew it out. "Are you sure you want to do this?"

"If it will help you find out the truth and protect Paige and the baby, I do."

NINE

The stress of having Stephanie in town and still not knowing why she had come back was taking its toll on Paige. Even while at home, she kept looking over her shoulder expecting to see her ex-friend standing behind her with a maniacal smile on her face, ready to do something to Paige that couldn't be undone. Her heartrate had ticked up a few notches as she busied herself with prepping dinner and she felt like she couldn't breathe. Setting down the knife and carrot in her hands, Paige headed into the living room. Perhaps a nap would help.

As she reached the living room entrance, a knock echoed into the entry hall.

Paige's stomach did a nervous flip flop and she stopped in her tracks. "Who is it?" she called, realizing she should have remained silent and let whoever was at the door leave.

"It's me," Clarissa said.

Paige let out a relieved sigh, walked over and opened the door. "Hi, Clary, come in."

"I got the feeling you needed me. Are you all right?" The older woman looked into Paige's face with concern.

"I was going to take a nap. I've been feeling unnerved all day... looking over my shoulder, hearing noises."

Clarissa took Paige by the hand. "Then come and sit down. Rest. Do you want me to make us some tea?"

"That would be nice. Thank you." Paige sat down on the sofa, swung her legs up onto it and Clarissa covered her with the burgundy throw blanket hanging on the end.

"I'll be right back." Clarissa headed to the kitchen.

Within minutes she was back with a tray containing a pot of tea, jug of milk, sugar bowl and two mugs. She almost dropped the tray when she glanced across at Paige. "Oh, my Lord!"

Paige was folded over, her face red, and clear liquid dripping onto the wooden floor. "I – I think I'm in labor."

Clarissa set the tray down on the coffee table, tugged her cell from the pocket of her dress and dialed 911.

Eli raced along the hospital corridor heading to the labor ward, his heart thumping against his ribcage. This was it. Their baby was on its way. They would soon be parents to a beautiful baby boy or girl. Eli didn't mind which gender the baby was as long as it was healthy. When he reached the nurse's station, a nurse recognized him immediately. "Sheriff Blackwood, I'm Paige's midwife, Jennifer, come with me please."

Eli followed the nurse along the quiet passage to a door at the end. Birthing suite 5. "Where's Doctor Shields?"

"She won't be needed unless there's a complication. And I don't expect there will be. I am well trained in delivering babies. There's no need to worry." She smiled. "You'll need to put these on before you go in and wash your hands as well." She passed him a green surgical gown, paper head covering and a mask.

"Thank you," Eli said. "Where do I wash my hands?"

"There's a basin in the room. Clean all the way to your elbows and dry on paper towel. I'll be back in a minute." She rested a comforting hand on his arm. "Your wife is doing well. And your grandmother is with her at the moment."

Eli breathed a relieved sigh, realizing his gut had been wound as tight as a guitar string. He eased the door back and stepped into the suite, giving Paige and his grandmother a wave as he headed over to the basin to wash his hands. "How are you doing, sweetheart?" He glanced over his shoulder.

A wave of pain hit her and she cried out.

Eli dropped the paper towel into the trash and rushed across the room, sitting down beside her on the opposite side of the bed to his grandmother, and taking Paige's hand in his. "Remember your breathing exercises." He blew out some short sharp breaths and Paige followed his lead. "You've got this."

Paige's labor had been relatively short for a first birth, and it had all gone according to plan with no complications. Both she and Eli couldn't take their tear-filled eyes off of their beautiful baby boy. He was perfect. They had chosen the name Tristan Elijah Blackwood for him.

Clarissa had stepped out of the suite when the delivery became imminent and was now coming back to meet her great grandson. "Oh, he's beautiful!" Tears welled in her eyes as she gazed at the sleeping baby. "How are you feeling?" she asked Paige.

"Now that it's over I'm feeling ok. Thank you for bringing me to the hospital and staying with me until Eli got here."

Clarissa waved the comment off. "That's what family is all about."

The nurse came into the suite. "We're moving you to a private room in a moment or two. You can have visitors then."

That was Eli's and Clary's cue to leave the birthing suite.

The nurse looked up at Eli. "I'll come get you once Paige is settled in. Why don't you take a seat in the waiting area?"

Eli kissed Paige and his new son on the forehead then took Clarissa by the arm and left the suite.

Archer, Rosemarie, and Cooper arrived at the hospital a short time later. They found Eli and Clarissa in the waiting room and joined them.

"So?" Archer asked.

"We have a beautiful son."

Archer shook Eli's hand. "Congratulations. That's wonderful news."

Rosemarie sat down next to Clarissa. "What did you call him?"

"Tristan Elijah."

"I love it," Rosemarie said, swiping at a tear slipping down her cheek. "Can we see Paige and the baby?"

"In a bit. She's been moved to a room and we're just waiting until we can go in."

Cooper shook Eli's hand. "Congrats on the baby, boss."

"Thanks, Coop."

The midwife came into the waiting area. "Ok. You can visit now. But only two at a time."

Eli stood up. "I'll just go in and let Paige know you're all here, then you can go meet Tristan." He followed the nurse along the hallway.

Later in the evening, after everyone had left and it was just Eli, Paige, and their baby boy, Eli sat holding his son, enamored with him. "He is beautiful, isn't he?" he said.

Paige opened her eyes as she lay in bed resting and smiled. "Yes, he is."

"I can't believe I'm a father." He looked at her with tears in his eyes. "Thank you for this precious gift."

She reached across and rested her hand on his arm. "You're going to be a wonderful dad. And the gift is yours and mine. We created him together. So thank you too."

Eli leaned across to Paige their foreheads touching. "I love you so much."

"I love you too."

A knock on the door startled them and their gazes moved to it.

The midwife entered the room. "Sorry, but visiting hours have been over for a while now. Why don't you go home and get some rest, Sheriff Blackwood. Tomorrow is another day." She smiled.

Eli didn't want to let his son go. He was afraid he'd wake up and it would all be a dream. He eased Tristan out of his arms into the clear plastic cot beside the bed and stood up. Turning to Paige, he planted a firm kiss on her lips, leaned down and gently placed a soft kiss on his son's head, then walked over to the open doorway. "See you tomorrow."

"Dads have an exemption of sorts," the nurse told him. "You can come in early in the morning if you like."

"Thanks. I will." He glanced across the room. "Goodnight, sweetheart."

"Goodnight." She blew him a kiss.

TEN

Eli woke with a jolt. Turning over, he expected to see Paige beside him. She wasn't. She had given birth to their beautiful baby boy, Tristan, and was in the hospital. He lay on his back staring up at the ceiling, a smile spreading across his face. He was a dad. A noise downstairs caused him to spring up in bed. *What was that?*

He threw the covers back, eased his tall frame off the mattress, slid open the drawer on the bedside table and retrieved his pistol. Tugging on a pair of jeans, he picked up the weapon and headed for the stairs. *There. Again.* Stopping at the top of the staircase, Eli stood in silence, his Lycan hearing listening for where the sound had come from. Nothing. Had he imagined it? He didn't think so.

He took a step down, stopped and listened.

Nothing.

He continued down the stairs to the entry hall.

Scanning the living room he found no one. No one in the dining room either.

He eased his body along the hall to the kitchen doorway. It stood ajar.

Eli frowned. This was like the dream he'd had a few nights ago.

With his heart thumping against his ribs, Eli crossed the kitchen to the back door. He swung it open and stepped out onto the patio, his eyes roaming the yard. Still nothing.

The back door slammed shut behind him and he swung around, pistol raised, his breathing ragged.

Reaching for the handle, he twisted the knob but the door wouldn't open. He jostled it, pushing against the door. It was locked.

A noise in the yard caused him to swing around and he saw Stephanie standing in the center holding something in her arms.

Eli opened the screen door, descended the three wooden steps and stopped on the concrete path, his mind trying to make sense of what he was seeing. *What is she holding?*

His eyes widened when the epiphany hit him.

Tristan…

Eli hurled himself out of bed, his heart pounding, his breathing short and sharp, his eyes roaming the room.

Eli couldn't sleep. He decided to get dressed and head downstairs. What had the dream meant? Was it some kind of premonition? Would Stephanie try to take their baby? She hadn't known Paige was pregnant. It had been a shock to her when she found out. Instead of doing what she'd planned, whatever that was, would her plans change now that she was here? Eli wouldn't let anything happen to Paige or their son. He would make sure they were safe.

Sitting at the kitchen table drinking a mug of coffee, he thought about what he could do to protect his family. Clary could do only so much. He needed to organize a safe house for them. He remembered Ruby McLaren had moved to Bellehurst to become part of a coven of witches there. She'd been there for a few months now and had emailed him telling him she was the happiest she'd ever been. He was glad. Could that be the place he needed to send Paige and his son for protection? Something to consider and discuss with Paige. He knew better than to make plans without her participation.

A knock on the door pulled his mind back into the moment. He stood up and walked through the entry hall to the front door.

"Hey, come in." Eli swung the door back and Brent and Abbey stepped inside. "When did you get back?"

"Just a couple of hours ago," Abbey told him. "How's Paige doing?" She leaned in and gave Eli a hug. "Congratulations."

"Thanks. Paige is good, so is Tristan. He's... amazing."

"Can we visit?" Brent asked.

"Sure. Visiting hours are ten till two and four till eight. Head on over anytime during those hours. I'm on my way back now. Dad's get a bit of leeway."

"Do you have a picture?" Abbey asked, eager to see her new grandson.

"Yes, I do." Eli tugged his cell from the pocket of his jeans and scrolled through his photos. Turning the phone around, he said, "Here."

Tears welled in Abbey's eyes. "He – he's beautiful."

"Yeah, I know." Eli smiled. "He is."

"I can't wait to meet him."

"You're a grandmother now. How does it feel?"

"Comforting. I'm so glad Paige has you and now Tristan. I only wish her dad had been here to meet him." She showed the photo to Brent.

"Yeah, it would've been nice for him to have a granddad."

"We'd better let you go." Abbey handed the phone back to Eli.

"Maybe I'll see you there later then."

"You will."

Eli showed Abbey and Brent out, then tugged on his jacket and closed the door behind him. "Ok. I'll see you later."

"Give Paige our love."

"I will."

After visiting with Paige and Tristan, Eli headed up to the church. The team had gone in and done a thorough sweep of the building and had taken samples of some kind of accelerant. Of course, Eli had known the fire had been deliberately lit but he had to file a report. Driving up the steep incline, he found the carpark empty. Odd. Someone was meant to be here to go over what was found at scene.

Eli pulled the Jeep up near the front entrance and sat, his gaze moving over the sooty damage. His eyes moved from the church to the dashboard clock, 11:45AM, and he wondered where Harold Newman was. He checked his phone for any missed calls or messages, as he'd had his phone turned to silent while at the hospital. Nothing. Eli drummed his fingers on the steering wheel, deciding to give the guy another few minutes before heading back to the station.

Movement in his left hand peripheral vision caused his head to turn in that direction.

No one.

He hadn't imagined it.

Eli pinched himself to make sure it wasn't another dream. It wasn't.

Midday was almost upon the town and he made the decision to drive back to the station. He'd call Harold later in the day to find out why he didn't show up.

As he started the engine, he glimpsed movement again in the left hand side trees.

Turning the patrol off, he tugged the key from the ignition, flung open the door and made a dash for the woods.

His hearing picked up fast moving treads on the leaves and brush heading further into the forest. He broke into a run following the sound.

The footfalls were becoming more and more distant until he couldn't hear them anymore.

He stopped, stood, listened.

Nothing.

"Dammit!"

Eli raised his chin and inhaled a deep breath taking in the smells around him.

Wolf.

Could it be one of Matthias's pack? The two remaining members had said they wouldn't join Eli's pack and he had respected their decision. Could one of them be wandering around Moon Grove? And, if so, why? Were they responsible for the fire, not Stephanie?

ELEVEN

Eli had spoken to Betty at the Moon Grove Inn to find out Stephanie's meal schedule. Paige's ex-friend, it seemed, was having most of her meals there in the dining room and was due for lunch at midday. Archer sat across the street in his convertible, eyes glued to the white double-story building, waiting for the clock on the dash to hit noon. He would enter the inn and take a table near the woman to see if she sensed him. If she didn't, or if she feigned not knowing what he was, he would know. Supernatural creatures were very aware of each other's presence and he would be able to pick up her Lycan vibrations, *if* she was a wolf.

Archer knew Eli wouldn't suspect her without probable cause and he would do whatever it took to keep Paige and her baby safe, even if it meant putting himself in harm's way. Eli had given him a description of the woman and warned him to be careful. He knew he'd be safe in the café of the inn, but also knew that once he made himself known to her he would also be in her sights. He didn't care. This situation could potentially be a matter of life and death for someone he felt deeply about, and he planned to make sure that didn't happen.

Right on midday, Archer took the key from the ignition of his Mercedes Benz, obsidian black convertible, set the alarm and crossed the road. He had called and booked a table, so he was expected. As he climbed the front steps and walked up to the wood and glass door he spotted Stephanie heading into the dining room. *Perfect timing.* A satisfied smile spread across his handsome face as he pulled open the door and stepped into the foyer.

She had chosen a table by one of the multi-paned windows with a view of the street. He would take the one behind her. Walking through the dining room, he made sure to pass by her table as close as he could, without seeming conspicuous, to see if he got a reaction. He didn't. Either she hadn't picked up on him or she was human. Perhaps Eli had been wrong.

After ordering a meal and keeping a close eye on the woman sitting only a few feet away, Archer wondered again if, perhaps, Eli had been wrong with his suspicion of her. She didn't appear to be anything other than a human. Nothing about her gave him the impression she was a wolf. If the sheriff's father had scratched her, there would be a definite aura and vibe coming from her and Archer wasn't getting either.

He wiped his mouth on the white linen napkin, placed some bills in the bill fold, stood up and passed the woman's table as a final attempt to pick up on something. Nothing. He continued out the entrance to the café, said goodbye to Betty standing at the reception desk with a new client, and headed out the door. All he could do was tell Eli he didn't think Stephanie Harris was of Lycan genes, unless she had some kind of trick up her sleeve to shield herself completely.

When Eli stepped into the Tribune office and saw the look on Archer's face his stomach flipped over under the silver belt buckle on his jeans. "So how did it go?"

Archer came around his desk, hand extended. "I'm sorry, Eli, but I couldn't pick up anything from her. If she is a wolf she's hiding it well."

Eli gave a heavy sigh. "I appreciate you checking her out for me. I was certain I'd figured her out. If my father had scratched her and she'd turned then that would be a reason for her to be back in Moon Grove. A reason to exact revenge."

Archer gave the situation some thought for a moment. "What if I engage with her?"

Eli frowned. "What do you mean?"

"Strike up a conversation. Try to get closer to her. See if spending time with her will offer something tangible."

Eli shook his head. "No. You'd be putting yourself in danger by doing it, especially if my suspicions are correct. Which I still believe could be the case." He rubbed a hand across his chin. "I just don't understand how she could be concealing it."

"Maybe she had a witch put some kind of cloaking spell on her supernatural abilities."

"You could be right. She's had two years to immerse herself in our world. Perhaps she has done something like that." Eli turned on his heel and headed for the door.

"Where are you going?" Archer called after him.

"To see Clary."

Clarissa gave her grandson an odd stare. "You think Paige's friend has some kind of masking spell on her to prevent other supernatural creatures from detecting her true nature?"

"I know how it sounds. It was Archer's idea. Is that possible?"

Eli's grandmother brought a hand to her chin, her eyes moving to the cross-stitched table cloth and gave it some serious thought. "I – I'm not sure. Maybe."

"How can we find out?" Eli finished the last of his coffee and set the mug down on the coaster.

"I'll have to check my spell books. In all the years I've been a witch, and that's since the day I was born, I've never heard of a spell that could do that." She raised her hand. "That's not to say there isn't one. I just haven't come across it before."

"You'll find out?"

"Of course, my boy, if it'll help."

"Did you find out anything else about the reason Stephanie's here?"

"No. The cards are being stubborn."

Eli gave a heavy sigh. "I've been thinking about sending Paige and Tristan to Bellehurst."

"Oh? Why?"

"Ruby's living in a coven there and she's sent me a couple emails telling me how great her life is now. She feels like she's part of a sisterhood. Maybe they could help us keep Paige and Tristan safe until we can work out what Stephanie's agenda is."

"Yes, I heard from Ruby too. I'm so glad she's feeling better about... everything. She deserves some happiness in her life. Have you spoken to her?"

Eli shook his head. "No, not yet. I want to run it by Paige first. If I make that kind of decision without her input she'll be upset with me."

"And I wouldn't blame her. You need to keep the lines of communication open with Paige. You need to tell her of your suspicions about Stephanie too. Paige has a right to know."

Eli folded his arms and let out a long sigh. "I know you're right, but why worry her any more than she already is about the situation?"

"Because if she finds out any other way, and also finds out you knew and didn't tell her, how do you think she'll feel?" Clarissa picked up her cooling coffee and took a generous sip.

"Ok, I'll talk to her once she's back home. That's if we don't arrange for her and Tristan to go spend time with Ruby and her coven."

"Go talk to her then. Organize it. She and the baby need to be somewhere safe."

"Has Archer been to see you?"

Clarissa shook her head. "Not yet. He called and offered his assistance but we haven't met to discuss it further."

"Ok. I talked to Cooper and he's in as well."

"Good to know."

Eli stood up. "I'd better go. Did you want to come with me to visit Paige and Tristan again?"

"I want to keep at the cards to see what information they'll offer. Is she due to be released soon? Maybe I can visit with her at home before you send her and the baby off to Ruby's. If Paige wants to go, that is."

"I hope she will. I need to get Paige and Tristan somewhere Stephanie can't just turn up on the doorstep and expect to get what she wants. Whatever that is." He headed for the front door.

Clarissa followed. "Give Paige my love and tell her I'm working on a way to solve this problem."

"I will, Gran." Eli leaned down and kissed his grandmother on the cheek.

She play slapped him and gave him a faux scowl. "You know I hate being called that."

"I love you." Eli walked across the lawn to his patrol.

Clarissa waved and mouthed 'I love you too'.

Eli reversed onto the road and headed toward town instead of toward the hospital. He had a stop to make before he went to visit his wife and son.

Climbing the front steps of the inn, Eli wondered if he was doing the right thing. If he antagonized Stephanie it might make her more determined to set her plan in motion sooner, if she hadn't already. But he had to be sure of his suspicions about her. Something inside him told him he was on the right track; he just needed a way to prove it.

He pulled open the door and walked into the foyer. No one was at reception. Rather than go see Betty, he climbed the carpeted staircase two at a time up to the second floor and wandered along the hall to room 12. He stood outside for a moment or two contemplating whether to knock or to leave. He raised his fist and knocked three times. No answer.

"Stephanie, it's Eli Blackwood. I need to speak to you."

Nothing.

He leaned in and pressed his ear to the door. No movement. She wasn't in her room. As she didn't know anyone in Moon Grove, apart from Paige, he wondered where she could be.

The dream Eli had had the previous night crashed into his head and his gut shrank into a tight ball of nerves.

Without hesitation, he raced down the stairs, burst through the front door and ran across the street to his patrol. Once inside, he got on the radio. "Rosy, come in?"

"Ten four, Eli. What can I do you for?" She chuckled, not usually her form to use trucker speak on the radio. But she had to try it.

"Is Cooper in the office?"

"He sure is. Do you want to speak to him?"

"No, I want you to send him to the hospital *now*."

Rosemarie's blood turned ice cold. "Eli, what's wrong?"

"Rosy, just tell Cooper to get over to Paige."

Cooper got on the radio. "Leaving now, boss. I'll put the siren on."

"Eli, what's going on?"

"I can't explain right now. Just stay close to the radio."

"Ok. Keep us informed."

"Will do." Eli replaced the handset, turned on the siren and sped along the highway.

TWELVE

Cooper raced along the hospital corridor to Paige's room. No one was there. He gazed up and down the hallway at patients, staff, and visitors but she was nowhere to be seen. He thought about checking the nursery and went back to reception to find out where it was. Once he had the location, he zig-zagged through patients and staff heading down the corridor and around the corner. He pressed his face to the glass and scanned the sleeping babies in the room. Tristan was there, but not Paige. *Maybe she's taking a shower or in the ladies room.*

The deputy made his way back to Paige's room and peered inside. Still not there. As he headed back to reception, Eli rushed up to him.

"How's things here?"

Cooper stood with hands on hips. "Tristan's in the nursery sleeping, but I haven't been able to find Paige. I thought she might be taking a shower while she can or..."

Eli stepped up to the nurses' station. "Excuse me."

A woman in her fifties with gray hair swept up into a soft bun, wearing a pink uniform and black rimmed glasses pulled her eyes away from the computer screen.

She gave him a pleasant smile. "Can I help you with something, Sheriff?"

"Uh, yes, I'm looking for my wife, Paige. She's not in her room or in the nursery with our son. You wouldn't know where she might be, would you?"

"Let me check to see if she has any tests or other appointments." The woman pressed a couple of keys on the keyboard. "What's your wife's name?"

"Paige… Paige Blackwood."

"I don't see anything scheduled for today. Perhaps she's taking a shower while the baby's sleeping. Or she may have gone out to the sitting area outside."

"Where's that?"

"Past the nursery, straight ahead, then make a right and follow the hall to the door at the end."

"Thank you." Eli and Cooper headed for the sitting area.

Eli's gut was wound as tight as a drum. He had a terrible feeling in his solar plexus, one he hadn't been able to shake since he had that dream about Stephanie holding Tristan. He picked up his pace.

When the pair reached the frosted glass door, Cooper pushed it open and they stepped outside, Eli's gaze roaming the people sitting in the sun. Paige wasn't there.

"Where is she?"

"We'll find her, Eli." He held the door for his boss then followed him in. "I'll ask someone to check the bathroom."

"Thanks, Coop. She has to be here, somewhere."

"Yeah, she does." Cooper marched off ahead of Eli back to the ward's reception desk.

A nurse went into the couple of bathrooms on the ward to check if Paige was in either of them. She wasn't. "I'm sorry, I've checked both of the women's bathrooms and she's not there. I also checked the toilet stalls."

"Well, thanks for your help." The nurse turned to go back to the desk.

"Uh, can I ask you one more thing?" Eli walked up to her. "If Paige isn't here, where is she? She couldn't and wouldn't have left without our son."

"I – I don't know what to tell you, Sheriff Blackwood. She should be here. We'll check other wards to see if she might have gone to take a shower there. She could have if the bathrooms were occupied."

"Thanks, I'd appreciate it."

Cooper stood, head slightly raised, and inhaled a deep breath into his nostrils. The smells around him were potent: the astringent sterile smell of pine disinfectant, floral arrangements, coffee, and one other… Wolf. "Eli."

"What is it?"

"I smell wolf."

"Probably. There're bound to be other wolves hiding in plain sight. We have no idea how many there are in the localized area."

Cooper shook his head. "No, this is different."

Eli turned to him and frowned. "How so?"

His deputy took another drag of the air around them. "It smells like… *you*."

After several of the nursing staff and security doing a thorough sweep of the hospital and turning up nothing, Eli got on the radio again. "Rosy, come in."

"I'm here, darlin'," the receptionist responded.

"Can you contact Archer Hamilton and ask him to come out here?"

"Still no sign of Paige?" Rosemarie's stomach was in anxious knots.

"Not so far. Would you text me once you've contacted Archer?"

"Sure will, hon. I'll call him right now."

Eli gave Cooper a sideward glance. "I've got a bad feeling about this. I think Stephanie has abducted Paige."

"Wait. What?"

"She came here with a vendetta. I suspected she was scratched by my father when he attacked her in the Ghost Train at the Christmas Fair a couple of years ago, and I think she was his intended victim. He knew he was setting the scene for something dire down the track, and now it's here."

Cooper folded his arms and frowned as his mind tried to process what Eli had just told him. "So, you believe Paige's friend was scratched when she was stabbed so she'd turn into a werewolf? And then, one day, when the time was right, she'd show up in Moon Grove to exact revenge?"

"That about covers it, yes."

"Holy smoke." Cooper scratched the back of his head. "That is plain crazy."

"Whatever it is, Paige is in danger and we have to find her."

THIRTEEN

Paige came to in the trunk of a moving vehicle, hands bound behind her back, a strip of duct tape across her mouth and a blindfold over her eyes. Her heart leaped in her chest and crashed against her ribs. *Oh, my God! Tristan.* She tried to wriggle backwards to see if she could maneuver her arms through her legs so they'd be in front of her but there wasn't enough room. Tears stung the backs of her eyes as she thought about her baby son at the hospital. And Eli. *He must be frantic with worry by now.*

The car turned a sharp left onto a bumpy stretch of road and Paige wondered where they were going. What had happened back at the hospital? She willed her foggy brain to think. *Come on, come on, remember.* Nothing would adhere. Tears spilled down the sides of her cheeks now. Her eyes widened as a frightening thought popped into her mind. *Stephanie.* It had to be her. Was she the one driving the car? Or did she have someone else abduct her from the hospital? Paige was sure she was right.

The car made another sharp left and continued traveling along another bumpy stretch of road – or a dirt track. Were they out in the woods? Or some other woods? Paige had no idea how long she'd been unconscious. Was it even the same day? A burning lump lodged itself in her throat and more tears spilled. She prayed Eli would be looking for her. The thought caused her stomach to go hollow. But how would he find her? He had no idea where to start looking.

Eli and Cooper left the Jeep and headed back into the hospital. After speaking to the head of security about checking cam footage for the floor, he and his deputy were led to the security surveillance epicenter. On the way there, Rosemarie had texted Eli to let him know Archer was on his way and should arrive at the hospital within the hour. She also texted that she hoped they found Paige safe and well. Eli pocketed his cell as they entered the secure room, a wall of computers lining the side wall and desk, every angle of the hospital in view.

He shook hands with the two guards sitting at the desk and asked them to run back through the footage for the day's monitoring, focusing on the obstetrics ward, and if nothing showed up there, all other wards. He also requested footage for their loading dock, in case it was the way the abductors got Paige out of the hospital unseen.

Cooper would remain to go through the footage with the security team and relay anything significant back to Eli.

As Eli walked through the hospital foyer, heading back to the Jeep, Archer rushed through the automatic doors.

"Have you found out anything yet?" he asked, his face etched with concern.

"Not yet. Coop's with security going through today's footage. If anything shows up he'll contact me."

"That's it?"

"What else would you suggest?" Eli folded his arms.

"Paige's ex-friend has to be behind this."

"Yes, there's no doubt about that."

"Do you think she did it or had someone else do it for her?" The pair stepped outside and headed for Eli's patrol.

"Hard to say. Although she seemed to be in Moon Grove alone."

"You kept track of her?"

"Yes, I wasn't going to risk Paige's life."

"Who would've thought something like this would happen at a hospital."

"I know. She would've had to have changed her initial plan because she'd had no idea Paige was pregnant. She's shrewd and resourceful."

"So what do we do now?"

"Follow me back to Clary's. We need to find out if she's learned anything more from the cards. She told me they were being stubborn. Let's hope they play nice now, because without their help we have no way of finding Paige."

The car came to an abrupt stop, the engine continuing to idle. Had they arrived at their destination? If so, where were they? Paige swallowed hard when the engine died and two doors opened and clicked shut. She held her breath waiting for the trunk to pop. It didn't. She could hear two sets of footfalls crunching gravel. Heavy rubber-soled boots by the sound of it. That meant it wasn't Stephanie who had taken her. Even so, it didn't mean she hadn't orchestrated the abduction.

The footsteps grew distant and Paige heard male voices but couldn't make out what they were saying. What if it wasn't Stephanie? What if it turned out to be another supernatural assault on Moon Grove with her as the decoy? Paige struggled to free her hands but they were bound tight. She felt a trickle of warm blood run down her left arm. She couldn't even shift into wolf form to save herself. And they had to know that.

What would happen to her? Did the pair that brought her out here have orders to kill her? More tears welled in her eyes and spilled down the sides of her face. Would she ever see her baby or husband again?

FOURTEEN

As he drove toward his grandmother's house, Eli got on the radio. "Rick, Taylor, come in." He'd turned on the siren and strobe lights as he sped along the highway for Moon Grove. Perhaps a misuse of government property, but this was a matter of life and death.

Taylor came back. "Yeah, boss, what's up?"

"How's the surveillance going at the inn?"

"No movement," she told him.

"You're sure about that?"

"Yes. We've been sitting out here since the sun came up and the suspect hasn't left the building."

"Keep a close eye on her. I want to know everywhere she goes today."

"Sure thing, boss."

Eli gave a heavy sigh. He'd assigned Rick and Taylor to surveying the inn, telling them Stephanie Harris was a person of interest. As there wasn't a lot to do in town at the moment, they jumped at the opportunity to stake out the inn. But by the tone in Taylor's voice just now it seemed they were bored. Nothing he could do about that for the time being. He needed eyes on Stephanie.

"What do you think this stake out is all about?" Taylor asked her partner.

"I don't know. I saw Cooper hightail it out of the office earlier today after Eli was on the radio. He headed for the hospital. Isn't the boss's wife in the hospital? She just had a baby so she'd still be there, wouldn't she?"

Taylor shrugged. "Don't know. They tend to send new mothers home as soon as possible these days. Not like when my mum was younger."

"Oh, ok. So maybe it wasn't about her then."

"Maybe."

Rick's gaze returned to the inn. "Hey, look."

Stephanie Harris came out of the front door, walked down the path to her rental vehicle and climbed in.

"Let's see where she's going." Rick started the engine.

Once the white hatchback was on the move, Rick pulled away from the curb, keeping a comfortable distance between them.

"Looks like she's heading for the highway," Taylor observed.

"Yeah, it does."

"Should we let Eli know?"

"Nah, let's find out where she goes first. Then we'll have something to tell him."

"Ok. Good plan."

Once on the highway, Stephanie put her foot down and sped toward Bellehurst.

Rick eased the accelerator down in an attempt to keep up. He didn't want her to realize she was being followed. They had taken his car on the stake out so as not to look conspicuous and it appeared to be working out.

After traveling south for approximately thirty minutes, Stephanie took an exit ramp.

Rick slowed down as he came off the ramp because he didn't want to catch up to her right away. Leave a little distance between them. He indicated, made a right and continued along the road. "This seems to be taking us out into the country. I wonder where she's going."

"Well, only one way to find out." Taylor pointed through the windshield. "Hey, she's taking that dirt road."

"I can see." Rick pulled onto the shoulder for a minute.

"What are you doing? She'll get away."

"Trust me, will you." He eased the car off the shoulder and took the dirt road.

Taylor frowned. "Where'd she go?"

"She has to be ahead of us."

"I hope you're right, otherwise we've lost her and Eli will not be happy about that." Taylor folded her arms and scowled at Rick.

"Hey, I didn't want her to make us and the whole thing blow up in our faces."

"Yeah, well, maybe she did and that's why she's disappeared."

"Where could she go except straight? There are no turns or anything along this road."

"I don't know, but it seems we've lost her."

"Let's just keep heading in that direction and see where we end up. Ok?"

Taylor threw her hands up. "But…"

"No buts. She has to be ahead of us, like I said. There's nowhere else she could've gone."

"Let's hope so or our butts will be toast."

When Eli pulled the Jeep into his grandmother's drive, Archer stopped at the curb and climbed out of his convertible. As usual, the front door opened and Clarissa came out onto the porch. "Any news? she asked, wringing her hands together.

Eli shook his head. "No, nothing yet."

"Good morning, Clary," Archer said as he stepped up beside Eli.

"Morning, Mr. Hamilton." She motioned to the open doorway. "Please come in."

Clarissa stepped into the entry hall followed by her grandson and the editor and the trio went into the living room.

"I've been working with the cards all afternoon and they're still being stubborn about that masking spell and whether or not Stephanie is a wolf."

"She is." Eli told her. "I don't know how she's disguising it, but Cooper could smell her at the hospital."

"How do you know it was her?" Clarissa frowned into his eyes.

"Because she smells like me. Cooper was confused at first, but once he knew the story of what happened it made sense to the both of us."

"Oh my. So Elijah scratched her when he stabbed her... but for what purpose?"

"This very situation we're in right now. He knew it would only be a matter of time before things came to a head back then. He knew someone would end him and he wanted to be sure he implemented some kind of impending danger for Paige. He was determined not to have our bloodlines united." He took his grandmother's hands in his. "Clary, I need your help more than ever now. Can the cards tell you where Paige is?"

"I don't know about the cards, but I can do a locator spell."

"You'll need something of Paige's?"

"Yes."

"I'll be right back." Eli opened the front door, hurried along the path, crossed the road and entered their home. Within minutes, he was back with one of Paige's hairbrushes. "Will this do?"

"It should." Clarissa removed a few strands of Paige's hair, walked over to the bookshelf and picked up the map of the surrounding area, unfolded it, laid it out on the coffee table and sat down on the sofa. She dropped the strands of hair onto the map and, closing her eyes, chanted an incantation. When she opened them nothing had happened. "Oh, that can't be good."

Eli lowered himself onto one knee. "What's wrong?"

"Well, the strands of hair should have traveled to Paige's location. I mean, stretched out to wherever she is, but they haven't."

"So what does that mean?"

His grandmother gave him a sorrowful look. "She may not be with us anymore."

Archer moved closer to the pair. "Are you saying she might be…?"

"I'm not sure what it means. A person's living energy is the method with which we locate them."

"But you could be wrong, couldn't you?" Archer asked.

"Anything is possible." Although Clarissa couldn't be sure.

FIFTEEN

With church undergoing renovations Eli couldn't hold a snap meeting there, so he had contacted everyone and asked them to meet him at the station. Cooper was still at the hospital so Eli would fill him in later. As Rick and Taylor were on surveillance, he knew it was safe to hold the meeting at the office. Right now, he needed to get his pack and anyone else who could help out into the surrounding woods searching for Paige. When he entered the station house, Daniel, Ethan, Braydon, and Joshua were already there. He'd received a text telling him Abbey and Brent were on their way. Archer came in behind him and stood with Daniel and his guys, while Rosemarie busied herself offering refreshments. She didn't know what else to do. She had tried to do a location spell for Paige and had come up with nothing. She knew that wasn't a good sign and wouldn't mention it to Eli.

Daniel came up to Eli. "I'm sorry this has happened. How's your son doing?"

"He's safe at the hospital. Security is with him to make sure he remains that way."

"That's good. What can we do to help?"

"I'll explain it once the others get here." Eli pushed through the swinging gate on the partition, headed to his office and closed the door. He needed a moment. Pulling the blinds for some privacy, he walked over and sat down behind his desk, resting his head in his hands. "Where are you, sweetheart?" He didn't believe she was dead. Maybe she was in a place that couldn't be located by magic. At least he hoped so. Tears stung the backs of his eyes and slid down his face. What would he and their son do if...? No, he couldn't think like that. He had to stay strong for Paige. They *would* find her.

Betty and Hal had arrived at the same time as Abbey and Brent. They wanted to offer their support too.

Eli came back into the office. "Thanks, everyone, for being here." He gave a thin smile to Betty and her husband. "I appreciate you getting here on such short notice." His gaze roamed the concerned faces around him. "We haven't been able to locate Paige with magic so I need your help."

"Whatever we can do," Betty said.

"Thank you, I appreciate it." Eli stood with hands on hips and was about to tell the group what he had planned when the door opened.

"Hey, Eli, need some more help?"

"Ruby? What... how did you know?"

"Clary." Ruby entered the office followed by the rest of the coven: Jasmine, Erica, Crystal, Beatrice, Lacy, and Dahlia. "These ladies want to help you too."

Once again, tears stung the backs of Eli's eyes and he blinked them away. "I can't thank you enough. Please come in."

The coven of seven moved further into the office.

"Ok, now that we're all here... I think the only way we're going to locate Paige's whereabouts is to do a search of the surrounding area and towns. And I mean as wolves, for those of you that are. For the rest of you, look in all the unusual, unexpected locations. Derelict buildings, abandoned cabins in the woods, caves, underground sewage drains, anywhere someone could hide a person so they wouldn't be found. Time is running out so we need to move on this quickly."

Brent raised his hand. "It's going to be dark in a few hours. Do you want us, the wolves I mean, to keep searching once the sun goes down?"

"Yes, I do. It's our only chance to find her before..." He rubbed a hand over his face. "Let's just get out there and do the best we can, ok?"

Everyone nodded.

"Keep in touch by text or call if you need to. If you find anything – anything at all I want to know about it. Understood?"

Again, everyone nodded.

"Ok, thank you, let's get out there."

Archer came over to Eli. "What do you want me to do?"

"I had a thought and I want to check it out."

"Ok. Where are we going?"

"I'll fill you in on the way."

As they traveled out of town, Archer stiffened in his seat. "This is the way to Matthias's cabin. Why are we going out there?"

"I know Stephanie was at the hospital but no one saw her. I don't believe she kidnapped Paige. I think she had help."

"Ah, you think she got in touch with Samuel and Heath to elicit their assistance?"

"Yes, I do. The more I think about it the more it seems to cohere."

"They did have a grievance with you but do you really think they would stoop that low?"

"Desperate men, desperate times. They believe I got Matthias killed so, yes, I think it's more than possible."

"Your powers of deduction far outweigh mine and I'm a journalist. I'm meant to pull things like this together." Archer folded his arms. "You really think they would do something like this?"

"As I said, they want to exact some kind of recompense for their Alpha."

"Man. This is deeper than I thought. Now we have three desperate supernatural creatures wanting to exact revenge. It could get ugly."

"That's what I'm afraid of."

SIXTEEN

When the sleek, blue Greyhound bus pulled into the depot on the outskirts of Moon Grove three passengers alighted. The town wasn't what you'd call a quintessential tourist destination, but these three hadn't come to the rural township for fun and recreation. They were here for a different purpose. The driver followed the trio down the four metal steps, stuck a key into the lock of the luggage compartment and lifted the door up. The three passengers tugged their bags free, thanked the driver and made their way along the sidewalk, heading for the Moon Grove Inn where a reservation had been pre-arranged for them.

The air in small towns always smelled sweet, but this one had a distinct scent to it – a supernatural one that the three passengers were acutely aware of. As they wandered along the sidewalk, people on the street eyed them with discreet curiosity, the looks on their faces displaying bewilderment. Why were these three individuals in their town? They seldom had visitors to Moon Grove so what did these new arrivals want?

Once at the fence line of the inn, the trio walked the path to the front steps, climbed onto the porch, and entered the double-story white building. The inn had once been the home of one of Moon Grove's prominent families, and was built in the late 1800s, circa 1892 or there about. The elegant rooms featured antique Victorian furnishings and had working fireplaces for those cold winter nights to keep the rooms warm and comfortable.

"Cozy," one said.

"Yes, isn't it?" said the other.

"Let's get settled in," the third visitor suggested. "Then we can take a look around."

One dinged the domed bell on the reception desk, the high-pitched sound lingering in the atmosphere.

A young woman came around from behind the staircase and smiled when she saw the three standing at the counter. "Hi," she said, "my name is Sophie. How can I help you?"

"Hi, we have reservations."

"Oh, ok. Can I have your names please?"

"Yes, of course. I'm Stephen Knox." He turned and pointed to his first companion. "This is Hunter Fleming, and that's Harper McKenzie."

Sophie keyed the information into the laptop. "Yes, here we are. You're in rooms nine, ten and eleven on the second floor." She lifted three keys from off their hooks and handed them to her guests. "Enjoy your stay."

After coming from a big city where most hotels had card keys for their room doors, the trio was surprised when they were each handed a key – a brass key with a numbered leather tag. Quaint.

Climbing the stairs, they located their rooms and set about unpacking before heading out for something to eat and to survey the quiet township. Moon Grove was exactly as described, all except for the curious residents.

Once they were settled in, the three met in the downstairs foyer and decided to stay in for their meal. Choosing a table by one of the three windows, they sat and perused the evening's dinner menu. Everything sounded homey and appetizing.

"What are you having?" Stephen asked.

Harper ran her gaze over the contents of the menu. "Hard to decide. It all sounds so delicious."

"What about you, Hunter?"

"I'm so hungry I could eat a horse... literally." He chuckled. He wasn't joking. "But I think I'll have the chicken pot pie instead."

"Hey, that sounds good," Harper said. "I think I'll have the same." She placed the menu back in the center of the table.

"Ok, then, chicken pot pie it is." Stephen got up and walked over to the server to order their meals and coffee then returned to his seat. Gazing out the window, the semi-dark street looked picturesque with its old-fashioned lamp posts with flower baskets hanging from them and trees dotted along the sidewalk. "This place is cute, don't you think?"

"Yes, it is. Pity..."

"Don't, Harper, not now." Stephen's serious gaze met hers.

Harper's cheeks flushed and she looked down at her hands on the white table cloth. "Sorry."

"Let's enjoy the pleasant moments while we can."

SEVENTEEN

Night had set in as Eli and Archer trudged through the trees to the cabin in the woods. After everything that had happened during their battle with Scarlet and her witches, and the loss of life they had all suffered, he understood why Samuel and Heath were antagonistic toward him. What they had forgotten was that Matthias had made the decision to fight, he hadn't been coerced into it. It had been his choice. And his pack had gone along with that decision.

When the pair got close, Archer suggested he do a whip around to see if he could hear Paige's voice or at least learn how many might be inside. Eli agreed. He'd wait behind one of the tall pines until Archer returned, which would only be a matter of minutes. An owl hooted somewhere in the distance and it caused Eli's hackles to rise. Another sound made him spin around and someone's fist connected with his nose.

Eli came to with someone slapping his left cheek. Hard. "Hey, Blackwood, wake up."

Samuel.

Eli opened his eyes, his vision hazy, and blinked several times to clear his focus. He was seated on a wooden chair, his hands secured behind him. His gaze roamed the interior of the wood cabin. Where was Archer?

"What are you doin' out here, Sheriff?"

"I have a situation and I came to ask for your help," he lied.

"Yeah? What kind of situation could possibly need our help?" Samuel eyed his companion with a smirk then returned his gaze to the sheriff.

"Paige is missing and…"

"You think we give a damn about your wife?" Heath folded his arms.

"I would hope that as wolves we could join forces to find her. That's what most packs would do."

"We aren't most packs. In fact, we aren't a pack at all anymore because you took it away from us." Samuel stepped closer, leaned in, his nose almost touching Eli's and scowled. "Or have you forgotten that?"

"I apologized for the loss of your members. There isn't much more I can do. Matthias made the decision to fight. It was unfortunate he died in battle. But like I said back then, he would be remembered for his bravery."

"Right." Heath spat on the floor in front of Eli's feet.

"You do realize you're committing a criminal offense by holding me hostage."

"We're not holding you hostage. You're free to leave any time you want."

"All right, then untie me."

"Now why would I do that?"

"Because you don't want to spend time in jail, do you?"

Eli stood his ground. Even though he was anxious, he wouldn't show fear.

"That would only happen if they find you." Heath chuckled.

"So, what? You plan to kill me?" Eli prayed Archer was somewhere nearby as the pair had not realized he hadn't come alone.

Archer had seen what had happened to Eli and he was on his way back to the patrol to radio for help. Who would be there? It was late. Would Rosemarie still be at the station? Would Cooper? Maybe the rookies? He slid into the passenger seat, picked up the handset and depressed the button with his thumb. "Hello? Anyone there?" Crackling static. He pressed the button again. "Hello, Rosemarie, are you there?" Nothing. "Dammit!" He tossed the handset onto the driver's seat. He could take the pair of wolves by surprise, he supposed. But he'd have to lure them outside to do it.

Archer climbed out of the Jeep and made his way back through the tall pines to the cabin without a sound, the advantage of being a vampire. When he got closer, he peered in through one of the windows. Eli was tied to a chair and the two were antagonizing him, playing games with him. Archer circled the cabin and tried the back door. Locked. Of course. He headed around to the front of the wooden structure.

Searching the ground for a medium-sized rock, he found one lying near the fence and picked it up. He'd toss it in the direction away from himself and wait to see if one or both of the wolves came outside. He eased his body back to the window, peering in again and watched as Samuel back-handed Eli across the face. He tossed the rock.

The wooden door flew open and one wolf came out.

He stood with hands on hips and surveyed the perimeter. "Can't see anyone," he told Samuel.

"Go make sure. Maybe the sheriff didn't come out here alone."

Heath sighed. "Why don't you go do it?"

"Because I told you to."

"I'm not your servant, Sam. You'd do well to remember that."

Samuel stalked across the room to Heath and stood with hands on hips. "Or what?"

"Nothing. You just need to remember we don't belong to a pack anymore and you're not my Alpha." He headed out the door and into the woods in the direction Archer had thrown the rock.

Samuel gave a heavy sigh and crossed the room to Eli. As he did, Archer sneaked into the cabin, closed the door and rushed the wolf, tackling him to the ground. He punched Samuel in the face, blood spraying from his nose, setting off the bloodlust in Archer. The editor's canines elongated and he growled.

"Archer, don't!" Eli said.

The vampire turned to look at him, his mind and body wracked with a blood frenzy. He wanted to rip the wolf's neck open and drink him dry.

"Archer, you've got this."

The editor turned to look at Samuel. He raised his fist and brought it down hard knocking the wolf out.

"Untie me before Heath gets back."

Archer whipped across the room and tore the restraints from Eli's wrists. "Thanks for stopping me from killing him."

"No problem."

The pair heard crunching footfalls coming closer.

"Quick, let's get out the back before he comes in." Archer headed for the rear of the cabin.

"Wait, I need to check the rooms for Paige."

Eli did a quick run through but found no sign that Paige had been there.

The two men raced through the cabin, unlocked the back door, and disappeared into the trees.

On the drive back to Moon Grove, Eli quizzed Archer. "Where'd you go when you left me?"

"I circled the cabin as I said I would and found only Samuel and Heath inside. While I was checking the other rooms from outside, they must've realized you were there and Samuel came out to find you."

"Their hearing is far more acute than mine, if that's the case." Eli hooked onto the highway and pushed his foot down on the accelerator.

"I'm sorry. I wanted to make sure Paige was or wasn't inside before I came back. If she wasn't, there would have been no reason to bother them."

Eli gave a heavy sigh. "Yeah, you're right. Sorry. This whole situation has got me even questioning my own actions."

"I understand."

"She's been gone for over twelve hours, Archer. The longer it takes…"

"Don't think like that. We're going to find her. Do you think those two had anything to do with Paige's abduction?"

"I'm not ruling them out at this point. They seemed cagey. That could mean something."

"It could just mean their hatred for you runs deep. Sorry, but it's true."

"I know. But the way Samuel was looking at me and smirking… I think he knows something, even if he's not directly involved."

"Then, maybe we should find out what he knows."

EIGHTEEN

Do you have any idea where we are?" Taylor asked Rick. "I think we're lost." She glanced at the digital dashboard clock. "We've been driving around here for hours." She stared through the windshield into the intersecting circular beams of the headlights, the dirt road and legions of trees the only things she could see. "We need to find our way out of here. Stephanie is long gone and we lost her trail."

Rick gave a heavy sigh. "She had to have come this way. There's nowhere else to go."

"That we know of. Can we turn the patrol around or do we have to back up all the way out of here?"

"Nah, I'll get it turned around." He maneuvered the four wheel drive doing careful, calculated movements so they didn't get stuck in the mud and finally got the wagon heading back the way they had come. "Ok, let's get outta here. I'm mad at myself for stalling back on the road. I just wanted to give her a bit of a head start otherwise she would've known for sure we were following her."

"It's not your fault. I think she knew. And I think she had a way out that we missed somewhere along that dirt road."

"You're probably right. She's shrewd. I wonder why Eli has her as a person of interest."

Taylor shrugged. "Why don't you ask him? If we have to keep an eye on her we have a right to know, don't we?"

"Yeah, nah, you know what Eli's like. If he wants to tell us he will and if he wants to keep it under wraps he will. And it seems this is on a need to know basis and we don't need to know."

"That's what I mean. We're not privy to any of the important information. We're kept in the dark. Remember what happened when we queried him about the animal we saw that night? He told us it had to have been a dog of some kind when you and I both know it wasn't. Something about this town doesn't add up and we're never going to find out about it if we're stuck at our desks." A thought popped into Taylor's mind. "What if she lit the fire at the church? Stephanie, I mean."

Rick gave her an incredulous frown. "Why would she?"

"I don't know. But don't you think it's odd that she arrives in Moon Grove and the same night there's a fire at the church?"

He shrugged. "A coincidence."

"You think? I'm not so sure. We need to keep digging. I know we're going to find something."

"Well we're going to have to do it on our own time because we're chained to our desks until further notice." Rick headed for the highway, pushing the accelerator to the floor.

When the pair pulled into the parking lot of the station they were surprised to see Eli's patrol there. Rick had brought Taylor back to pick up her car and then they were each going home. "I wonder what he's doing here so late." Rick turned off the engine.

"Maybe he's catching up on paperwork or something." Taylor opened the passenger door and got out.

Rick came around the back of the wagon to her. "What paperwork? There'd only be paperwork if we had any incidents, which we haven't."

"Then, I don't know. It's none of our business." She walked over to her car and opened the door. "I'm heading home. See you in the morning." She glanced at her phone screen. "Which is only a few hours away. Goodnight."

Rick's gaze moved from the lit windows of the station house to her. "Yeah, goodnight."

"Don't go doing something that will get you into trouble." Taylor climbed into her car.

"I won't." Rick scowled.

"Ok. See you tomorrow." She closed the door and started the engine.

Rick stood and watched her leave before walking up the steps onto the front porch of the station. He was curious to find out why Eli was at the office so late. He tried the door, unlocked. Unusual. Pulling it open he stepped inside, his gaze roaming the semi-lit room. No one else was there. He heard voices coming from Eli's office and wondered who was with him.

Making his way across the room and through the swinging gate of the partition without a sound, Rick eased his tall frame up as close as he could to the fish bowl. The blinds were still drawn so he wouldn't be noticed.

"Those wolves need to be taught a lesson about respect," Archer said.

"Look, they've been through a lot, losing Matthias the way they did. I get it. They're angry… and confused."

"If you think they know something about Paige's abduction then we have to find out what they know. I can arrange that."

"So you said. How?"

"You don't want to know. It's best if you don't, being an officer of the law."

Rick took a step closer. What were they talking about? Wolves needing to have respect? What did that mean? And Eli's wife has been abducted? Why didn't he tell them?

"Stephanie has to be the one who orchestrated the abduction. She has a vendetta against Paige for what happened to her. My thought is she hired Samuel and Heath to help her."

"How would she have known about them?"

"Word travels fast in supernatural circles. I can only assume she immersed herself in that world back in Washington to make sure she was well prepared. I did a bit of checking and I learned her parents were killed. Maybe she had something to do with it."

"You think she murdered her parents?"

"Not on purpose. The first time someone turns – the urge to kill is uncontrollable. It would've happened on impulse."

"I wonder how the police handled it."

"I'm trying to get copies of the reports. I'd be curious to know that myself."

Rick took a step backwards. Supernatural circles? The first time she turned? What was he talking about? The epiphany suddenly hit him. Wolves? Werewolves! Rick's heart hammered in his chest and he turned to leave.

"I wouldn't do that if I were you," a voice said behind him.

Rick swung around, eyes wide.

Eli came out of the office and stood next to Archer. "What are you doing here?"

"I – I came back to pick up something I forgot," he lied.

"What did you hear?" Eli folded his arms.

"Nothing. I only just got here."

"Don't lie to me, Rick." Eli walked across to him. "Tell me what you heard." He grabbed his deputy's arm and led him into his office. "Sit."

Rick did as he was told. "I swear, I didn't hear anything. I just…"

"Yeah, so you said. Why don't I believe you?"

"I – I don't know."

"Out with it. You're not leaving until you tell me."

Archer leaned against the bookshelf under the window and folded his arms. "I could…"

Eli raised his hand. "It's ok. Rick's going to tell me himself. Aren't you?"

Rick contemplated his options. Continue to lie which would get him into more trouble or come clean and see what happens. Not great choices. He decided on option two. "Ok. But before I do I want to tell you that Taylor and I followed Stephanie Harris out along the highway toward

Bellehurst, and she got off and headed into the woods there. Unfortunately, we lost her but that might be a place of interest, seeing your wife has been taken."

"Spill." Eli propped himself on the corner of his desk, arms folded.

"I heard most of what you were talking about. And I came to the conclusion you were talking about werewolves. What else could it be?" He shrugged.

Eli's and Archer's eyes met. This was the day Eli hoped would never happen. He knew Archer could erase Rick's memory of what he heard tonight but maybe it was time to come clean and let his deputies in on what goes on in his town. "What makes you think we were talking about werewolves?"

"You said something about when Stephanie turned the first time she killed her parents."

Eli remained poker faced. "What else?"

"That Matthias's wolves needed to be taught a lesson about respect."

Eli nodded. "Ok." Maybe he did need Archer to wipe Rick's memory after all.

"Who's Matthias?"

"He was a friend who was killed a few months ago."

"Oh, I'm sorry." Rick's nervous gaze moved to Archer then back to Eli. "I didn't mean to pry."

"Yes, you did. You and Taylor have been doing just that since you got here."

"That's not…"

"True? You know it is. The problem I have is whether I can trust you with the information."

"You can. I swear."

"I'll need time to think it over." Eli gripped Rick's arm. "In the meantime, you're spending the night here in the cells."

"But, boss," Rick whined.

"I need you to do as I ask. It's only for a few hours."

Rick gave a heavy sigh. "Ok." He knew he deserved it. He'd snuck up on Eli and learned something he shouldn't have by being sneaky. "Will you be here too?"

"I will. Let's go."

After securing Rick in a cell, Eli walked Archer out.

"I can erase the memory if you want me to."

"Yes, I know you can. But it's been tricky trying to keep the secrets of Moon Grove from him and Taylor. They've been suspicious since that wolf ran in front of their patrol that night."

"So what are you going to do?"

"I think it's time to sit them down and have a long talk with them. If that doesn't work then you can use your mojo on them."

"Ok, if you think it's wise."

"I don't know what I think at this point. I've got too much on my plate. This only adds to it."

"Well you know where I am if you change your mind about telling them. I can be here in no time and make the kid forget he heard anything."

Eli rested a hand on Archer's shoulder. "Thanks. I may take you up on it. We'll see."

Archer crossed the parking lot and climbed into his convertible. "Leave the wolves to me. I'll handle it. I'll let you know what I find out."

"Thank you." He gave the editor a wave, watched him leave, then headed back inside. Would Rick and Taylor respond well to what he had to tell them? He would have to wait and see. He headed through the station to the holding cells and leaned against the wall across from Rick's cell with arms folded. "If I tell you what you want to know I need to know you'll keep it as privileged information."

"You can trust us, Eli. You can."

Eli's right eyebrow arched. "Can I indeed. Is that why you've been investigating the town and asking questions for the past few months behind my back?"

Rick stood up. "Look, we were curious about Moon Grove because there's a vibe here. Both Taylor and I have felt it. We knew there was something about the town. And the night we saw that wolf it only solidified our suspicions."

"So why didn't you come to me?"

"Because you wouldn't have told us anything. I think you were trying to protect us… and I appreciate it, but we can't do our jobs if we don't know what's going on in this place."

"Fair comment, I suppose. And, yes, I was trying to keep you safe."

"We know." Rick stepped up to the bars. "You *can* trust us. I give you my word on that."

Eli pushed himself away from the wall. "We'll see. Get some sleep. I'll talk to you both in the morning."

NINETEEN

The next morning, Stephanie came downstairs at around 7:30AM and took a seat in the dining room at her usual table by the window. She liked to have a view of the main street. Moon Grove was a pretty town and it appealed to her sense of calm. And she was calm. She had accomplished what she had planned to do despite one unexpected hitch and everything seemed right with her world. She smiled as she picked up the breakfast menu and perused the day's specials.

Before she had arrived in the quaint little town she had been involved in something otherworldly and had had to get away for a while, for her own protection. She felt safe here. For how long she was unsure, but while it lasted she would make the most of it. Stephanie continued to gaze out of the multi-paned window until a voice behind her caused her to swing around.

"Coffee?" Betty offered, coffee pot in her hand.

"Uh, yes, thanks."

Betty turned the cup over on its saucer and poured the steaming brew into it. "Are you ready to order?" She pulled a pad and pencil from the pocket of her clean white apron. "No need to come over to the server."

"I appreciate that. Thank you." Stephanie smiled. "Bacon and eggs, sunny side up, and a serving of buttered toast."

"Coming right up." Betty made her way through the tables and into the kitchen.

There were only a handful of guests having breakfast in the dining room so the place was relatively quiet. Stephanie was glad. It would be nice to eat breakfast in peace before she headed out to finish what she'd started.

Stephen, Harper, and Hunter stepped into the dining room and took a seat close to the entrance. They wanted to remain inconspicuous to those around them, but to one in particular. As she sat by the window unaware they had come to the town for her, Stephen's eyes watched as the waitress set down the woman's breakfast and check. Stephanie had double-crossed their boss and he was not a happy man – well – demon. He had sent them to Moon Grove to bring her back to face the consequences of her actions, but if that failed they had orders to dispatch her. Stephen hoped that wouldn't be necessary and that she would cooperate with them.

When Stephanie had killed her parents, which had been a terrible and unfortunate accident, their boss, who was attached to the PD had cleaned up her mess. She'd owed him. But when he had called on her to do another job for him she'd packed up and disappeared. It had taken almost a year to sniff out her trail and here they were. She was a feisty one, hence the reason their boss had sent the three of them to Moon Grove. She would not go down easily.

The trio ordered breakfast and enjoyed their meals as they continued to monitor the wolf from a distance. When the time was right they would make their move.

TWENTY

Eli entered the station house, set the donuts down on the kitchen counter and turned on the coffee maker before heading to the cell block. He'd gone out to pick up some breakfast before he let Rick out of the cell and then sat his deputies down for a serious discussion about the town. As he reached the cells he found Rick still sleeping. "Hey, Rick, wake up."

His deputy turned over, rubbing the sleep from his eyes, and swung his legs off the cot. "Morning, boss."

Eli unlocked the door. "Get cleaned up. There's some breakfast in the kitchen."

"Thanks." Rick shuffled past his boss and made his way to the bathroom.

Eli wandered back into the office just as Rosemarie and Taylor were coming in.

"Morning, ladies," he greeted.

"Mornin', darlin'," Rosemarie said, her face grim. She couldn't hide how she felt, although she tried.

"Morning, boss," Taylor returned. "Rick here?"

"Yeah, he's in the kitchen. I want to see you in my office in ten. If you're hungry there's some breakfast out there and the coffee's hot."

"Thanks." Taylor pushed through the partition gate, holding it for Rosemarie, then headed down the short passage to the kitchen.

Rick was munching on a donut when she came in.

"You look like hell," Taylor told him. "Didn't get much sleep?"

"No. It was a rough night." He poured two mugs of coffee and passed one to her. "Here."

"Thanks." Taylor eased the mug from his hand and took a cautious sip. "Eli wants to see me in ten."

"Yeah, me too."

Taylor's eyebrows came together. "Do you know what it's about?"

"It's better if he tells you."

"Rick."

Her partner raised a defensive hand. "I can't. He'll explain everything."

Taylor gave an exasperated huff, turned and headed back into the office.

Rick hated not being able to say anything, but he'd already spent one night in the cells and didn't plan on doing it again.

Eli closed the office door, walked across the room and took his seat. He leaned forward, resting his clasped hands on the blotter, his gaze moving from Rick to Taylor. "Something happened last night and we need to talk about it."

Taylor glanced at Rick then returned her gaze to Eli. "What happened?"

Eli looked at Rick. "You want to tell her?"

Rick's cheeks flushed. "Uh, not really but I guess I don't have a choice."

"What did you do? I told you to stay out of trouble." Taylor folded her arms.

"Yeah, I know." He gave his partner a sheepish glance. "And I wish I'd taken your advice."

Taylor frowned at Eli. "What happened?" she asked again.

"Rick felt the need to sneak in here and listen in on a private conversation between me and Archer Hamilton."

Taylor's head spun toward him. "Rick!"

He raised defensive hands. "I'm sorry."

"Rick gets impulsive sometimes, but he means well." She couldn't believe she'd just said that, under the circumstances. He'd been caught out and nothing would change that.

Eli leaned back in his office chair and folded his arms. "You two have been suspicious of this town and its residents pretty much since you arrived. You've both gone out of your way to investigate Moon Grove behind my back and have riled up some of the folk here."

Taylor's face paled. "We – we only…"

"Yes, you only wanted to know the truth. Well, today you're going to find out what that truth is."

Taylor gave Rick a sideward glance then looked at Eli. "What does that mean?"

"I'm going to explain some things to you. Things that must remain confidential."

The deputy nodded. "Ok."

"Ok doesn't cut it, Taylor. I need your solemn word that what you learn here today stays with you and you alone."

"It will. You have my word." She looked at Rick again. Had he already made that promise?

After their meeting with Eli, the deputies had been sent out on patrol to have a chance to discuss what they'd been told. Taylor felt vindicated because she knew there was something – something unusual about Moon Grove, and now she knew what it was.

Rick pulled the patrol into the curb opposite the playground and turned off the engine. "My head is spinning. Can you believe it?"

"It's something I never thought I'd find out... not in a million years. Eli's a werewolf. So is Cooper, which explains a lot, and Rosemarie is a witch. It's scary and awesome!"

"I guess. We live in a magical town."

Taylor swiveled in her seat. "No, Rick, it's a supernatural town."

"Yeah, ok." He ran his hand over his face. "I wonder what it feels like."

"What what feels like?"

"Turning into a wolf."

"Maybe you should've asked Eli that question."

"Now we know the animal we saw that night was a werewolf."

"Yeah, we do." A warm tingling feeling coursed through Taylor's body. "It's amazing."

"So what do we do about it?"

Taylor gave Rick a curious stare. "What do you mean?"

"I mean now that we know the truth do we become part of it?"

"Are you saying what I think you're saying?"

"Yeah, I am. Eli needs us. We could become part of his pack."

"I – I don't know about that." Taylor grimaced. "I don't think I'm ready to tear someone to shreds and eat their liver."

"They don't eat people's livers."

"Of course they do. They rip people to shreds and devour their flesh and blood."

"Eli doesn't. Neither does his pack. They live off the land, eating animals."

"Ok, yeah, but…"

"Don't you want to do something incredible with your life?"

"That doesn't mean becoming a werewolf."

"Well, we could always become vampires. Like Archer Hamilton. Then you'd only have to drink blood."

"Gross!"

"Think about it. Ok?"

Taylor wasn't sure she wanted to give it any thought at all. What about her family? Would she ever be able to see them again? Could she hide something like that from them? She could still do her job as a human, as long as she knew what she was up against. And, for her, that seemed the right thing.

TWENTY ONE

The search for Paige proved fruitless and Eli paced his office wondering what they could do to find her before it was too late. If Stephanie had her, and he believed she did, time was of the essence. It was obvious to him that the woman planned to get rid of Paige and it was only a matter of time... time they didn't have.

Rosemarie came to the door. "Eli, what can I do to help?" She stepped into the office and came up to him.

"I honestly don't know, Rosy. Clary has tried locator spells and consulting the cards and neither has provided anything useful. I'm worried we may already be too late."

The receptionist rested a comforting hand on her boss's arm. "Please don't think like that, hon. We have to stay strong."

"Cooper found nothing in the hospital security footage, which means Stephanie was there in disguise and we didn't pick up on it. We know she was definitely there because Cooper could smell her Lycan scent. And the only movement in the loading dock was a laundry truck taking trolleys of laundry from the hospital. Nothing unusual about that."

Rosemarie gave it some thought for a moment. "What if Paige was in one of the laundry trolleys? Maybe they got her out of the hospital that way."

Eli's serious gaze moved to her. "Why didn't we think of that before now?" He raced around his desk, dropped into the seat, and pulled up the security footage. Scrolling through, he came to the loading dock. Zooming in, he checked the two men loading the laundry trolleys onto the truck. He zoomed in more, pushed some keys on the keyboard to sharpen the video and zoomed in even more. "It's them."

Rosemarie gave him a perplexed frown. "It's who?"

"Samuel and Heath, Matthias's pack members. They're working for Stephanie."

"Oh, my Lord." Rosemarie brought her hand up to her mouth.

"You're amazing." Eli flew from his chair, kissed Rosemarie's forehead, and rushed out the door.

Eli charged into the Tribune office like a man on a mission. When Archer saw him, he came around his desk. "What's wrong?"

"Samuel and Heath abducted Paige from the hospital by hiding her in a laundry basket."

"What?"

"Rosy made the suggestion, and when I checked the footage again I found it was them. Can you do whatever you were going to do to find out where they took her?"

"Absolutely. Do you want to go out there now?"

103

"They might not be at the cabin. They're most likely guarding Paige somewhere else." Eli paced. "But where?"

"Stephanie wouldn't know the lay of the land like they would, so it would have to be somewhere they'd know about. Can you think of anywhere?" Archer asked.

Eli racked his brain. He didn't know enough about the comings and goings of Matthias's pack to even begin considering where they had taken his wife. "I don't know. It could be anywhere."

"Perhaps they took her somewhere close to Bellehurst, considering the hospital is there," Archer offered. "What's out that way?"

Eli stopped pacing. "There's the old medical center. We went out there before when Gregor took Paige, remember?"

"Would they know about the place though?"

"Maybe. It's kind of a landmark for urban explorers and teens wanting to party. And it's far enough away from anything. No one patrols it anymore."

"Then, perhaps we should check it out again. At least it's a start."

"You're right. Let's go."

The dilapidated medical center hadn't changed at all. Well, perhaps there was more graffiti and smashed windows, but apart from that it still had a creepy, sinister vibe. Eli pulled up on the drive, turned off the engine, and stared out the windshield. It had been over a year since they were here fighting Gregor Petrov. He had been an ambitious ancient vampire wanting to become a super hybrid by drinking

Paige's blood, which he did. Rather than it turn him into a super vampire, it transformed him into a monstrous beast that had killed most of Eli's pack.

Archer eyed the abandoned building with apprehension. "Ok, let's do this."

The pair left the Jeep, trudged up the rocky overgrown incline to the partially boarded up front entrance, and climbed through the jagged holes in the double glass doors. The distinct musty stench of rotting paper and stagnant water drifted into their nostrils as they trod through the damp reception foyer. Broken waiting room chairs were turned upside down, patient files strewn across the linoleum floor soaked in muddy pools of rainwater, and new colorful spray-painted tags: Demon, Serpent, and Cougar were splashed across the walls behind the reception desk. Their eyes roamed the gloom.

Archer stood with hands on hips and did a 360 degree turn. "Where do you want to start?"

"Where else?" Eli told him.

They headed for the basement stairs.

Stepping into the pitch black corridor that led to the morgue, neither needed any light, their nocturnal vision expanding so they could see more clearly. They pushed through rusted wheel chairs and trolleys lining the passageway and headed into the bowels of the building.

Archer listened for a heartbeat or any other sound, but there were none. "I don't think Paige is down here, Eli. I don't hear a heartbeat."

"Ok, maybe we can try upstairs."

The pair turned to leave but a sound further down the corridor echoed up at them.

"What was that?" Archer whispered.

"Good question." Eli drew his weapon. Let's go take a look."

TWENTY TWO

Clarissa opened the front door to find Ruby and a group of women she knew were witches standing on her doorstep. It had been several months since she'd seen the young witch and it was good to see her again. "Come in, come in. Welcome."

Ruby and the rest of the coven stepped into the entry hall, Ruby giving the older woman a hug as she did. "It's good to see you, Clary. How have you been?"

"Fine, dear, just fine. I'm so happy you're finally settled and with people you can relate to." Her eyes roamed the faces of the other women. "Please have a seat in the living room. Anyone want tea, coffee?"

"We can't stay long," Ruby told her.

"Oh, so why are you here?"

The women walked into the living room and took seats on the sofa and in the armchairs. Clarissa remained on her feet.

"We want to help find Paige. What can we do?" Ruby sat on the arm of an armchair.

"I've consulted the cards and have tried several location spells but have come up with nothing. To be honest, I don't know what else to try."

One of the women spoke up. Jasmine. "Perhaps our combined powers would offer some insight."

Clarissa raised her hand to her chin and gave it some thought. "It's possible, I suppose. I'm prepared to try anything at this stage, if it will help find Paige."

Ruby stood up. "Do you still have something of Paige's here?"

The older woman nodded. "Her hair brush."

"Ok, good." Ruby ran her gaze around the other women. "Let's give it a try."

Eli and Archer gave each other a frowning stare. Who would be down here, Eli wondered. The pair made their way along the corridor in the direction the sound had come from. If Archer couldn't hear any heartbeats what was hiding in the dark? Eli's heartbeat kicked up a couple notches and he gripped the pistol in his hand even tighter. If whatever it was turned out to be supernatural, a bullet wouldn't suffice.

Archer gripped Eli's arm so he'd stop and placed his hand on the sheriff's forehead. "I think we should get out of here and leave whatever is down there alone."

Eli could hear the words in his head. 'How are you doing that?'

"I have certain tricks up my sleeve. Let's go."

"No. If it's something dangerous we need to deal with it."

"Ok, if you really think it's necessary."

The pair continued moving forward.

Eli swallowed hard.

The sound echoed along the passageway again.

When they reached the door leading into a storage room they noticed it standing ajar. The sound had to be coming from inside.

Eli motioned with his head and Archer nodded.

Raising his hand, Eli counted to three with his fingers. One. Two. Three. The pair burst into the dark space.

The sound of scurrying and squealing echoed around them and both men let out a relieved sigh.

"Rats."

"Thankfully. Come on, let's get out of here," Archer said.

"Yeah, let's."

"Wherever Paige is it has to be underground or somewhere magic can't reach her," Ruby said. "Or…"

Clary raised her hand. "Don't say it. Don't even think it."

"I'm sorry, Clary, but there's no way to pick up her life force, and I'm not sure what that means."

"I know." The older woman frowned and her eyes filled with tears. "She's alive. I know she is. She's a fighter."

"Being a fighter is one thing but being in a position where you can't fight is another."

Clary gave a heavy sigh and sat down in a now vacant armchair. "She has to be alive. She has a son to raise."

"Then we have to figure out another way of finding her." Ruby was adamant.

Clary wrung her hands together. "We're running out of time."

Eli called another meeting at the station to do a follow up on the search. Everyone that had participated had checked in, but he wanted to make sure nothing had been overlooked. Abbey and Brent were the first to arrive, followed soon after by Daniel and his friends who were now part of Eli's pack. Ruby and the witches didn't attend, although Ruby had called him to let him know they were working on another way to try to locate Paige. He was grateful.

Betty and Hal were busy with the inn but had sent him a text message to confirm they hadn't found anything while out in search of Paige. They wished they could have done more.

Cooper came into the office and his eyes widened when he saw Rick and Taylor sitting at their desks. *What are they doing here?* He crossed the office to Eli and asked if he could speak to him in private. The pair went into Eli's office and closed the door.

"Why are the rookies here?" Cooper stood with hands on hips.

"Sorry, Coop, with everything that's been going on I haven't had a chance to catch you up." He motioned for his deputy to take a seat and perched himself on the corner of his desk. "Rick and Taylor know. We had a meeting and I told them about Moon Grove."

Cooper's eyebrows rose. "Why would you do that?"

"Because Rick overheard a conversation I was having with Archer and I decided it was time to be up front with them." He folded his arms. "They live here. Work here. So they have a right to know what's going on here."

Cooper gave it some thought. Eli was right. At least now he wouldn't have to sneak around them all the time. He could be himself. "Ok, fair enough. Do they want to be part of the pack?"

"Not that I'm aware of. We have enough pack members as it is and I don't think it would be fair to ask that of them."

"But what if they ask you?"

"That's a bridge I'll cross if and when it happens." Eli stood up. "Let's get this meeting underway."

TWENTY THREE

Stephanie drove her rental vehicle out to the location she had traveled to previously when those two deputies followed her and thought she didn't know she was being tailed. Her eyes met her reflection in the rearview mirror and she smiled. Did Eli Blackwood really think she was that stupid? She turned onto the dirt road and continued driving for about a mile before stopping. She stepped out of the hatchback, walked over to a clump of tall bushes attached to a gate and pushed it open.

Climbing back in, she started the engine, drove through, stopped, got out and secured the gate before continuing on. The old concrete drain had proved useful in hiding Paige. Stephanie knew Eli's grandmother was a witch and would try to locate her hostage using magic, but wouldn't be able to because the empty drain was at least thirty feet deep and had a heavy steel trap door over it to prevent anyone from falling to their death. Down below, there was a grated metal cover over the length of the drain preventing Paige from getting free. Stephanie had left strict instructions for the wolves not to leave Paige alone.

Her ex-friend was resourceful and she needed to be sure she wouldn't find a way to escape.

She pulled the car to a stop and spotted the tent beside the well. Samuel and Heath had set up camp here. She tugged the key from the ignition, opened the driver's door and climbed out, slipping out of her heels and into a pair of rubber-soled hiking boots.

Samuel flung back the flap on the tent and stepped out. Heath behind him. "Finally. How much longer do we have to stay out here?" Samuel folded his arms and scowled at the woman.

"For as long as necessary. I'm paying you so you'll do what you're told." She glowered at him.

"We have other things to do. And this was meant to be a partnership not an authoritarian arrangement. We could always leave. Then you'd have to deal with it yourself." Samuel didn't like being told what to do. He was a free wolf now.

Stephanie knew she had to appease the angry wolf. She gave him an agreeable smile." You're right, I'm sorry. But I am paying you well so I really need you to be here until the job is done."

Heath stepped up beside Samuel. "So why don't you just do it already? Get it over with?"

"I have my reasons."

"Yeah? Well you need to move it along before Eli Blackwood comes looking out here. He's bound to eventually, especially as you were followed out here by those rookie cops." Heath ran his hand over the stubble on his face and stared into her eyes. He was sick of the woman giving them orders.

Samuel eyed her from head to toe. Slim with curves in all the right places. Attractive enough, but she had a mean streak. "What's with them?" He pointed to the brown lace up hiking boots she had on.

"I'm going in."

His eyes widened. "Why would you do that? She doesn't know you're even involved."

"She knows." Stephanie walked across the tall grass to the circular drain buried in the ground. "Can you lift that for me, please?" She had to remember her manners or the pair of wolves might trap her with Paige and leave them both here to die.

Samuel and Heath followed her over. One moved to either side of the three foot concrete cylinder and the pair grunted as they hefted the heavy metal circle off the top of the drain.

"Are you sure you wanna do this?" Heath asked.

"I am." She climbed over the rim onto the black metal ladder. "Keep your cell handy in case I need one of you."

Something had changed. Ruby rushed into the kitchen, grabbed Clarissa by the arm and pulled her into the living room. "I think we've got something," she said, excited.

Clarissa wiped her hands on the dish cloth she was holding and stood in the entry. "What is it?"

"We got a brief glimmer. Paige is still alive." Ruby's face lit up.

"Do you know where she is?"

"Yes, somewhere in the woods close to Bellehurst."

"Those woods are vast. Can you narrow it down?"

"We'll try. It's a start, Clary. At least we know Paige is all right for the moment."

"Tristan needs his mother. We have to find her."

"And we will."

Stephen, Harper, and Hunter had followed the woman out to the remote location and had seen the hidden gate she had driven through. It was only a matter of time before she left and they would wait it out back on the main road. Why would she come all the way out here? What was she up to? They'd heard about the sheriff's missing wife. It was all over town. Could Stephanie have something to do with it? Maybe they should hike through the woods and find out. It would be leverage they could use to get her to go back to Washington with them.

Stephen maneuvered the rental around, lucky it was a compact car, and headed back to the main road. He'd park the hatchback under some trees and the three of them would shift and take a run through the woods.

"Ok. Let's see if we can find her," Stephen said.

The trio shifted into wolf form and bounded into the trees.

As they got closer to what looked like a camp site they stopped and surveyed their surroundings. There were other wolves here.

Stephen motioned with his large head and the three split up, circling the site.

Was this where the Blackwood woman was being held captive?

The trio remained hidden in the trees as they watched Stephanie climb out of what appeared to be a drain. After she was on land again, she stood with her hands on her hips and did a 360 degree turn. "Hey, where are you?"

The flap on the tent flew back and two men stepped out. "We're here," one said.

"Ok. I'm heading back to Moon Grove. Keep up the good work and I'll see you tomorrow."

"This needs to get done," the same guy told her.

"It will be done when I'm ready to do it." She glowered at him.

"Like I said, we don't have to be here."

"If you're not here you won't get paid. Simple as that." Her cooperative demeanor had vanished.

The pair of wolves stared at her as she climbed into her rental and drove away.

The three wolves watching disappeared into the trees. They knew where to find her.

TWENTY FOUR

Eli had spent part of the day at the hospital visiting with his new son. As he held the precious bundle in his arms, tears stung the backs of his eyes. *Paige should be here enjoying these moments with our son. Where is she?* A nurse came into the nursery to check on the pair and smiled when she saw the baby boy sleeping peacefully in his dad's arms.

"I'll leave you to it," she said, backing out of the doorway, the door whooshing closed behind her.

"I'm going to find your mom, little guy. I promise you that."

The door opened again and Rosemarie stood in the entrance. "Is it ok to come in?"

Eli nodded. "Of course."

Rosemarie crossed the nursery. All the other babies were with their mothers. "How's he doin'?"

"As well as can be expected."

"Cooper's outside. He wants to talk to you."

"Oh, ok." Eli eased himself out of the armchair and placed his son gently into his crib.

The pair left the nursery, heading to the waiting area.

When Cooper saw them coming along the corridor he stood up. "Hey, boss, how's it going? How's the boy?"

"He's doing ok. What did you want to talk to me about?"

"Your grandmother's been trying to get in touch with you."

Eli tugged his cell from the pocket of his shirt and checked it, frowning. "I had it on silent and didn't even notice the vibration.

"Too busy being a dad," Rosemarie said.

"Yeah."

Eli's gaze moved to his deputy. "Did she tell you why she was calling?"

"She said the witches had a glimmer of Paige, whatever that means, and she wants you to come to her house."

"I'll let the nurses know I'm leaving and head straight over. Where are you going now?"

Cooper looked at Rosemarie then back to Eli. "I'm going to take Rosy back to the station and then go out on patrol."

"Ok. I'll see you there later."

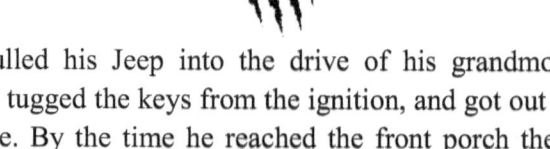

Eli pulled his Jeep into the drive of his grandmother's home, tugged the keys from the ignition, and got out of the vehicle. By the time he reached the front porch the door opened and Clary was beckoning him to hurry inside. "Come in, come in."

"What's this about a glimmer of Paige?"

"Come into the living room." She took his arm and ushered him inside.

Eli gave Ruby a brief smile when he spotted her sitting on the arm of the sofa.

"We've picked up Paige's energy in the woods outside Bellehurst. At this stage, it isn't giving us an exact location but…" Ruby told him.

"We covered part of the woods there but it's quite vast." Eli crossed the room to the coffee table and the map laid out on it.

Jasmine came up to him. "We had to combine our energy to get this far and we'll continue to do what we can to find your wife, Sheriff."

"I appreciate your help. When you have anything, please let me know."

"We will."

Clary looked up at her grandson. "Do you have time for coffee?"

"Maybe later." He headed for the door. "I'll come by tonight with some take out. Sound ok?"

"That would be lovely, Eli." She smiled. "But you'll have to bring enough for everyone."

"They're staying here?"

"Only until they find Paige."

"That could take a while."

"I know. That's why I suggested you bring enough food for us all."

"Ok, will do." He gave his grandmother a kiss on the forehead and left them to it. He had to get back to the station and have his pack head out to do another sweep of the woods.

As the sun slid into the distant orange horizon, Eli wondered if the search would prove useful this time. Without a definite location for Paige's whereabouts, it was difficult for his wolves to pinpoint exactly where she would be in the vastness of trees and land. Was she ok? He hoped so. He checked his watch. 7:08PM.

Eli pulled himself out of his office chair and headed for the door. He had to pick up the Chinese he'd ordered from the Jade Dragon and drive over to his grandmother's. They hadn't spent a lot of time together lately, so it would be good to sit and talk for a while and perhaps even find a more accurate location for Paige in the process. He wanted her home.

As he drove toward Clary's his cell jingled. Pressing the button for Bluetooth, he answered. "Eli Blackwood speaking."

"Hello, Sheriff. I think I might know where your wife's being held."

Eli screeched the Jeep into the curb. "Who is this?"

"Who I am is irrelevant. Do you want the location or not?"

"Ok. Where is she?" Eli drummed his fingers on the steering wheel, his gut tight. Could this be a hoax?

"I think we should meet."

"You want to meet but you don't want to give me your name?"

"You'll get it when we're face to face. Can you come to the inn?"

Eli glanced at the food sitting in bags on the passenger seat. "I can be there in half an hour."

"Good. I'll see you then."

"Wait. How will I recognize you?"

"I'll find you." The line went dead.

Eli dropped the food off at his grandmother's, telling her he had a lead, and headed back into town. Pulling into the curb outside the Moon Grove Inn, his eyes roamed the double-story white wood building. Giving a heavy sigh, he tugged the key from the ignition, climbed out of the Jeep and headed along the path. When he reached the front entrance, the door opened and a man around Eli's age stepped outside.

He extended his hand. "Hello, Sheriff, I'm Stephen Knox."

Eli shook his hand and studied the man's face and demeanor. "You're a wolf?"

"Yes."

"You said you know where my wife is?"

Stephen motioned to the white metal table and chairs along the porch. "Shall we?"

Eli eyed him for a moment, then walked ahead of him and took a seat, Stephen sitting opposite him.

"I haven't seen you before. Are you here on vacation?"

Stephen shook his head. "No. I think we have a mutual enemy. Stephanie Harris." He leaned back on the chair and clasped his hands across his abdomen.

Eli's right eyebrow arched. "You're here for Stephanie Harris?"

"Let's just say my boss wants her brought back to Washington to discuss an important matter."

"Ok, fair enough. Your issues with her have nothing to do with me." Eli shifted on his chair. "So do you want to tell me where you believe my wife is?"

"Better yet, I'll show you."

"Can you meet me at the station? I'll pull a team together…"

Stephen shook his head. "Just you and me alone."

"Why?"

"You go trudging out there with a team and you're likely to get your wife killed. Sorry to be so blunt, but it's the truth."

Eli gave it a moment's thought. "Who's with her?"

"There are two wolves out there. We didn't actually see your wife… we saw Stephanie and I came to the conclusion she had something to do with your wife's disappearance."

Eli knew who the wolves were. He wasn't sure how comfortable he was going out to a remote location with another wolf he knew nothing about, but he didn't have a choice.

TWENTY FIVE

Stephanie sat on her bed with her laptop in front of her and stared at the list of unopened emails. Azzaron was relentless in his pursuit of her, attempting to wear her down so she would give in and fall back into his clutches. A single tear left a moist trail as it slid down her right cheek and she brushed it away. She had to remain one step ahead of him or her life would be over. She had been grateful for his help when she'd inadvertently killed her parents the first time she turned into a wolf. But she had repaid him over and over again until she'd had enough. Now she was on the run from him and it would be only a matter of time before she was found. She had to get this situation sorted and move on.

The problem was she was enjoying watching Paige suffer. Her having been pregnant when Stephanie had arrived had proved to be a plus in her plan. Taking her away from her newborn son was the pain she wanted her ex-friend to feel. And Paige was truly feeling it. She smiled at the thought and a surge of satisfaction poured over her.

She snapped the lid of her computer shut, slid it onto the nightstand and got underneath the covers. She would sleep well tonight knowing Paige was hungry, thirsty, cold, and alone out in the drain in those woods. There had once been a homestead on the property, the remnants not far from where she had Paige captive. The old farmhouse had fallen in on itself and there was nothing left of the barn and paddocks. It had been the perfect location.

Stephanie turned over, snuggled beneath the warm, crimson floral duvet, and drifted into sleep with a smile on her face.

When Stephen told Eli to pull off the road, Eli's hackles rose. The road they were on led from the highway into Bellehurst and nowhere near the location his companion had described. "What are we doing here?"

"We're leaving the Jeep and going in on foot."

"As men or wolves?"

"Which do you think would be the better choice?"

Eli sighed and started to undress. He hadn't brought along a change of clothes, not expecting to have to shift into wolf form for this search.

Stephen followed suit. "Ok, let's go."

The pair of large wolves bounded through the legion of trees. Once on the perimeter of the site, Stephen stopped and motioned with his head. Eli followed.

When they came upon the clearing with the drain no one was there.

Eli changed back to human form. "Are you sure this is the place?"

Stephen turned to human form as well. "Yes. Stephanie climbed out of that drain today. It's obviously where they were holding your wife."

"Paige."

"What?"

"Her name is Paige."

"Oh."

Stephen pointed across the clearing. "There was a tent set up over there."

The pair crossed the dirt patch, Eli lowering himself onto one knee to check the remains of a camp fire. "Looks like no one's been here for a good couple hours."

"I'm sorry, Sheriff. I had hoped we'd be able to save your... Paige."

"Yes, me too."

They shifted back to wolf form and headed to the car.

While traveling back to Moon Grove, Eli came to the decision he was going to wake up Stephanie Harris and make her talk.

"I wonder where they moved her to," Stephen said.

"Your guess is as good as mine right now." Eli stepped on the gas pedal. He needed answers and he was going to get them.

"Can I make a suggestion?"

"What?"

"Don't go to see Stephanie. Keep her under surveillance and see where she goes. If you alert her to the fact you know what she's been doing, you'll never find out where Paige is."

"How…?"

"You're a distressed husband. It's obvious."

Eli's frowning gaze moved to his passenger then back to the road. "What are you… a mind reader?"

"No. But it's what I would do given your position. I have friends with me. We might be able to help."

"And?"

"There are no strings. We want Stephanie and you want your wife back. Simple."

Eli dropped Stephen outside the inn, Stephen telling him he'd be in touch. As he drove toward home, he prayed they weren't too late and that Paige hadn't been killed. Hence, the reason the camp site was empty. His stomach went hollow at the thought. What game was Stephanie playing? His instincts were to go and make her tell him where Paige was. But Stephen's words rang in his head. Perhaps she suspected the location had been compromised and moved Paige somewhere else. He continued along the street and when he arrived at their house, he threw open the door of the Jeep, got out, and crossed the road. Even though it was late, he had to find out if the witches knew about the change of location. He climbed the front steps and pounded on the door. "Clary, open up."

Ruby opened the door. "Shh. Your grandmother's asleep."

"Not anymore," came the reply from the staircase.

"Sorry." Eli rushed inside. "They moved the location. Did you pick up anything?"

"What are you talking about?" Ruby folded her arms.

"We found where Stephanie had Paige but when we went out there she'd been moved. At least I hope she's been moved."

Clarissa came down the stairs. "The girls have been working for hours trying to get a better reading from the map but it's still just a flicker."

Ruby and Clarissa went into the living room. Eli followed.

"We lost the glimmer for a brief period of time, but it's back so Paige is still alive." Ruby sat down on the sofa next to Jasmine and Dahlia. "We think they transported her in a vehicle that is lined with something magic can't penetrate."

"So you suspected Paige had been moved and you didn't think to let me know?"

Ruby scowled. "We wanted to give you something significant, not just washy pieces of information."

Again, Eli apologized. "I'm sorry. I know you're doing your best."

"And I know how distressed you are so I'll cut you some slack... this time." Ruby gave him a thin smile. "Go home. Get some rest. You're no good to anyone if you're exhausted. As soon as we have anything I'll call you. Ok?"

Eli wanted to wait. He knew he wouldn't sleep, regardless. He needed to be doing something – anything to find out where Paige was, but he knew Ruby was right. "All right. I'll try to get some sleep. Please, as soon as you know anything..."

Ruby nodded. "I'll call."

Eli kissed his grandmother's forehead. "Sorry I woke you."

"It's all right, dear. We're all worried about her."

Eli left his grandmother's, crossed the street, and headed for the front porch of their home. He tugged the keys from the pocket of his jeans, pushed one into the lock, opened the door, stepped into the dark empty house and burst into tears. They had to find Paige alive. Their son needed her – *he* needed her.

TWENTY SIX

The next morning, a knock echoed into the entry hall pulling Eli from a fitful dream. He'd fallen asleep on the sofa, not wanting to spend another night in a lonely bed, and hadn't set the alarm on his cell. He swung his long legs over the side of the sofa, sat up, and rubbed a hand over the stubble on his chin. He needed a shave. Climbing to his feet, he went to answer the door. He snapped back the lock and tugged it open.

"You look like hell," Abbey said, eyeing her son-in-law from head to toe. "Didn't get much sleep?"

"Uh, no, not really. What's up?" He moved aside and Abbey entered the house.

"I was wondering if you have any news." She ran her gaze around the entry hall and living room. "Do you want me and Brent to do another run?"

"I'm waiting on some intel. Once I have it I'll call another meeting." He wished the church renovations were completed. Meeting at the office wasn't ideal.

Abbey's left eyebrow arched. "Oh? What kind of intel?"

"Ruby and her coven are trying to locate Paige. They had a glimmer of her energy last night but it wasn't enough to give a location."

"Interesting. Do you think they can locate her?"

"I'm hoping so." He closed the door. "Want some coffee?"

"Sure." Abbey followed Eli into the kitchen and took a seat at the table.

Eli poured coffee into two mugs and brought them over to the table, setting one down in front of her before sitting opposite. "The coffee's hot but it's yesterday's. Where's Brent?"

"He went to talk to Cooper. I think they're planning to do a run together." She raised a hand before Eli could protest. "They both feel they need to do something to help you."

"Fair enough."

"What are you going to do about Tristan?"

"He's staying put until this ordeal is over."

"Do you think that's a good idea? He needs to be in his home. With you."

"Abbey, I don't have time to be with him every minute of the day right now. He's safer where he is."

She couldn't argue with that. "Ok. You're right."

"Thank you."

"What about this Stephanie woman? How can she be doing this to someone who she used to call a friend... a best friend?"

"She's angry about what happened to her and blames Paige."

"And you're sure she has her?"

"One hundred percent sure."

"Then why don't we pay her a visit and make her tell us where my daughter is?"

"Because we'll never find Paige that way. She's already been moved…"

"What?" Abbey popped up off her chair. "How do you know that?"

"I got a call from someone that found the location but when we went out there the place was deserted. They'd moved."

Abbey frowned. "Who's the someone?"

"Stephanie got herself into some kind of trouble in Washington and needed help. The guy I spoke to was sent here to take her back there."

"Great. What if they take her before we find out where Paige is?"

"He and his friends want to help. Then they'll take Stephanie and leave Moon Grove."

"Which means she could get free and try this again."

That was a good point. And a hitch they didn't need.

"You're right." Eli stood up. I need to go talk to the guy.

"I'm coming with you."

"He may not help if I bring you with me."

Abbey gave a frustrated huff. She needed to be doing something to help locate her daughter, but Eli could be right. And right now they needed all the help they could get. "Ok. But call me when you finish. Please."

Eli nodded and rested a hand on his mother-in-law's arm. "I will."

He walked Abbey out, grabbed his jacket, and flew out the door. He had to speak to Stephen.

Stephen came down the staircase and walked up to Eli, hand extended. The sheriff shook it. "Let's get some coffee."

The pair entered the dining room and sat by one of the windows. Betty spotted them and came over to their table. "How are you holding up? What can I get for you?"

Eli smiled up at her. "I'm doing the best I can right now. Thanks for asking." He glanced at Stephen then to her. "I think it's just coffee."

"Ok. I'll be right back." Betty crossed the café to the server, picked up a full pot of coffee, and brought it over to the table. She poured two cups and left.

"What did you need to see me about?" Stephen asked.

"Once this is done, and you take Stephanie back to Washington, I need your word she won't get free to do this again."

Stephen straightened on his chair, leaned in and clasped his hands on the white table cloth. "I can guarantee you she won't be back to cause any more trouble."

"How can you be so sure?" Eli frowned.

"Because my employer has plans for her."

Eli's frown deepened.

"You did say what issues we have with her was none of your concern."

"Yes, I know, but…"

"Trust me when I say you don't want to get on the wrong side of my boss. He's a demon to deal with." He meant that literally and Eli got the message.

"Ok. I get your point."

"Good." Stephen leaned in closer. "I will make you a promise that Stephanie Harris will never set foot in Moon Grove again, once this mess is sorted."

"Thank you."

"No problem."

After the meeting with Stephen, Eli walked along the sidewalk to the Tribune office. He hadn't spoken to Archer since they'd been out to Matthias's cabin. He entered the store, the bell jingling above the door, and was surprised to find the editor's desk vacant. Where was he?

Eli walked the length of the office and along the short passage to the printing room. He spotted Archer talking to one of his staff at the printing machine and wandered over to the pair. "Hey."

The editor turned around. "Hey yourself." Archer rested a hand on Eli's shoulder. "How're you doing?" The pair headed back to the office.

"As well as can be expected, I guess. It's been almost two days, Archer, and we both know the first 48 hours are critical in finding anyone alive."

"Remember we're not dealing with a human psychopath."

"No, and that's what worries me."

"What I meant was Stephanie obviously has plans for Paige before… well, so we have no idea what her timeline is like."

"A psychopath is a psychopath, no matter whether they're human or supernatural. You never met my father."

"How's Ruby and her coven doing with the location spell?"

"They got a glimmer of Paige's energy but not enough to locate her. But I did have some help with finding the first location."

Archer frowned. "What do you mean by first location?"

"There are people in town who were sent here to escort Stephanie back to Washington. They're wolves. One of them contacted me and said he knew the location where Paige was being held. Unfortunately, by the time we got out there they'd moved."

"Was it Samuel and Heath?"

"Yes, but they're working with Stephanie as I suspected."

"And now we have no idea where they've taken her?"

"No, none."

Archer sat down at his desk, motioning for Eli to take a seat.

Eli paced. "Like I said, we're running out of time."

"We're going to find her."

"I wish I had your confidence."

"These wolves that are in town, how can they help?"

"I'm not sure yet. One thing I do know is once this is over they're taking Stephanie and she's never coming back."

"Do they plan to kill her?"

"I didn't ask, and to be honest I don't want to know."

"They work for a demon that Stephanie double-crossed or ran away from and were sent here to take her back to him."

"That doesn't sound good."

"Her problems are not my concern. Paige is. And Stephanie knows where she is."

Stephanie pulled up at the drain site, her eyes roaming the area through the windshield. *Where is the tent? Why is the metal cover off the drain?* She threw open the door and climbed out of the car, her gaze searching the trees. *No one's here.* She ran over to the open drain and called, "Paige, Paige are you down there?" Her voice echoed up at her. She turned around, her eyes once again roaming the trees surrounding her. "Samuel? Heath? Are you here?" she called out. Nothing. *Where could they be?* All of a sudden the penny dropped. They had taken Paige somewhere else and had double-crossed her. She let out a massive roar. Startled birds in the nearby trees scattered into the air at the sound. *They will pay for this.*

TWENTY SEVEN

S amuel and Heath carried the limp body of Paige into the cabin and set her down on the cot against the wall by the fireplace. They had driven around for hours before heading here so that they were sure they weren't being followed. Heath built a fire and lit it, the warmth spreading quickly around the confined space. This cabin was one of three that Matthias had set up in case the pack had needed to get out of town fast. Somewhere now only he and Heath knew about.

Samuel stood with hands on hips watching the sheriff's wife. She was a mess. They had been ordered not to feed her or give her any water, and she had sat in her own excrement for the past two days. He wasn't sure how he felt about that. Paige had never done anything to Matthias when he'd been alive, in fact, she had stood up to him and showed her true female Alpha determination when Eli was kidnapped by Remus and his demented council members. Samuel had a certain amount of respect for her. Even so, what was he going to do about this situation? He and Heath were party to Stephanie's plan to kill Paige

Blackwood. They were as much to blame as she was. They would go to jail for this.

Heath came over to him. "What are we going to do with her?"

"I haven't figured that out yet." Samuel gave his companion a sideward glance. "She's done nothing to us. But we are involved in the abduction and holding her captive. That's a felony offense."

"Maybe we could let her go?"

"She saw us, Heath. She knows who we are."

"Stephanie made us do it."

"No, she enticed us with money – a lot of money to do it. There's a difference."

"Yeah, ok, but she didn't pay us."

"Doesn't matter."

"What if we contacted the sheriff? Made a deal?"

"After what I did to him? Do you really think he'd want to make a deal with us?"

"Yeah, to get her back he would."

"I don't think that's an option."

"Well we can't kill her."

Samuel paced. "I haven't decided what I'm going to do with her yet."

"Sam."

"Just let me think, will ya?"

He'd used chloroform to get her into the truck once she was out of the drain and it would be wearing off soon. She needed a bath, some water and some food. Maybe Heath was right. Maybe the sheriff would make a deal for his wife's life.

"Hey, Heath, there's an old metal tub out back. Would you have a look at it and see if it'll hold water?"

Heath gave him a horrified look. "You're not going to drown her, are you?"

"Of course not. If I wanted to do that I could take her down to the creek. I was thinking she could take a bath in it."

"Oh, good idea. Yeah, sure, I'll go check it out." Heath opened the door and stepped outside into the chilly air. The wind had picked up, rustling the leaves loudly on the trees surrounding the cabin.

Paige started to stir, a groan escaping her lips.

Samuel's gut tightened and he wondered whether he was doing the right thing. Ending her would keep them out of trouble. He let the thought go. For the moment.

The door opened and Heath dragged the metal tub into the center of the single room. "It's water tight."

"Good. Let's heat some water."

Another groan left Paige's lips.

"She's gonna be awake any minute," Heath said.

"Yeah, I know. Hey go grab that duffle bag in the truck. I think there's some clothes in it that'll fit her."

"Nothing's gonna fit her. It's all too big."

"Well it's better than the alternative."

Heath gave him a cheeky grin.

"Just go get it, will ya?"

"Ok."

Paige's hands were tied in front of her and she had a salty tasting gag in her mouth. She turned over and spotted Samuel standing next to the cot. She gasped air in through her nostrils and her eyes widened.

Samuel tugged the wad of cloth from her mouth. If she screamed out here no one would hear her. She didn't.

"Where are we?" she asked.

"None of your concern."

"Why did you bring me here?"

"Still none of your concern." Samuel folded his arms.

"What…?"

Heath came into the cabin with the black canvas duffel bag. "You're awake."

"Yes."

"We're getting a bath ready for you. And there might be something in here you can wear." He tossed the bag across the floor. It landed with a thud next to the cot.

Paige's eyes roamed the single room. "Where's Stephanie?"

"She's not here."

Once there was enough hot water to half fill the tub, Samuel cut the restraints on Paige's wrists and helped her to her feet. "After you get cleaned up we'll organize some food for you."

"Why are you doing this?"

Samuel shrugged. "Better than the alternative, don't you think?"

Paige nodded. "Thank you."

"Don't thank me yet. I'm still not sure what we're going to do with you."

That sounded ominous.

"If you talk to Eli I'm sure he'll make a deal with you."

"We've been talking about that," Heath said.

Samuel elbowed him in the ribs.

Heath frowned. "What?"

"Shut the hell up."

"Why?"

"Because anything you say can and will be used against you in a court of law. You've watched cop shows. Don't you get it?"

"Oh, right."

"We'll be right outside that door," Samuel told Paige, pointing to the only door in the room. "Don't try anything or you'll regret it. Understand?"

Paige nodded again. "Understood. I appreciate you letting me get cleaned up."

Samuel shrugged. "Yeah, well, you stink... so."

"Did you know I had a baby boy? Tristan. He's in the hospital."

Stephanie hadn't told them about that.

Samuel tried to keep a poker face but Paige could tell he hadn't known. "Congratulations."

"Thanks."

"Get cleaned up. We'll be out there."

The pair stepped onto the porch and closed the door.

"Sam, we have to let her go. She's got a kid."

"Shut up, will ya?" This just made things a hundred times worse.

"The boy needs his mother. We have to do something."

"And what would you have me do? Drive her back to Moon Grove and drop her off at home?"

Heath shrugged. "Why not?"

"Are you nuts?"

"The little kid needs his mom, Sam. You know it. I know it. That bitch didn't tell us because she knew we wouldn't't've gone along with it."

"Harsh words, pal, harsh words." Samuel's head was aching. He didn't want to think or talk about it anymore.

TWENTY EIGHT

Rosemarie eyed the two young deputies sitting at their desks and wondered what they thought of it all, now they knew Moon Grove's secrets. Would they want to become part of their supernatural world? Or would they want to remain human? She stood up. "Would either of you like some refreshments?" she said, crossing the office to the door leading to the kitchen.

Taylor looked up from her computer and smiled. "That'd be nice, Rose. Thank you."

"What about you, young fella?" Her eyes moved to Rick.

"Are there any donuts left out there?"

"There sure are."

"Then, yeah, coffee and donuts sound great. Thank you."

"Coming right up." How could she broach the topic with them? Just come out and ask or go around it somehow? She busied herself with making the coffee and plating the donuts, then carried the tray back into the office, setting it down on the low-level filing cabinets next to the partition. "Help yourself."

Taylor and Rick got up from their desks, crossed the office, and poured themselves a coffee. Rick plated a couple of jelly donuts and went back to his desk. Taylor took her mug of coffee and one cinnamon donut and returned to hers.

Rosemarie poured herself a coffee, plated a pink iced donut and sat down at her desk. "Um, can I ask you something?"

"Of course, Rose. What is it?" Taylor's gaze moved to her.

"Are you guys ok with what you know about the town?"

"Yeah, sure," the deputies said together.

"Have you given any thought to becoming part of it?"

"Rick has, but I'm still undecided." Taylor took a cautious sip of her coffee.

Rosemarie's eyes moved to Rick. "So you want to become a werewolf?"

Rick shrugged. "Yeah, why not? I could do more good if I had those abilities, you know?"

"It's not an easy transition."

"I figured as much. But I live here so why not become part of it, part of Eli's pack?"

"But you may not always live here, hon. What if you wanted a career move?"

"Nah, I like it here. The town's grown on me."

"What about you, Taylor?"

"I don't think I could eat raw meat of any kind. I'm a vegetarian."

"If you became a wolf you wouldn't be. It goes with the territory. But I completely understand if you didn't want to do it. It's a *big* decision, and one that can't be reversed."

Taylor thought it was time for a topic change. "So you're a witch, right?"

"Um, yes I am."

"What's it like? Do people ask you to do stupid things like give them the winning lottery numbers or make a love potion? That kind of thing?"

"No, they don't because I only just came out a few months ago and only a handful of people know what I am."

"Oh, why?"

"Because of those very reasons. I didn't want people asking me to do silly things. I take my gift very seriously."

"As you should. What kinds of things can you do?" Witchcraft fascinated her and now she could talk about it with an actual witch.

Rosemarie gave it some thought. "Well... let's see... I can locate people that are lost or missing, given the right tools. Please don't say anything to Eli, but, I tried to find Paige and it didn't work. I'm not sure why."

"Don't worry, Rosy, we won't," Rick assured her.

"Thank you. I appreciate it."

"Maybe you could show us something," Taylor said. "Not now, of course, but some time."

"Maybe."

The door opened and Cooper stepped into the office. He gazed around at their faces. "Morning, did I miss something?"

"Oh, no, hon, we were just conversing." Rosemarie gave him a sweet smile.

"Ok, cool." He spotted the coffee and donuts and headed to the filing cabinets. "Yum, I'm starved."

Rosemarie glanced at Taylor and Rick. "Another pitfall of being a wolf. Always hungry."

Archer walked Eli back to his Jeep. "Do you think my suggestion about getting close to Stephanie might prove useful?"

Eli shook his head. "Even if it did it's too dangerous. I don't want anyone else putting themselves at risk."

"But…"

"Archer, trust me on this. The woman is demented. One scratch from her and you're history. I need you here. Please don't go doing something…"

"Stupid?" Archer frowned.

"Life threatening."

"Ok. But I think it would give us the advantage because she doesn't know me."

"That you know of. What if she's watching us from somewhere right now?"

Archer's gaze roamed the street. Could Eli be right? "All right. I'll do what you ask. For now."

"Archer?"

"I still think it could offer something."

"Yes, your death. If she discovered the truth."

The editor swallowed hard. "Ok, ok. Go. I'll stay here."

Eli climbed into the patrol and wound the passenger window down. "Give me your word."

He didn't answer.

"Archer, I'm serious."

"Yes, all right, you have my word I will not engage with her."

"Thank you. I have to go see my son. Talk later."

The editor waved him off. "Yeah, sure."

Archer didn't like going behind Eli's back, but he had to do something to help. As Eli had said, it had been two days and time was of the essence. As he walked up the path to the front door of the inn he thought about the dangerous aspect of getting up close and personal with the woman. If he was going to get anything out of her he'd have to lead her to believe he was interested in her romantically. Not initially, of course, but soon into the interaction. He opened the door and stepped into the foyer. Betty gave him a brief smile and wave from the reception desk, and he took a seat in the dining room. He knew Stephanie's schedule.

As he sat gazing out of the window, he checked his watch. It was almost midday. She should be making an appearance soon.

Once Betty was finished checking some of their guests out, she came over to his table. "How're you doing, Archer?"

"I'm well, thanks for asking. How about you?"

"Worried about Paige, as is everyone who knows her."

"Yes. It's a terrible situation."

"It is, especially with the baby and all. What can I get for you?"

"I think I'll have the Caesar salad and a Coke."

"Coming right up." Betty headed to the kitchen.

Archer's gaze moved to the staircase, which was visible from where he was sitting. No sign of her. Yet. He checked his watch again. 11:59AM. Unless she'd made other plans, she should be coming down those stairs at any moment. And there she is.

Archer watched her saunter across the café and sit at her usual table. He'd seen her there before so he knew that's where she liked to sit.

Betty returned with his meal and drink. "It's on the house."

"No, Betty, you can't do that."

"I can and I am. Enjoy."

Before the editor could protest any further, Betty turned on her heel and disappeared back into the kitchen.

Stephanie spotted him and her facial expression changed from unenthusiastic indifference to pleasantly surprised. "What are you having?" she asked him.

"The Caesar salad. It's good here."

"I might give it a try." She smiled. "I'm Stephanie, by the way."

"Hello. I'm Archer, Archer Hamilton. I'm the…"

"Yes, you're the editor and chief of the Moon Grove Tribune."

Archer swallowed hard. Could she know he was friends with Eli? "That's right. How did you know?"

"I saw you here on a previous day and I asked about you."

That could be a bad thing, especially if she spoke to someone other than Betty or Hal. "You did? Well I'm flattered." He smiled. "Who did you ask?"

"Betty. She was a wealth of information."

"She was?"

"Mm hm." Stephanie gestured to the vacant chair across his table. "May I join you?"

"That would be very nice." He motioned to the chair. "Please." It seemed things were looking up. His plan was working.

TWENTY NINE

Daniel and his three friends were out in the woods close to Bellehurst. They'd decided to do their own search for Paige, hoping to uncover something, but so far it hadn't yielded anything useful. They had come out here in human form to roam the legion of tall pines just in case they did come across something and needed to make contact with Eli to get help out to them. Being in wolf form was a faster way to travel but proved difficult in situations like this one.

Ethan raised his head and inhaled a deep draft of air into his nostrils. "Hey, I got something."

Joshua, Braydon, and Daniel hurried over to him. "What is it?" Daniel asked.

"I smell traces of chloroform."

Daniel paced then turned around. "Maybe they knocked Paige out to move her to a new location so she wouldn't know where they were taking her."

"Good point," Braydon said.

"Can you track it?" It was tricky because often the wispy trail of scent would fade out. Daniel hoped this one wouldn't.

"I can try. Come on, this way." Ethan marched off ahead of the trio, past the open drain, down a dirt trail that had tire tracks along it.

"Hey, wait up," Joshua called.

Ethan waved them on. "If we don't keep moving I might lose the scent."

The others hurried to catch up to him.

"Let's stick close together," Daniel told them. "There are a couple of wolves guarding Paige, so we want to find them before they see us coming."

"Ok, then stay close." Ethan kept moving.

"Wait," Braydon called. "We need a plan."

"We can't devise a plan without knowing where they are, what's out there, and how many more might have joined them by now."

Daniel made a valid point.

"So we get there, stay hidden, do a sweep of the place, if there is a place, and go from there," Ethan offered.

Braydon folded his arms. "They'll sniff us out."

"Not necessarily. We'll need to move in fast and take the pair of wolves down."

"They belonged to Matthias's pack, remember? Those mothers are tough. They won't go down without a fight."

"Not if we catch them off guard." Daniel paced again. "We're kind of going in blind. Maybe we should suss out the place first and then come back prepared. That way we'll know who's there and what we need to do to get Paige out."

"Makes sense." Ethan rubbed his hand down the back of his head to the nape of his neck. "The only problem is Paige has been away from her baby son for two days, dudes. The sooner we can get her back to him the better."

Daniel's gaze moved to him. "Eli said he's doing ok. So let's just focus on a plan that will work."

"Dan's right. We can't mess this up," Braydon told him.

Ethan nodded. "Ok, so let's go and suss out the place. At least it's a start."

The group continued along the dirt trail following the tire tracks. After an hour, they came upon a tiny wooden cabin set amongst the trees.

The four bobbed down behind the tall grass.

"Ok, I think this is it." Ethan's eyes roamed their surroundings. "I'm still getting a thin whiff of chloroform."

"Good. Let's spread out and do a perimeter sweep." Daniel headed off to his left, Ethan to the right, Braydon at the front of the cabin, and Joshua out back. After several minutes, they met back at their original point.

"Anything?" Daniel asked.

"No. Nothing to indicate anyone's here. The place is too quiet," Ethan told him.

"Maybe they've moved on. I don't hear any other heartbeats except ours." Joshua stood up.

"Ok. Let's move in with caution." Daniel led the way through the waist high grass, keeping low. Just in case.

When the four reached the cabin, they kept close to the ground and made their way up onto the porch, Daniel easing himself up to the door to listen. Nothing. He turned his head, his eyes roaming the other's faces and whispered, "On the count of three. One. Two. Three."

The group burst into the cabin.

No one was there.

In the center of the single room stood a metal tub half filled with dirty water. It also looked like a fire had been lit at some point.

"Maybe this was a rest stop," Joshua suggested. "Looks like someone took a bath in that." He pointed to the tub.

"Yeah, you could be right," Daniel said. He walked across to the fireplace. There was still some warmth in the ashes. "They haven't been gone too long." He turned to Ethan. "Can you get anything else from the air?"

The group stepped outside.

Ethan raised his head and took a deep draft of the surrounding air in through his nostrils once again. He shook his head. "No, nothing."

Daniel's gaze roamed the ground. "Search for tire tracks."

"Over here." Everyone rushed across to Joshua, who was crouched down checking the damp leaves. "See here?" He pointed to the mulched brown dead leaves. "Something has flattened them into the mud. Even though there're no tire tracks as such, I'm confident the vehicle went that way. "He pointed in a south westerly direction through the trees.

"Wait. If the truck's heading in that direction doesn't it lead to the council mansion?"

"Braydon's right." Daniel frowned. "Why would they take Paige there?"

THIRTY

Eli climbed the concrete circular stairs up to the double black front doors of the council mansion and stood for a moment before knocking. Alistair had given his word the governing body would remain transparent and not cause harm to any, and yet, here he was about to knock on the door to question his nemesis about Paige's whereabouts. He took a step backwards, close to the bannister, and ran his enquiring gaze around the grounds. No truck parked anywhere, the cars in the multi-car garage classic limousines with heavy tint on the windows and gleaming metal adornments.

He'd waited until sundown to travel over here as the vampires would have been sleeping. They were of the old school variety bloodsucker, never venturing out into the sun during daylight hours for fear they would disintegrate into a pile of ash if they did.

Eli crossed the black and white checker tiled front porch and was about to lift the brass dragon knocker when the door opened and Alistair stood in the open doorway. "To what do we owe the pleasure?"

He didn't have time for pleasantries. "I'm sure you already know about Paige's abduction. I'm here to ask you some questions."

Alistair gave him a curious frown. "Eli, what could we possibly know about your wife's disappearance?"

"A truck carrying her came this way."

"And you think they stopped here to, what, drop her off?"

"Maybe."

Alistair stuck his black hooded head out of the doorway to ensure the sun was behind the aubergine horizon then stepped out onto the porch. "We made a pact, you and I, that this town would be governed in a far different manner to Remus's, and yet you come here accusing us of having a hand in the kidnapping of your wife?"

"I'm not accusing you of anything, I'm examining every possibility." Eli stood with hands on hips.

"That may be, but I can assure you we have absolutely nothing to do with Paige's disappearance. Nothing." Alistair gave Eli an insulted stare. "I cannot believe you would even consider us in this."

Either Alistair and the governing body had nothing to do with Paige's concealment, or the vampire was an accomplished actor.

"Can I check the premises?"

"Did you not hear what I said?"

"I heard. I just want to be thorough."

Alistair's stern gaze remained on Eli for longer than it should before he agreed to allow the sheriff access to the mansion. "Very well. You may enter. But I want you to know this has seriously affected the relationship we've forged."

"So be it." Eli stepped across the threshold.

Alistair followed him in and closed the door. "I suppose you'll want to start in the basement."

"No, I'd prefer to check the bedrooms first, if you don't mind?" Eli walked across to the carpeted staircase. The mansion had some serious renovations since the battle they'd had with Scarlet and her coven. Part of the building had been burned; the other had many of its ornate windows blown out. To look at it now, you would never know. He gripped the dark wood bannister and began the climb. The mansion was three stories high with a turret at the top that gave a view of the surrounding countryside, its expanse traveling for miles.

"Is that necessary? Some of the members are still in repose."

Eli turned around. "The sooner I get it done the sooner I'm out of your hair."

"Very well. Follow me up. I want to open the doors so as not to alarm anyone."

Eli motioned for Alistair to go ahead of him. "Fine with me."

When they reached the first landing, Alistair began at the first door on the left. There were four doors on this floor, two on the right and two on the left that led into individual self-contained suites.

Alistair knocked lightly. "Frederick, I'm coming in." He swung back the door so Eli could scan the area behind the black wood door. Nothing except a sleeping vampire.

They finished the first floor and moved up the stairs to the second level.

"As you can see, so far there is no one here but us."

"That doesn't mean she isn't here somewhere."

On the second floor, Alistair proceeded with the same routine as before. Knocking, announcing himself and Eli, and opening the door. And again on the third level.

Eli hadn't realized Alistair had extended his governing body. There were more bloodsuckers than he'd like in the mansion.

Once done with the upstair floors, Eli headed for the basement. He knew the layout of it as he'd been a prisoner here not all that long ago.

"I can assure you again Paige is not here. I have no knowledge of where the vehicle you spoke of has taken her but she is not in the mansion."

"I'll still do a sweep of the basement. If that's all right?"

"It's incredibly inconvenient, but if you must."

"I must." Eli opened the door leading downstairs, stepped onto the first tread and turned around. "Are you going to follow me down or wait here?"

"I will escort you. Wouldn't want you getting lost down there, would we?"

The pair descended the dark staircase, neither needing any light to see by.

After being ushered out of the mansion by a disgruntled Alistair, Eli headed back to Moon Grove. It wouldn't be light for much longer and he wondered how Paige was holding up. His phone vibrated on the center console and Eli pressed the Bluetooth button. "Daniel, any more news on Paige?"

"Not at the moment, no, but I was just at the Moon Grove Inn picking up some home cooking and I saw Archer with Stephanie Harris. They seemed to be having a friendly conversation. It kinda looked like they'd settled in for the day."

Eli gave an exasperated huff. "Thanks for telling me. I'll head there now."

"What happened at the mansion?"

"No sign of a truck or Paige, I'm afraid. If we don't make some headway on this soon... well, I don't know what to do next."

"We're continuing the search. I'll let you know what we find."

"Thanks, Daniel, you don't know how much I appreciate it."

"I think I do." He rang off.

Eli was angry. Archer had given him his word he would not engage with Stephanie and had gone behind his back to do just that. What had he been thinking?

Eli parked the Jeep down the block away from the inn. He didn't want to alert Archer to his presence until he got inside. He walked by several businesses on his way along the sidewalk and when he reached the hedged fence of the Moon Grove Inn he stopped. He tugged his cell from the pocket of his shirt, keyed in the inn's number and waited. "Betty, hi. Can I place an order to go? I'd like the Roast pork meal with extra potatoes and gravy. I'm almost there, how long will it take? Ok. See you in five minutes." He dropped his phone back into his shirt pocket and continued along the sidewalk.

When he stepped into the inn's foyer he glanced around the dining room and spotted Archer and Stephanie at a table by the window. Had they been sitting there since noon? Betty came over to the entrance with a covered plate. "Here you go." She handed him the meal.

"How much do I owe you?"

She waved the comment off. "Absolutely nothing. You do this town a great service and we appreciate you."

"Thank you. I'll return the plate tomorrow."

"Whenever you're nearby will be fine."

Archer spotted Eli and knew he was in trouble, but he couldn't just get up and leave Stephanie sitting at the table. Eli tipped his hat at him and headed out the door. They would have words at some point, the editor realized, but not now.

THIRTY ONE

L ater that night, Samuel and Heath entered the cabin they had shared with their dead Alpha, Matthias, and other pack members. The pair had come back to grab some clothes and a couple of shotguns before heading out. Samuel had injected Paige with a sedative so she'd be out for a couple hours, maybe longer. His conscience had gotten the better of him since he'd discovered she was a mom to a new baby boy. A boy that would one day be a wolf, just like them.

He threw some clean shirts, underwear, and a couple pairs of jeans into a duffel bag and flung it over his shoulder, then walked through the cabin to Heath's room. "Come on, make it snappy. We don't want to hang around here too long. Who knows where the sheriff and his pack are."

"Ok, ok, I'm goin' as fast as I can." Heath zipped up the bag and tugged it off the bed. "Let's go."

The pair tossed their bags in back, climbed into the truck and drove away. Unaware they were being watched and pursued.

When Archer walked back to the Tribune office Eli was waiting for him. They needed to talk. "Hey, Eli, it's getting late. Can't it wait until tomorrow?" He gave him a sheepish glance as he unlocked the wood and glass door and stepped into the store front.

Eli didn't mince words. "You promised me you would not engage with Stephanie Harris."

"I know, but…"

"There are no buts, Archer. This is serious. You could get yourself killed."

"I won't."

"If she finds out what you're doing you might."

"I'm being cautious."

Eli paced, stopped, turned around. "Did you find out anything? It seems you two were sitting in the café all afternoon."

"No, not yet. But I will. Give me some time to build a rapport with her first."

"We don't have that kind of time."

The editor sat down at his desk. "I'm working on it. We did broach the topic. She feigned sadness and said she hoped we'd find Paige alive and well." He folded his arms and leaned back in the plush office chair. "You know, I had a feeling something was wrong."

"Oh? Like what?"

"She seemed out of sorts about something. She covered it well, but I definitely got that vibe from her."

"Maybe the next time you talk to her you can press her for a bit more information."

"I plan to."

"So when are you seeing her again?"

"Tomorrow for lunch."

"Don't go falling for her."

"I wouldn't dream of it. She's the enemy. I haven't forgotten."

"Good. Make sure you don't. Paige's life depends on it." Eli walked back to the door. "I'll be in touch."

"Eli?" Archer called.

"Yes?" He glanced over his shoulder.

"I'm doing this for Paige."

"Keep that in mind when you're having lunch tomorrow." Eli pulled open the door, the bell above his head jingling, and headed around the corner to his Jeep. Once inside, he gave his grandmother a call. "Hey, Clary, how's that location spell coming along? Any luck?"

"I wish I had good news for you, dear, but unfortunately I don't. Everything the coven has tried has failed."

Eli gave a heavy sigh. "Ok, well, they gave it their best. That's all they could do."

"How are you? How's my great grandson doing?"

"I'm tired, Gran." He sighed again. "Tristan is thriving. He's gaining weight and eating well."

"Then that's all you can hope for. I'm looking forward to spending time with him again when all of this is over."

"Maybe you can come to the hospital with me and visit."

"I think I should be here for when Ruby calls with any news. It's important."

"Ok. If you change your mind let me know." He didn't understand why his grandmother was reluctant to go back to visit his son at the hospital. "I'm heading home to try and get some sleep. Another day of doing it all over again tomorrow."

"I know. The girls have gone back to Bellehurst, but they say to tell you they'll keep working on it."

"Next time you talk to Ruby tell her I appreciate everything they're doing, will you?"

"Of course, dear. Go home, get some rest."

"Goodnight, Clary."

"Goodnight, Eli."

Paige woke up in the dark, her groggy gaze roaming the unfamiliar surroundings. *Where am I?* She attempted to sit up but realized she was bound to the bed, the ropes on her wrists traveling down the side of the mattress to the metal base below. "Hello?" she called, wondering if Samuel and Heath were in another room. No answer. She wriggled her wrists to determine how tight her restraints were. Could she loosen them? She kept twisting her arms back and forth in the hope she'd get free. The friction of the ropes burned her skin and she knew if she continued the rough fibers would tear her flesh. Paige let out a huge, frustrated sigh and lay there defeated. *How am I going to get back to my son and Eli?*

Tears slid down both cheeks as she thought about Tristan. Would she ever see him again? Adrenalin kicked in and she tugged and tugged at the ropes holding her captive. If she could get free she could run, although she had no idea where she was. She heard a crack and the rope on her left arm loosened. She tugged some more. It gave way and came loose. Sitting up and turning over, she fought with the other tight rope until it loosened. She was free.

Slipping out of the room into the dark hallway, Paige realized she was in a house. Not an abandoned one, a home someone lived in. She eased her trembling body along the passage and peered around the corner of the open doorway. No one. Where had her minders gone? She didn't care; she had to make a run for it before they came back. Crossing the shadowed living room, she moved the curtain aside and gazed out at the night. A suburban street. She frowned. *Why would they bring me here?*

Samuel's hackles rose as he peered into the rearview mirror and spotted what looked like another car without its headlights on following them. "Hey, Heath, check the rear windshield. Is that a car or my imagination?"

Heath unclipped his belt and swiveled on the seat. "I don't see anything."

"Like I said, must be my imagination."

"Yeah, must be." Heath clipped in his seatbelt and gazed out of the front windshield. "How long before we get there?"

"Another hour or so."

"I think we're doing the right thing."

"Yeah, me too." Samuel stepped on the gas and the truck lurched forward.

They were leaving.

Someone would eventually find Paige Blackwood in Bellehurst and set her free, if she didn't figure out a way to do it herself. They had been lied to by Stephanie Harris and that did not sit well with Samuel. He hoped she got what was coming to her. He once again had the feeling they were being followed. His eyes returned to the rearview mirror but it was so dark out he couldn't make out if there was a car behind him or not. He put his foot down. They needed to get to where they were going.

The Rocky Range Bridge and the turn off was only a mile up ahead. Samuel would be relieved when they arrived, knowing no one would find them there. He smiled to himself. It felt good to do the right thing. And, besides, Paige had never done anything to warrant being killed. Not in his book.

The bridge came up fast. "We're on the home stretch," Samuel told Heath.

As they drove onto the wooden bridge, something rammed the back of the truck and it veered to the right.

Samuel peered over his shoulder. "What the hell!"

Heath's gaze jerked to the back windshield. "What was that?"

"Don't know. Let's get off this bridge." Samuel leaned on the accelerator.

Another hard bump.

The truck swerved.

An even harder bump.

Samuel couldn't keep the vehicle straight on the bridge. He pressed the accelerator to the floor, hoping to get some distance between them and whoever was trying to run them off the road. The black four wheel drive came up on the driver's side of the truck and rammed the door. It rammed it over and over.

The truck skidded across the road, crashed through the wooden railing and toppled over the edge. It hit the rocky creek bed with a loud, crumpled metallic crash and exploded into flames.

THIRTY TWO

P aige roamed the empty house, wandering into one of the bedrooms. She opened the closet and skimmed through the clothes hanging there. What she wore right now wouldn't be appropriate for outside. She had on a pair of boxer shorts belonging to either Heath or Samuel and no bra underneath an over-sized, red checked flannel shirt. *Whose house is this?* There was an assortment of women's clothing hanging on the hangers.

She crossed the room to the dresser and opened the top drawer. It contained underwear and bras. Paige picked up a pair of panties – they looked like they'd fit – and slid them on, then she tried one of the bras. Almost a perfect fit. It would have to suffice for now. She wandered back to the closet and set about finding an outfit to wear. She tugged a soft pink button down shirt off one hanger and a pair of jeans that looked like they'd fit off another. Fossicking through the remaining clothes, she found a brown leather jacket that she slipped on. Her gaze perused the shoes sitting neatly on the closet floor and chose a pair of black boots. They were a bit bigger than her foot size but they would do. It felt good to be dressed and warm.

She checked the nightstand drawers for a phone or some money but there was none. Would there be in the kitchen? She wandered along the hall and through the living room to the kitchen tucked in the right hand corner of the house. Opening drawers and cabinets, Paige rummaged through the contents in the hope of finding what she was looking for. She spotted an old metal canister on the top shelf of the overhead cupboards. There. Hopefully.

Tugging a chair out from under the table, she slid it across the faux wooden linoleum floor and climbed onto it. She reached up and pulled the canister off the shelf, set it down on the kitchen counter, and climbed off the chair. When she opened it her heart gave a little leap of joy. There had to be at least two hundred dollars in it. She would make a mental note of the address and send the money back once she was home safe. She tucked the bills into the pocket of the jacket she had on and searched the place for a landline.

There didn't appear to be a home phone anywhere, so she wouldn't be able to get in contact with Eli until she left the house. Her heart rate kicked up a notch or two at the thought. She was going home to her husband and son. A tear of pure joy slipped down her right cheek. She couldn't wait.

As she reached the front door, and about to open it, a key slid into the lock and it clicked back.

Paige sucked in a shocked breath. She had to get out of here. She rushed across the living room and into the hallway. Maybe the laundry had an external door. She pushed open a couple of doors but they weren't the laundry. The door near the kitchen. She snuck back along the hall, pushed it open and stepped inside, closing it again, her heart hammering against her ribs. She heard a voice.

"Paige? I know you're here." Stephanie.

How does she have a key to this place? The epiphany hit her. The house belonged to her ex-friend. Nothing she'd said to Samuel and Heath had made any kind of impact. They were just following orders.

She remained silent.

"Paige!" Stephanie yelled. "Come out and face me. *Now.*"

Paige eased herself across the laundry to the back door and tried the knob. Locked. How would she get free?

Eli's cell buzzed on the bedside table next to him and he reached across, snatched it up and pressed it to his ear. "Sheriff Eli Blackwood speaking," he said sleepily.

"Sheriff Blackwood, this is Sheriff Steve Mossman of the Bellehurst PD. Sorry to wake you, but we have a situation."

Eli sprang up on the bed, threw back the covers, and stood up. "What kind of situation?"

There's been an accident on one of the old State Highways. A truck has run off the Rocky Ridge Bridge and exploded into flames. The fire brigade has just put it out and our guys are investigating as I speak. It looks like the occupants died on impact. Lucky for them or they would've been burnt alive. Poor devils. The license plate gave us the name Samuel Keegan. I believe you've had dealings with this individual in the past.

Eli's heart pounded in his chest. "How many people were inside?"

"What?"

"How many people were in the vehicle?"

"Uh, I'm not sure at this stage. But I can find out for you." The cop frowned.

"I'm on my way."

"There's really no need for you…"

"I'll be there soon." Eli rang off. What if Paige was in the truck with them?

It took Eli an hour to get out to the bridge. By the time he arrived what remained of the bodies had been bagged and put into the coroner's van. Eli pulled his Jeep off onto the dirt shoulder, threw open the door, got out and marched along the road to the entrance to the bridge. "I'm looking for Sheriff Steve Mossman," he said as he reached the yellow crime scene barrier.

The only cop at the scene turned around and raised his hand. "That would be me." He walked over to Eli, hand extended. Eli shook it. "You didn't have to come all the way out here, Sheriff Blackwood. We've got it under control."

"Did you happen to find out how many people were in the truck?"

The cop raised his index finger. "Just a moment, I'll find out for you." He made his way along the bridge to the coroner's van and spoke to a guy dressed in white hooded coveralls. While they spoke, the cop kept glancing over his shoulder at Eli. He came back. "There were two males."

"That's all? Just the two men?"

"Yeah, that's what I've been told. Why?"

"It's nothing. Just another case I'm working on. I thought the two might be connected."

The cop stood with hands on hips. "Anything we can help you with?"

"Thanks, but no." Eli shook the cop's hand again. "I appreciate the information."

"No problem."

Eli headed back to the four wheel drive and climbed in. His heart had slowed down. Now that he knew Paige hadn't been in the truck. But where was she? Only three people knew the answer to that question, and two of them were dead.

Paige had nowhere to hide. She was trapped.

Stephanie passed the closed laundry door and made her way down the hallway.

Paige wondered if she could make a run for it. Was the front door locked? She waited until Stephanie's footfalls grew distant, opened the door and peered out. No sign of her. She must have gone into the bedroom to check.

Paige eased herself out of the laundry, sneaked across the living room to the front door and attempted to open the lock. It wouldn't budge. Stephanie had key-locked it from the inside. Of course she had. A noise behind her caused her to swing around. Her ex-friend was standing in the entrance of the living room pointing a pistol at her.

Stephanie motioned with the gun. "Over there."

Paige crossed the living room and sat down on the sofa.

"So they thought they could hide you away and I wouldn't find out." Stephanie crossed the living room, gun still pointed at Paige, and stopped in front of her. "They thought they could double-cross me and get away with it. Ha, I showed them."

"What did you do?" Paige asked, her voice almost a whisper.

"What I had to do." She gave another chuckle. "They won't be telling anyone anything anymore."

"You killed them?" Paige's breath caught in her throat.

"Damn right I did. No one does that to me without consequences." She moved around the armchair opposite Paige and sat down, the pistol still pointed at her ex-friend's head. "And I watched them burn."

Paige's heart hammered in her chest and her body trembled but she did her best not to show fear. That's what Stephanie wanted. "How did they burn?"

"I ran them off the bridge and the truck plummeted into the creek and exploded. What a sight." She popped up off the chair and paced. "But someone traveling from the opposite direction came along and called 911. I told them I'd just got there and wasn't sure what had happened. And like fools they believed me. Just like that." She clicked her fingers making a loud snapping sound.

"This house, is it yours?"

"No, it was Matthias's."

"But there are women's clothes here."

"He had a girlfriend that died and he couldn't bear to get rid of her stuff. Poor lovesick fool."

Paige wondered how Stephanie had the key but didn't ask. She didn't want to anger her any more than she already was.

"I suppose you're wondering how I came by the keys." She tugged them from the pocket of her jacket and jingled them. "I stole them when Sam and Heath weren't looking. They were a spare set anyhow." She stuffed them back into her pocket. "They never noticed." Seeming bored by the conversation, Stephanie stopped talking and walked over to the window. It would be daylight soon. She turned to look at Paige. "Get up."

Paige did as she was told.

"This has gone on long enough." She waved the gun in the direction of the hallway. "Move."

Paige crossed the living room and stopped at the open door.

Stephanie shoved her in the center of her back. "Go down to the bathroom."

Paige's eyes roamed the hall. "Where's that?"

"The last door on the right." Stephanie shoved her again.

"Why are you taking me to the bathroom?"

Stephanie gave a humorless chuckle. "Why else? Less mess to clean up."

This was it. Her ex-friend was going to kill her. Paige had to think of something… fast.

THIRTY THREE

Ruby and two of the members of their coven, Jasmine and Dahlia, drove at break neck speed to get to where they were going. They'd picked up more than a glimmer once they were back in Bellehurst and were traveling to the location that had appeared on the map. It was a single story house in a tree-lined street not far from where they resided. When they reached the address, Ruby cast a spell over the street to prevent anyone hearing what might happen inside. "Let's get into the house quickly," she told her companions.

The witch trio wandered around to the back of the property and Jasmine used an incantation to unlock the laundry door. They stepped into the house with caution.

Ruby raised her hand, motioning for her sisters to stop for a moment. She could hear a voice coming from along the hall. She turned to look at them. "Ok, that way," she whispered, as they eased their bodies into the hallway and along to an ajar door.

"You ruined my life," the woman said. Ruby assumed it was Stephanie Harris. Who else would it be?

"I had nothing to do with what happened to you." Paige.

"Your husband's father cursed me when he scratched me. I never asked for this."

"I'm sorry he did that to you, Steph, I truly am, but killing me won't change it."

Stephanie gave a demented chuckle. "Maybe not, but it'll make me feel better."

Ruby moved closer to the door, raising her finger to her lips. She stepped across to the opposite side and made hand gestures to her companions. They were going in. She counted down without a sound, three, two, one, and burst into the room, using an incantation to freeze Stephanie on the spot.

Paige leaped from the bathtub, rushed up to Ruby and wrapped her arms around her. "Thank you, thank you, thank you."

Ruby eased Paige away from her. "You're welcome." Her eyes moved to Stephanie and she walked over and tugged the gun from her hand. "Let's bind her and throw her in the back of the van. I'm sure Eli will want to have a word with her about all of this."

Jasmine and Dahlia stepped into the bathroom and used zip ties to secure Stephanie's hands and feet, then tilted her backwards and carried her out to the waiting car.

"How are you?" Ruby asked Paige.

"I thought she was going to kill me. I thought this was it." A tear slipped down her left cheek. She swiped it away. "I thought I'd never see Eli or our son again."

Ruby gave her a tight hug. "Well, your safe now. Let's get you home."

The pair walked along the hallway, out through the laundry door, Ruby pulling it closed behind them, and headed for the van. When they reached it both witches were lying in the driveway, blood everywhere, and Stephanie was gone.

Paige and Ruby's wide eyes met. "Not as safe as you thought," Paige said.

Flashing red and blue strobe lights lit up the street as the bodies of Rubies friends were tagged, bagged, and lifted into the coroner's van to be taken to the Bellehurst morgue. Paige and Ruby had been questioned by the cop on duty while other cops did a sweep of the surrounding area in search of Stephanie. So far, they had come up empty handed.

Another set of flashing strobe lights screeched into the curb outside and Eli rushed from the wagon up the driveway to where Paige was sitting on the back step of an ambulance. When she saw him she threw off the thermal blanket and ran into his arms.

"Sweetheart," Eli said as he wrapped her in a tight embrace, never wanting to let her go ever again. He eased back, lifted her face up to his and planted a long hard kiss on her lips. "I have been so worried about you." His eyes roamed her body from head to foot and back again. "Are you all right?"

She gave him a wry smile. "I am now you're here. How's Tristan?"

"He's doing great. I can't wait for you to be with him again. He needs his mom."

"I can't wait to see him." Tears welled in her eyes. "I thought…"

Eli pulled her into his arms again. "Don't think about that now. You're safe."

She looked up into his concerned face. "Am I? Stephanie is still out there… somewhere."

That was true.

As Eli and Paige drove back to Moon Grove, daylight broke, the sun's golden rays peeking over the hazy gray horizon and peering through the trees. The silence in the patrol was deafening and Eli reached across to wrap his fingers around his wife's hand. "Hey, are you ok?"

Paige gave him a thin, tired smile. "I think so. I'm just worried about what Stephanie might do now."

"There're some other wolves in town from Washington. They were sent to take her back there. Apparently, she double-crossed a demon and he wants pay back."

"Oh, really?" Paige's eyes widened.

"Yes. I've had a couple conversations with Stephen Knox, one of them, and he's given his word that once Stephanie has been taken from Moon Grove she won't be coming back."

"That's a relief. But in the meantime, we have to find her before she does anything else." Paige wrapped her arms around herself and gave an involuntary shiver. Her once best friend scared her to death.

Stephanie was waiting at the front of the office for the Tribune to open. She wanted to speak to Archer. She needed his help.

When the editor turned the corner, fingering the keys in his hand, and spotted her, he pulled up short. "Morning, you're out early."

"I need to talk to you about something. Can we go inside?"

Archer could see she was distressed. What had she done? "Of course. Let me open the door and…" He sidled past her and unlocked the wood and glass door, pushed it back, and motioned for her to step inside. He followed her in and closed it behind him. "What did you want to talk to me about?" He walked down to his desk, dropped his satchel on the floor and took his seat. "Please." He gestured for her to sit down.

Stephanie sat, then popped up and paced. "Archer, I need somewhere to hideout for a while. Can you point me in the right direction?"

"Hideout? I don't understand." He leaned forward, resting his clasped hands on the desk.

"I've done something… something I'd prefer not to discuss right now, and I need to lay low."

He gave her a cautious smile. "Sounds ominous. Are you in some kind of trouble?"

"I just need a place to stay. Do you know of anywhere where I won't be found?"

Archer gave it some thought. If he offered her his place they would know where she was, at least. "I have a house in the woods that I rarely use because I'm so busy," he lied. "You're welcome to stay there for a while, if you like."

"Are you sure?"

"Of course I am."

She gave a relieved sigh, came around the desk and hugged him. "Thank you."

"No problem." He tugged the keys from his pants pocket and sat them on the desk. "I'll draw you a mud map."

After Stephanie left the Tribune office, Archer was on the phone to Eli. "I gave her the keys to my place so we'll know where she is."

"Good thinking. Thank you," Eli said as he turned onto the freeway heading back to Moon Grove.

"I knew my talking to her would pay off."

"Yeah, ok, you were right." Eli hated to admit it, but she'd played right into their hands. He'd let Stephen know her whereabouts and that would be the end of it.

"I didn't hear you," Archer joked.

"Ok, don't overdo it. I'm grateful for your help. Let's leave it at that."

Archer chuckled. "Ok. When are you and Paige getting back?"

"We're on our way now. Should be there in fifteen minutes or so."

"I can hear you, Archer," Paige told him.

"How are you feeling? Are you ok?"

"I'm… ok. But I'll be so much better when Stephanie is out of our lives for good."

"Eli, are you going to tell the three that are here to pick her up where she is?"

"What do you think? The sooner this nightmare is over the better."

"Agreed. Ok, I'll see you when you get here."

"You will." Eli pressed the Bluetooth button to end the call, his eyes moving to Paige. "It's going to be ok. We know where she is."

Paige gave a heavy sigh. "I hope you're right."

THIRTY FOUR

Paige climbed the stairs and headed to the bathroom. She wanted to take a long hot soak in the tub to clean off the past three days. It had been a horrible nightmare. One she thought she would never escape from. She had really believed that Stephanie would kill her, and if it hadn't been for Ruby and her witch sisters that could have been the case. She was so very sorry that the two women who had come to help her had lost their lives at the hands of her ex-friend. How could Stephanie have changed so much? It had to be Eli's father's Lycan genes. He was a psychopath and now so was she.

Eli had gone up ahead of her and ran the faucet, filling the bathtub with luxurious soapy bubbles. He had also lit some soothing lavender candles and set her phone to play some gentle music. He knew her so well. As she stripped out of the clothes she had on, she dipped a toe into the bubbles to test the temperature. Just right. Slipping into the wet warmth, she sighed, laid her head back and closed her eyes. She needed this before seeing her beautiful baby boy. She needed to be calm and relaxed, not stressed and anxious. It wouldn't be good for him.

MAGGIE ANDERSON

Eli had said he had to make a quick trip into town and would be back before she knew it. Paige assumed he'd gone out to grab some food for them; they would eat, and then head over to the hospital to pick up their son. She wanted him home. As she lay in the soothing water, her body and mind relaxed and she drifted off to sleep...

Something woke Paige with a start and she splashed bubbly water all over the bathroom floor as she jerked her body up into a sitting position, her arms flailing. She tried to calm her ragged breathing and slow her heart rate. What had she been dreaming? Why couldn't she remember? She tugged the towel off the rail, stood up, and wrapped it around herself then stepped out onto the bath mat. Where was Eli? Why hadn't he come in to say he was back?

Paige padded along the hallway to the stairs. "Eli? Are you down there?"

No answer.

How long had she been asleep?

She walked down the stairs and into the living room to check the wall clock. Over an hour. So where was her husband? Had he left a message on her cell? She climbed the stairs, rushed along the hall and into the bathroom to retrieve her phone. No messages or missed calls. She took her phone and wandered along to their room to get dressed. Maybe he stopped by Clary's. She keyed in her number. "Hi, Clary, is Eli with you? He said he had to go out for a bit but would be right back, and that was over an hour ago."

"No, dear, he's not here. Maybe he stopped at the station and got held up."

Paige hadn't thought of that. "You're probably right. I'll give the station a call. Thanks."

"Paige?"

"Yes?"

"I'm so glad you're back and I can't wait to spend some time with my little great grandson again."

"I appreciate that. Thank you. Well, as soon as Tristan's home you'll have to come over for a long visit."

"That would be lovely. I'll look forward to it." The old woman rang off.

Paige gave a sigh, wandered downstairs and into the kitchen to make a mug of coffee. She'd hardly had any food or water over the time she was missing and she needed to hydrate. Was coffee the best option? No, but she felt like she needed the boost. She decided not to call the station. She didn't want to be asked how she was doing. She'd been asked it enough for the moment. All she wanted to do now was hold her baby son in her arms and try to get life back to a new kind of normal. She was a mom.

Paige took her coffee and sat down at the kitchen table. After being gone for those three days it felt odd being back home. Stephanie had had Samuel and Heath treat her like an animal. No food, water, or fresh clothes until the pair grew a conscience and moved her to a safer location. Why had they done that? Had what she told them about her son caused them to change their minds about killing her? She shook the thought from her mind. The pair had double-crossed Stephanie and had paid with their lives. A shiver ran through her and she wrapped her fingers around the warm mug for comfort.

Being a psychologist, Paige recognized the signs for post-traumatic stress disorder or PTSD as it was known by. And she knew she couldn't battle it alone. She would have to make an appointment with her colleague in Bellehurst and take a trip over there to unload. If she left it untreated it would eat away at her, and she would most likely end up suffering a breakdown. Something she couldn't afford to do now she had Tristan to think about.

The front door opened.

"I'm in the kitchen," Paige called.

When Eli came to the kitchen door, Paige leaped from her chair and raced over to him, taking their baby son from his arms. "You went to pick him up and bring him home without me?"

"I wanted to surprise you." Eli planted a soft kiss on her forehead.

Tears welled in Paige's eyes as she gazed lovingly at their beautiful sleeping baby. "I love you both so much." She leaned into Eli and they stood together holding their son.

Stephanie couldn't believe her luck. She'd imagined some kind of shack in the middle of nowhere, but Archer's house was amazing. Floor to ceiling windows that gave a fantastic view of the surrounding woods, soft honey colored wood walls that lent a warm ambience to the place, a circular staircase leading up to bedrooms and bathrooms above, and her own personal chef. What more could she ask for? She was going to enjoy staying here for a while before deciding what her next move would be. She hadn't finished what she'd started and she planned to. She *never* left a job unfinished. Paige O'Connell... no, Blackwood, would pay for what happened to her at the hands of Eli's demented wolf father.

The butler came into the living room. "What time would you like dinner, madam?"

She hadn't asked his name because she didn't care. "Seven? Seven thirty?"

"Very good." Bronson turned on his heel and marched back into the kitchen.

She gave a satisfied sigh as she sipped her Cabernet Sauvignon after eating a delicious lunch. She could get used to this. They seemed to have a connection, her and Archer, and she wondered if it could become something more. It had been a long time since she'd had a man in her life and she felt that, perhaps, somewhere in the future, they could create something wonderful together. He'd helped her when she needed it. That was the perfect start. And she felt he liked her, so maybe once she got rid of Paige who knew what would happen between them?

THIRTY FIVE

Eli had set up a meeting with Stephen Knox at the inn that afternoon to discuss their next move. When Stephen came downstairs he had his two companions with him. He introduced Harper and Hunter and the four sat at a table by the curtained entrance to the dining room. This meeting would secure the completion of the situation with Stephanie Harris. The trio would pick her up, remove her from Moon Grove, and everything would return to normal.

"Thanks for meeting me," Eli said. "We need to get this situation sorted. How soon can you collect Stephanie and get her out of our town?"

"You tell us where she is and it will be done – immediately." Stephen leaned back on his chair and folded his arms.

Eli gave him a serious stare. "You don't expect any problems?"

"We're the best at what we do. We've been doing it for a long time. I can assure you nothing will go wrong."

"Famous last words, I'm afraid." Eli mirrored Stephen's movements.

"Sheriff Blackwood, you don't have to be concerned with our retrieval of Stephanie Harris. It will be done expediently. I give you my word."

"She's killed two wolves already. What makes you think you'd be any different?"

"We have certain... tools at our disposal. She will not get away from us."

Eli's right eyebrow arched. "What kind of tools?"

"Have you ever heard of the Forsythe cloak?"

"No, I haven't. What is it, exactly?"

Betty came across to their table. "Can I get you fine people anything? Coffee, tea, some afternoon tea?"

Eli looked up at her. "How about coffee all round?"

"Nothing to eat?"

Eli's gaze roamed the other faces at the table. "A plate of those famous cookies of yours."

Her face beamed. "Ok then. Be right back."

Eli looked across the table at Stephen. "You were saying?"

"The cloak is made of pure silver... a bit like chainmail... but it's imbued with magic. Once the cloak is thrown over the intended target it renders them unconscious until its removal."

"How old is it?"

"A few hundred years, give or take."

Eli's right eyebrow rose again. "Interesting. And it works on every wolf?"

"It does. Vampires and certain other supernatural creatures too."

"Then..."

Betty returned to the table with a tray of coffee and cookies. She set the mugs down in the center of the circular table along with the plate of cookies. "Enjoy."

"Thanks, Betty," Eli offered.

She smiled and headed back to the kitchen with the tray.

Stephen slid a mug of coffee toward himself. "You have a question?"

"How can you handle the cloak? Wouldn't it do the same to you?"

"I have a special pair of gloves that allows me to touch the cloak without any adverse effects."

"Kind of like the moonstone ring." Eli lifted his left hand and gasped. The ring wasn't on his finger.

"What is it?" Stephen asked.

"I was wearing the ring and now it's gone."

"Maybe you took it off to shower and left it in the bathroom," Harper suggested.

"No. The ring was fused to me."

"What do you mean?"

"Once an Alpha chooses to wear the ring it becomes part of them. It never comes off."

"Well, it can't be good that it has," Hunter said.

"No, it can't." Eli stood. "Can we continue this another time? Later today? I have to go."

Stephen stood up. "Of course, we'll be here."

Eli dropped some bills on the table to cover the afternoon tea and hurried out of the inn.

The patrol screeched to a stop in Clarissa's driveway, Eli throwing open the door and rushing up the front steps onto the porch. The door didn't open, which was unusual. His grandmother always knew when he arrived and came out to greet him. He knocked. No answer. He knocked again. Nothing. He tugged his keys from the pocket of his jeans and unlocked the front door. Swinging it open, he stepped into the entry hall. "Clary? Clary are you here?" Again, no answer. Eli did a thorough sweep of the house. His grandmother wasn't there. *Where could she be?*

He walked back to the front porch, glanced over his shoulder, then closed the door. A thought crossed his mind and he wandered across the street to their house. Entering the home, Eli found Clarissa in the living room with Paige and Tristan. He smiled. Three generations were in the house right now.

"Eli?" Paige got up and came over to him. "You're home early."

"Yeah, I need to talk to Clary about something." He took Paige by the hand and walked her into the living room.

"He's beautiful, Eli. And he has your eyes." Clarissa beamed.

"He sure is a handsome lad." Eli sat down in one of the armchairs.

"Something's wrong," Clarissa said. She could feel it now that her grandson had entered the room.

"Yes, something is *definitely* wrong." He held up his hand.

Clarissa gasped. "Where's the moonstone ring?"

"I have no idea. You tell me."

The older woman handed the baby back to his mother, got to her feet and walked over to her grandson. "How can the ring be missing? It fuses with its owner."

"I know all that, but it's gone."

Clarissa paced the living room. "I don't understand."

"Me neither."

"This, as far as I know, is unprecedented. Nothing like this has happened before. I'm not sure what to tell you." Clarissa brought her hand up to her chin in contemplation.

"Well we need to find out where it's gone. We don't want the likes of Stephanie or another wolf getting their hands on it. Who knows what could happen."

"I'll check my reference books in the basement and see what I can find. Usually, as you're aware, once the ring melds with its owner that's where it stays until said owner has passed on and it's handed to the next Alpha."

"Yes, I know."

Clarissa headed for the front door. "I'll look into it and let you know what I find out."

"Thank you." Eli watched his grandmother cross the street and enter her house.

Paige came up to him. "What could this mean?"

"I wish I knew." He leaned down and kissed his son on the top of his head.

"It makes no sense that the ring would just vanish like that." Paige frowned up at him.

"No, it doesn't but that's exactly what it's done." Eli had a bad feeling about that.

Later that afternoon, Eli met up with Stephen Knox again to discuss how they would capture Stephanie Harris. He explained that he wanted to be with them when they did so she would know he had instigated it. She needed to know that she couldn't come into their town and try to kill his wife without serious ramifications.

"Look, I know you want to be there, Sheriff, but it will only inhibit our task of retrieving her."

"I'll stay out of the way while you do what you have to do. I just want her to know that I played a hand in her capture."

Stephen gave a heavy sigh. "We don't usually do things that way, but if you feel the need so be it."

"Thank you."

"I guess it's only fair after everything you and your wife have been through."

"I appreciate your consideration."

The pair stood up and walked out of the inn onto the front porch.

"Can you be ready by sundown?" Stephen folded his arms.

"You want to go in tonight?"

"The sooner the better, wouldn't you say?"

Eli nodded. "Yes."

"Ok, then, meet us back here at seven thirty and we'll head over."

"All right. I'll be here."

The pair shook on it.

189

Eli made sure Paige and Tristan were safely tucked away at Clary's before leaving to meet Stephen Knox and his crew. He couldn't be worried about his wife and son being alone in the house while he was gone. If things went according to plan, and he hoped they would, Stephanie would be out of their lives forever after tonight. He pulled the Jeep into the curb outside the inn and climbed out. He hadn't given the team the location of Archer's home because he wanted to make sure he was part of her apprehension. Besides, he didn't know them well enough to put complete trust in them or their ability to capture her. And for that reason, he had his pack out there already on standby. Archer included. After all, it was his house.

As he walked up the path to the inn's front porch, the three came outside. They each had on protective gear and Stephen carried a metal case in his hand. The cloak, Eli assumed.

"Ready to go?" Stephen asked.

"Yes. Like you said earlier the sooner this is done the better."

"Ok, let's head out." The group walked down the path to a van sitting in front of Eli's patrol.

Hunter pressed the remote and the lights flashed. "Climb in."

Stephen opened the passenger door for Eli. "You can ride up front as you have to give me directions."

"Sure." Eli climbed into the passenger seat and Stephen closed the door.

Once everyone was in the van Stephen started the engine. "Which way?"

Eli pointed through the windshield. "To the highway. How long do you expect it will take?"

"Depends on how much of a fight she puts up. Usually, we're in and out in minutes... but with Stephanie... well, it might be a different matter altogether. She's a fighter."

That's what Eli was worried about. "So you do expect complications?"

"Not really, no. But we can never be sure."

Eli nodded and his gaze returned to the dark road ahead.

When the van hooked onto the highway, Stephen pressed his foot down and the vehicle lurched forward. "Give me plenty of warning before we have to get off, okay?"

"Sure, of course."

Once off the highway, Eli directed Stephen to take a left at the next road, then a right and follow it all the way out.

When they reached Archer's house, Stephen turned off the headlights and pulled the van onto the right-hand shoulder of the dirt road. He handed around communication ear buds to the other two members of his team. "Ok, let's move in quietly. We don't want to alert her to our presence."

His companions climbed out of the back of the van and came around to where Eli and Stephen were standing. "I'll take the back," Hunter said.

"I'll take the left side," Harper told them.

"And I'll go in the front." Stephen grabbed the case from off the floor of the van.

"What about the right side of the house? Someone should secure it."

Stephen's gaze moved to the sheriff. "Do you want to do it?"

"Yes."

Stephen reached into his pants pocket and tugged out another communication ear bud. "Thought I might need this." He passed it to Eli. "Ok, then, let's move in with caution." Stephen disappeared into the trees, as did the other two. Eli stuck the device in his ear and stood for a moment, his Lycan vision searching the surrounding woods for his pack. He could see their eyes glowing in the dark. Good. They had backup.

THIRTY SIX

Stephanie had eaten a sumptuous dinner, drank some top-notch wine, and was now luxuriating in a hot tub. She felt relaxed and comfortable and was pleased with her opulent surroundings. Archer didn't have bubble bath, so shampoo had sufficed, and Stephanie lay in the warm bubbles smiling. She had escaped the clutches of those amateur witches, felt no remorse for their deaths, and would soon leave Moon Grove when it was safe for her to do so. In the meantime, she would enjoy her stay at the editor's home, and, hopefully spend some more time with him as well. She could get used to this kind of lifestyle.

A knock echoed into the large marbled bathroom, pulling Stephanie out of her reverie. She gave a frustrated huff. "What is it?"

"Would you like any further refreshments before I retire, madam?" Bronson asked through the closed door.

She thought about it for a moment. "No, I'm good."

"Very well. Goodnight, madam."

Stephanie didn't answer. He was hired help, after all. She closed her eyes and slipped back into her self-indulgent notions. She liked Archer Hamilton. He seemed like an honest kind of man. Well… she knew what he was but it didn't bother her at all. Why couldn't a werewolf and a vampire have a relationship? As long as she remained in human form nothing harmful would happen. Stephanie thought about it for a moment and realized he might like her too. Why would he help her otherwise?

If they got together, perhaps he could continue his career in another town or city. She much preferred a city because small towns had nothing to offer. Her fantasy continued as she lay in the now cooling water. It felt good to think about something other than Paige Blackwood for a while, although something would have to be done about her before Stephanie left Moon Grove. That had been her sole purpose for coming to this one horse town in the first place.

"Can you all hear me?" Stephen whispered as he made his way through the shadowed woods to the front entrance of the double-story wood house.

"Yep," Harper said.

"Yeah," Hunter answered.

"Sure," Eli came back.

"Ok, good. Let's close ranks and get this done."

"Wait." Eli emerged from the trees onto the gravel path. "Archer has a man servant, Bronson, he'll be in his quarters at the rear of the house. Shouldn't we get him out first?"

"Dammit, Sheriff, why didn't you tell me that before now?" Stephen's tight voice came back through the ear piece.

"Sorry. I didn't think about it."

Stephen gave a grunt. "Ok, can you go around there and do that?"

"I'd have to go inside to get to his room."

"This changes everything. We can't have an innocent inside in case things go pear shaped."

"I thought you said…"

"I know what I said, but we're not dealing with a regular retrieval, as I mentioned. Stephanie is a ticking time bomb."

"Ok, so how do you want to play this out?" Eli was concerned for Bronson's safety. If he'd learned anything about Stephanie, she would use him as a shield or bargaining tool.

Another sigh. "We'll go in, you get him out and we'll deal with her."

"Ok. Good plan."

"Let's hope so." Stephen headed for the front door and met Eli there.

The other two would keep the exterior under surveillance until they got the word.

Stephen tried the door handle. Locked.

"I can help with that," Eli said, pulling a wallet from the back pocket of his jeans and opening it. A lock picking set.

Stephen's left eyebrow arched. "You're full of surprises, aren't you?"

"It comes with the territory."

After unlocking the front door and easing it open, Stephen went in followed by Eli. He made hand signals and the sheriff nodded, heading through the kitchen to Bronson's room. Opening the door, he found the man reading in bed and raised a finger to his lips.

Bronson frowned but went along with what the sheriff had instructed.

Eli escorted Archer's man servant out of the house, telling him to go and sit in the van, then headed back inside to Stephen.

He'd already done a sweep of the lower level of the house and was now heading upstairs.

Eli followed.

"Hunter, Harper, be ready to move in." Stephen climbed the circular stairs with caution.

Stephanie's eyes snapped open and her Lycan hearing pricked up. *What was that?* Had she heard something? Maybe it was that servant guy fossicking around downstairs. Rather than stay in the bath now that the water had cooled, she stood up, plucked the white Egyptian cotton towel off the rail and wrapped herself in it. Stepping out of the tub, she crossed the marble tiled floor, opened the door and peered into the hallway, her eyes moving from one end to the other. Nothing.

She closed the bathroom door, walked over to the mirror and wiped the condensation off it, then wrapped her hair in another smaller towel, threw the one she had around her on the floor, and slipped into her cherry red robe. Checking her phone, she realized she'd been in the bath for almost an hour and a half. It had felt wonderful soaking in the warm bubbles so why should she care how much time she wasted. *No, it wasn't wasted time it was me time.*

Something caused her hackles to rise. Stephanie turned from the mirror, crossed the bathroom again, opened the door and listened. *There. What was that?* A second door stood across the room, which she'd assumed was a linen cupboard, but decided to check it out. She raced over and pulled the door open and breathed a relieved sigh. It led into the master bedroom. Was someone in the house? And if so, who?

Stephanie wasn't taking any chances. She slipped into Archer's room, closed and locked the door. The tub was still filled with water so whoever went into the bathroom would know she was somewhere in the house, but wouldn't know exactly where. A thought popped into her head. Could it be someone Azzaron sent to take her back to Washington? How would he know where she was? *What a stupid question*, she thought. *He's a demon; it wouldn't be difficult for him to find me.* Or could it be the sheriff and his pack? Either way, someone was in the house and coming for her.

She raced across the bedroom to the closet. She had to find something to wear and find a way out of the house fast. Throwing open the door, she skimmed through the editor's clothes hanging neatly on the hangers. Stephanie tugged a pair of jeans off one hanger and a plain black sweater off another. Dark clothing would hide her well in the woods. She slipped off her robe, stuffed it in the closet, threw on the sweater and jeans, then searched the floor for something to put on her feet. Lucky for her, Archer's trainers were a good fit. She closed the closet.

How was she going to get out of the house?

Stephanie crossed the room to one of the two windows and peered outside. There was a narrow tiled roof below her. If she was careful, she could climb out onto it, close the window, and wait it out. Once whoever was in the house couldn't fine her they'd be bound to leave and search the woods, thinking she'd gotten away. Good plan. Easing one of the windows up, Stephanie stretch one long leg out over the sill and then the other, bobbed her head, and climbed out. She'd move to the far corner where the roof met the house and hide there in the dark until they left. Just as she was about to close the window she heard footsteps in the hallway. She threw down the sash, scurried to the corner, and squeezed herself into the shadows.

Stephen pushed open the bathroom door, his gaze roaming the room, and spotted the tub filled with lukewarm water. Stephanie had taken a bath which meant she was still in the house. He crossed the room to a second door and tugged on the handle. Locked. It had to lead into the next room. Stephen walked back to Eli and the pair wandered along the hallway to the adjoining bedroom. Stephen eased the door back and scanned the room. No one.

Both men stepped into the room, checking the closet and under the bed before moving to the double multi-paned windows and peering outside. Still no one.

"Let's check the other rooms," Stephen told Eli. "She has to be here somewhere."

The pair left the room and moved on to the next one.

After doing a thorough search of the house, Stephen deduced that she'd heard them and got out. She could be anywhere in the woods by now. He checked in with Harper and Hunter. "See anything?"

"Nope, nothing," Hunter replied.

"Harper?"

"That's a negative."

"Dammit! Ok. I think we're done here."

Eli gripped his arm. "We have to search the woods. She's out there."

"You know as well as I do if she shifted she could be miles away by now."

Eli gave a frustrated sigh. "We can't leave her roaming free. Paige's life is at stake here."

"I know and I'm sorry. But there's not much more we can do here tonight." Stephen pressed the communication device in his ear. "It's a bust. Let's head back to the van."

"This was meant to be a get in, get the job done, and get out. What happened?" Eli was angry.

"You happened, Sheriff. You didn't inform us there was someone else in the house and that delayed our process of capture."

"Hey, wait a minute, don't blame me for this." Eli stood with hands on hips.

Stephen's left eyebrow arched. "This was all you."

Eli frowned into Stephen's eyes. He hated to admit it but the guy was right. He'd screwed up their plans of an easy capture. He sighed again. "I'm sorry. What now?"

"We'll re-evaluate and go from there after I speak with my boss."

Eli's eyes widened. "You mean if he says not to continue you'll head back to Washington and leave Stephanie here for us to deal with?"

"I don't think it'll come to that. My boss wants her pretty badly so we'll see what he has in mind before proceeding."

Eli swallowed hard. If they left, Moon Grove would still be at the mercy of a deranged werewolf. And Paige and even Tristan's lives would be in danger.

THIRTY SEVEN

Eli escorted Bronson back into the house. He'd decided to stay for a while, waiting for Archer and the others to come inside. When the editor opened the front door and entered the living room, Eli and Bronson were sitting on the sofa together talking. He figured the sheriff was questioning his man servant about Stephanie's movements to see if he could ascertain where she might have gone.

The front door opened again and Eli's pack members, minus Daniel and his friends, wandered into the stair-cased entry hall.

"Where's Daniel, Braydon, Ethan, and Joshua?" Eli asked.

"They wanted to do a run through the woods to see if they could pick up Stephanie's scent," Cooper told him.

Abbey and Brent sat down on a couple of large, cream colored ottoman. "What happened here?" Abbey asked. "I thought this was going to be an easy catch and contain."

"Yeah, well, that was my fault. I omitted to tell them Bronson was in the house and we had to get him out before we could continue with the capture. Time was of the essence, and I blew it."

"If they were so expert at doing their job they would've worked around it," Brent told him.

"Thanks for the support, Brent, but I should've known better." Eli stood up. "I guess we'll head back to town." He turned to Archer. "Can I borrow the Tribune van?"

"Of course. You can drop it in the parking lot behind the office tomorrow and I'll give you a lift back to the station."

"Appreciate it. But my Jeep is outside the inn."

"Ok, then, just leave it in the parking lot."

"Who's riding back with me?"

Abbey and Brent raised their hands. Cooper too.

Eli walked across the living room to the front door and opened it. "Ok, let's go."

Stephanie heard a car start and climbed up over the slanted roof to take a look. A couple of Eli Blackwood's pack members were climbing into the back of the Moon Grove Tribune van, Eli in the driver's seat having a conversation with Archer Hamilton from the window of the vehicle. Archer had been involved in all of this. How could she have been so stupid to have trusted him? His charm had softened her heart and made her vulnerable. She thumped her fist on the terracotta tile beneath her hand. A crack traveled along it. Stupid, stupid, stupid. She was so mad at herself for not being more perceptive. Tears welled in her eyes and she blinked them away. She would not show weakness. Not now. The editor would pay for his betrayal.

After the van drove away, Stephanie made her way back to the unlocked window, climbed in and closed it behind her. She would wait for Archer to come up to the bedroom and then…

On the drive back to town, Eli's cell vibrated in his shirt pocket. He hit the Bluetooth button on the dash to answer it. "Find anything?"

"Nothing. No scent. No tracks," Daniel told him.

"So she could still be at the house." Eli pulled the van onto the dirt shoulder and turned it around, heading back to Archer's.

"We'll meet you there." Daniel rang off.

"What's up boss?" Cooper asked.

"Stephanie could still be at the house which means Archer's in danger."

"Pull over," Abbey said, her voice urgent.

"Why?" Eli glanced over his shoulder at Paige's mother.

"We'll shift into wolf form. We can get there a lot faster than this van."

Eli pulled off the road. "I'll continue back. Get into the house as fast as you can and locate Archer. I'll call him to warn him."

Abbey, Brent, and Cooper climbed out of the van and were gone.

Eli hit speed dial for the editor and waited for him to pick up. He didn't. Eli tried again. Voicemail kicked in. "Hey, Archer, I'm on my way back. We think Stephanie is still in the house. Get out of there."

When Eli screeched the van to a stop, Abbey, Brent, Cooper, and Bronson were waiting on the porch. The sheriff's stomach squeezed tight at the sight of their ashen faces. He threw the door open and raced across the gravel to the front steps, his heart pounding. "Where's Archer?" he breathed, a wad of nerves threatening to choke him.

"Eli, you don't want to go in there," Abbey told him, her voice low.

Eli climbed the steps, pushed past the four and entered the house. Blood was spattered across the tiles and on the white carpeted stairway. He glanced over his shoulder. "Where's the body?"

"Upstairs in the hallway," Cooper said. "Please don't go up there, boss."

Eli didn't listen. He climbed the blood-stained stairs two at a time, his gut doing queasy flip flops beneath the buckle on his belt. When he reached the landing he stopped. His friend had been torn limb from limb. Body parts lay strewn along the hall. He swallowed the rising bile in his throat and the urge to throw up and took a step forward, then stopped. This was a crime scene.

He stepped backwards, turned around, and headed down the stairs. This was Bellehurst's jurisdiction. The case would be investigated by Steven Mossman who knew nothing about the inhabitants of Moon Grove. How was he going to explain this?

The drive back to Moon Grove was silent, everyone processing what they had seen at Archer Hamilton's home. Steven Mossman, as it turned out, was more than aware of the supernatural element within the boundaries of their town and Bellehurst, and said he would do everything he could to help find the perpetrator, Stephanie Harris. Eli was grateful for the assistance, but warned the cop not to approach her if they got a location. She was dangerous.

Eli's thoughts wandered to Paige and how he was going to tell her about Archer. She had been so distressed already by her abduction and the murder of Ruby's witch sisters, how would this affect her now?

After dropping Abbey, Brent, and Cooper off, Eli parked the Tribune van in the newspaper's parking lot, walked along the sidewalk to his Jeep, climbed in and headed for home. He'd called ahead and asked Paige to stay at Clarissa's until he got there. With Stephanie on the loose, they had no idea what her next move would be. Would she flee the town or would she finish what she'd come to Moon Grove to do?

He pulled the patrol into their drive, then crossed the street to his grandmother's. As usual, the door opened before he reached it. Clarissa immediately saw the look on his face and stepped out onto the porch.

"Where's Paige?" Eli asked.

"She fell asleep on the sofa with Tristan in her arms." She touched her grandson's arm. "What's happened? There has been a death."

A single tear slid down Eli's right cheek. "Stephanie... killed Archer. Tore him limb from limb."

"Oh, Eli." Clarissa's eyes filled with tears. "Oh, hon, I'm so very sorry."

Eli sniffed back the urge to cry. "Thanks, Gran. Now all I have to do is figure out how to tell Paige."

Paige came out of the living room into the entry hall and walked over to the open doorway. "Tell Paige what?"

"Let's go inside. There's a lot to explain."

"Did that team catch Stephanie?"

"I'll explain all that in a minute." Eli gripped Paige's hand and walked her into the living room. Their son was asleep on the sofa and looked so innocent and peaceful.

"Maybe we can talk in the kitchen," Clarissa suggested. Eli nodded.

The three went in and sat down at the table.

"Eli, what happened tonight? Is Stephanie contained?"

"No, sweetheart, she's not. She managed to escape."

"Escape!" Paige popped up off her chair. "That means she'll be coming for me."

"I'll make sure that doesn't happen." Eli tugged gently on her hand and she sat down again.

"There's something I need to tell you. Something…"

"What is it, Eli? Just tell me." She frowned into his honey colored eyes. "Please. Surely it can't get any worse."

"We thought she'd left Archer's house. We did a thorough search and came up with nothing. She wasn't inside. Daniel and his guys did a run through the woods trying to pick up her scent or a trail but couldn't find any. When he called me we were on our way back to Moon Grove and it dawned on me that Stephanie was still at the house. Your mom, brother, and Cooper shifted and headed back there, and by the time I arrived it had all gone down."

"What had gone down?" Paige shifted uncomfortably on her chair, her heart rate kicking up a few notches, tears already welling in her eyes. "What happened, Eli?"

"She... killed him. She killed Archer."

Paige gasped, raised her hand to her mouth and burst into tears, sobbing uncontrollably.

Eli wrapped her in a tight embrace and held her, not knowing what to say to comfort her. They were both grieving the loss of their friend.

Clarissa filled the kettle with water and popped it on the stove. She'd make some tea. Some calming tea. What else could she do?

Tristan stirred and let out a soft cry and Paige eased out of Eli's arms and headed into the living room, sniffing back more tears. She scooped her baby into her arms and held him, shushing him back to sleep, tears threatening to spill again.

Eli came to the entrance. "Paige, I..."

"I know." She continued to rock their baby son.

Clarissa made the brew, sat three mugs on the table, and brought the teapot over. "Come and have some tea," she called.

Eli and Paige came back into the kitchen and sat down at the table again. Paige cradling their son close.

"I can't believe Archer is gone," Paige said, her voice almost a whisper.

"Me neither," Eli added. "I'm going to do everything I can to find Stephanie and make her pay for what she's done."

"It won't bring him back though."

"No, but it will avenge his death."

Clarissa poured the tea then took her seat. "Drink up. It's medicinal."

Paige and Eli each picked up a mug of the tea and took a cautious sip. It was hot.

"What are your plans to capture Stephanie?" Clarissa asked.

"I'm waiting on intel from the team that came here to take her back to Washington. Once they have word from their boss I'll know what I need to do."

"She could be long gone by then, Eli," Clarissa reasoned.

He glanced at his wife then back to his grandmother. "I don't think so. I think she'll want to finish what she started." He gave Paige a thin smile and rested his hand on her knee. She already knew that to be true.

"I wonder where she's gone." Clarissa brought her hand up to her chin as she always did while contemplating something.

Eli gave it some thought. "Daniel was following the truck's trail when Samuel and Heath took Paige out of the well and moved her. We thought they were taking her to the mansion but what if they had another location? Another cabin or house like the ones we've checked out already?"

"Yes, dear, but where?"

THIRTY EIGHT

Stephen Knox walked through the door of the police station the next morning. Something he wouldn't normally do, but he had to talk to Eli to explain why they were leaving Moon Grove. He felt a pang of guilt for not being able to capture Stephanie Harris. He now knew just how dangerous she was. Their boss had ordered them back to Washington. He assumed the sheriff would take necessary measures to capture and execute the wolf for what she had done. And with another county sheriff involved in the murder of the vampire, Azzaron wanted nothing more to do with the situation.

When Eli spotted him he came out of his office. "What can I do for you?"

"Can we talk in private?"

Eli pointed to the swinging gate. "Come on through." He walked back into his office and took his seat behind his desk. "You're leaving, aren't you?"

Stephen nodded. "I'm sorry, Sheriff. My boss doesn't want any further involvement with Stephanie Harris. She's a ticking time bomb, as I mentioned before, and he's done with her. Now that another county sheriff is involved it's too risky for him."

Eli gave a heavy sigh. "I appreciate you coming and telling me face to face."

Stephen sat down on the other side of the desk. "I wish I could help you, but no one goes against a demon. Our lives wouldn't be worth living if we did. He'd hunt us down and have us killed, like he tried to with Stephanie."

"Fair enough." Eli stood and came around the desk, hand extended. "All the best. We'll figure something out. We always do."

Stephen walked over to the door. "I have something for you. Come out to my car."

Eli's right eyebrow arched. "Ok." He followed him out to the parking lot.

Stephen opened the rear door of the van, reached in and handed the metal case to Eli. "This will come in handy."

Eli's eyes widened. "You're giving me the Forsythe cloak?"

"Let's just say it's a loan. I may come back to Moon Grove one day to pick it up." He smiled. "Good luck. You're going to need it."

"Thanks. And I hope we do see you again one day." The pair shook hands. Stephen climbed into the van and drove out of the parking lot.

Eli headed back inside. He and his pack had plans to make.

With the church renovations complete, Eli called their first meeting back in the building for 9PM that night. They had to move quickly or risk losing Stephanie altogether. What if she had abandoned her plan to kill Paige? After all, her life was on the line now. Steven Mossman the sheriff over at Bellehurst was attending tonight because Moon Grove needed an ally. He and two of his deputies that were supernaturally aware would arrive at any minute.

Eli checked his watch. 8:56PM.

Everyone else was waiting patiently for the sheriff to make an appearance, talking among themselves.

"Listen up," Eli said, clapping his hands together. "Before we get started I want to take a minute to honor our friend, Archer Hamilton. He was an honorary member of our pack who risked his life on many occasions to help us. He will be sadly missed. I've organized a memorial for him here in our church for Wednesday of next week. Normally, the body wouldn't be released until the crime has been solved, but because of the extenuating circumstances and the amicable relationship we now have with the Bellehurst PD, it has been arranged.

"We will meet here at 1:30PM next Wednesday and after the service head to Moon Grove cemetery to lay Archer to rest."

Paige swiped a tear from her cheek. She still couldn't believe Stephanie had killed the editor.

At that moment, Steven Mossman and his deputies walked down the nave.

Right on time.

"Ok, let's get this meeting started. We have a lot to cover." Eli stepped up onto the platform.

THIRTY NINE

The next morning, two men stepped off the bus at the Bellehurst Bus Depot and gazed around the city street. Where was she? They collected their bags and walked along the sidewalk to a parking lot on the corner, both sets of eyes roaming the cars for the one that had been described to them. There. The pair zig-zagged through the motionless vehicles until they reached the white hatchback.

Stephanie stepped out of the car and opened the trunk for them to stow their luggage and then the three climbed inside.

"I'm glad you're here." Stephanie ran her sun-glassed gaze around the two men in appraisal. They were both tall, broad, and very appealing to the eye. Her contact in Washington had done their job well. "How was the trip?"

"We're not here for pleasantries, ma'am, we're here to do a job," the one in the passenger seat replied.

"All work and no play makes a wolf a dull boy." Stephanie smiled and started the engine. She had protection now and more was on its way. She wouldn't go down without a fight.

Eli stepped into the station and his gaze roamed the empty office. *Where is everyone?* He crossed the room, pushed open the swinging gate and headed for the kitchen. Before he reached the doorway, he could hear voices echoing out into the passage. He walked up to it. "Morning, you four. Having breakfast?"

Rosemarie picked up the box of donuts and pushed it toward him. "Yes, want some?"

Eli perused the assortment of cakes, chose one, and removed it from the carton, Rosemarie handing him a paper serviette to sit it on.

"Want some coffee?" Rosemarie picked up a mug, sat it on the kitchen counter, took the coffee pot from its stand and poured coffee for Eli.

"Thanks, Rosy," he said, taking the mug from her hand. "I've got some work to do and then we'll do a quick brief on what we're going to do about this situation with Stephanie Harris."

"Ok, boss," the group said together.

Eli turned on his heel and headed for the fish bowl.

"Eli's sad. It's easy to see on his face," Taylor said.

"He has every right to be, hon. His wife was kidnapped and now his best friend is dead at the hands of the same person." Rosemarie took a sip of her coffee.

"Yeah, it's been tough." Rick took another bite of his jelly donut.

Cooper poured more coffee into his mug. "I wish there was something *we* could do to help him."

Rick sat his empty mug on the counter. "We could always go over to Bellehurst and do a search."

"Yeah, we could. But without any idea of where Stephanie Harris would be it'd be pointless and a waste of time." Cooper rinsed his mug and sat it on the sink.

"Then what?" Taylor frowned.

Cooper shook his head. "I don't know, but we have to do something."

Rosemarie rested her hand on the young wolf's arm. "Until we have more information we're stuck. Let Eli work it out. He needs to do this for himself as well as for the rest of us."

The deputy gave a heavy sigh. "I hate seeing him like this, Rosy."

"I know, hon. Me too."

Eli had just finished his coffee and donut when his cell vibrated on his desk. He picked it up, pushed the button, and pressed the phone to his ear. "Sheriff Blackwood speaking."

"Hello Eli, it's Steven Mossman."

"Hello, Steven, how can I help you?"

"I think I might be able to help you."

"How so?" Eli leaned back in his office chair and frowned.

"We came across a damaged black four wheel drive hidden in trees not far from the truck accident. Whoever left it there wasn't concerned about it being found. We got forensics out to dust the interior and came up with some prints. When we ran them through the database they came back with a result."

"Let me guess. Stephanie Harris."

"Yeah. How'd you know?"

"She told my wife she murdered those two men. They'd been working for her and I guess she wanted to tie up loose ends." Eli sighed.

"Damn. That's some crazy woman we got roaming around out there."

"You bet. She's deranged."

"I've been keeping tabs on who comes into our town and a couple suspicious looking dudes got off the bus this morning. I've got one of my deputies following it up. You don't suppose she's getting reinforcements, do ya?"

"From the little I know about her, and what I've seen she's capable of, I wouldn't put anything past her. She's out for revenge and she obviously wants to finish what she started before she moves on. Only thing is she won't be moving on."

"We need to get a handle on this as fast as we can."

"I'm with you on that one, Steven. Let me know what you find out about those two new visitors."

"Well, they haven't made reservations at any accommodation places in town so that tells me they're staying with somebody."

"Yes, but who… and where?"

"Leave it with me and I'll call you again when I find out."

"Thanks. Appreciated." Eli rang off, pushed his phone into the pocket of his shirt and walked out of his office. He stopped short when he reached the front door of the station house, realizing he couldn't go visit Archer at the Tribune because he wasn't there. He tugged open the door, stepped out onto the porch and headed for the parking lot.

Cooper came running up behind him. "Hey, boss, where're you going?"

Eli glanced over his shoulder as he pressed the key fob to open the Jeep. "I need some air."

"Can I come with you?"

"Why?"

Cooper shrugged. "I thought you could use the company."

"I appreciate your concern, Coop, but I need some time by myself."

"Ok." The deputy nodded. "But if you need anything…"

Eli gave him a thin smile. "Yes, I know."

Eli drove the patrol up the steep incline to the church and parked close to the double front doors. He turned off the engine, tugged the key from the ignition and climbed out, his gaze roaming the surrounding trees. Thinking back to the day of the fire, he realized the shadowed figure he'd spotted in the woods had to have been either Samuel or Heath doing the dirty work for Stephanie Harris. That woman had a lot to answer for and he would make it his mission to see that she did. Once they located and captured her she would be tried and executed under Lycan law. After what she had done there would be no reprieve.

He stood with hands on hips doing a 360 degree turn, inhaling a deep draft of the pine scented air and blowing it out in a long whoosh. His eyes filled with tears and spilled down his face. He hadn't liked Archer Hamilton initially because when he and Paige had split for a time she had started dating the vampire. But once they were back together and he learned more about the editor they had become tentative friends, at first, and then best friends as time moved on. He missed him. Moon Grove wouldn't be the same without him.

Walking up to the double wood doors of the church, he fingered his keys, found the one for the lock, opened the door and stepped inside. The silence was overwhelming and he sidled into a back pew and sat, more tears sliding down his cheeks. He realized it could have been much worse. Stephanie could have killed Paige too. He was grateful his wife and mother of their son was safe back home, but grieved the loss of his friend.

A noise behind him caused him to jerk out of his seat and swing around.

"Hello, Eli," Max said.

Eli moved out of the pew, rushed up to him, and gave him a tight man hug. "How are you holding up?"

Max stepped out of Eli's embrace. "As well as can be expected, I guess. I never thought my brother would die at the hands of a demented wolf."

"Neither did I."

The pair sat down.

"I'm so sorry, Max. When I realized that Stephanie had to still be in the house, I sent some of my pack members to try to prevent your brother's death. I called and left a voicemail message as well, in the hope he'd hear it and get out of there before…"

Max rested a hand on Eli's shoulder. "Hey, I don't blame you for any of it. I heard what happened with Paige. Archer told me. And I know he would've wanted to do all he could to keep her and your new baby son safe. It was his choice."

"I feel like I could've done more."

Max frowned at him. "Don't, Eli. You did all you could."

"I have the sheriff in Bellehurst assisting with the situation. It appears Stephanie's headed over there and is in hiding somewhere. It also looks like she's called in reinforcements. Steven's going to let me know the minute he has anything. We will apprehend her and execute her under Lycan law. I give you my word."

"I know you will. I wish I could offer my help but I'm here briefly to tie up my brother's affairs, attend his memorial, and then I have to head back. I'm working with the governing body now. I want to do something to honor my brother."

"That's an awesome opportunity for you. Congratulations."

"Thank you. It means I have to keep my nose clean."

"I understand."

"You know if ever you need the governing body's help…"

Eli nodded. "I'll keep that in mind."

FORTY

Stephanie pulled the hatchback up outside a cabin set among the trees and turned off the engine. "This is where you'll be staying until the others arrive. Keep a low profile. And stay out of trouble. Understood?"

Calvin, the front passenger, gave his companion a sideward glance then looked at her. "Whatever you say, *boss*." A sarcastic grin spread across his handsome face.

"And you can stop with the smart-alecky wisecracks. I'm paying you a substantial amount for your services. You'd do well to remember that." She handed him the keys. "Just be mindful of what I said. Keep out of sight. You've got everything you need inside. No sneaking off to bars or anywhere else. All right?"

The pair climbed out of the car.

"Like I said, whatever you say. You're running this show." Calvin opened the trunk and tugged his and his friend's bags out then closed the door with a bang.

Stephanie's body gave an involuntary jerk at the sound. She peered into the rearview mirror at the two wolves standing watching her leave as she pulled away, wondering if they were the kind of assistance she needed after all.

As she drove along the dirt track and out onto the main road, Stephanie thought about Paige. Nothing had gone according to plan and she needed to remedy that. She felt a twinge of remorse for killing Archer. She had liked him up until the moment she'd discovered he'd been part of Eli Blackwood's attempt to capture her. A casualty of war, she decided, and pushed the thought from her mind.

Whipping along the highway, Stephanie glanced at her reflection in the rearview mirror and smiled. She had gone back to the house in that beautiful tree-lined street. How stupid the Bellehurst cops were. They'd checked the place out initially, but hadn't come back to take a second look, believing that she was either long gone or hiding out some place else. When she reached the street, she pressed the button on the garage remote and as the door rolled up she drove in and closed the door.

She'd lay low until the other wolves arrived and then she'd brief them on her plan to destroy Eli Blackwood and Moon Grove. She had a secret weapon.

When Eli returned to the station, Rick waited until his boss was in his office then went over and knocked. Eli motioned for him to come in and close the door. "What's up?"

Rick crossed the room and sat down in front of Eli's desk. "I – I want to become a werewolf. I want to be part of your pack. I want to do something to help this town."

Eli took his seat. "This is a serious decision. Have you really thought it through?"

"It's all I've been thinking about since I learned the truth about Moon Grove."

"Nothing about the initial transition is an easy one. It's a painful process. Over time it does become easier." He frowned at his deputy for a moment. "Maybe you should talk to Cooper. Get his perspective on being a wolf."

Rick shook his head. "I know this is what I want."

"What about Taylor? Have you talked to her about your decision?"

"Yeah, I have. She thinks I'm nuts."

Eli's right eyebrow arched. "I'd like to say yes, but right now I've got too much going on to monitor your transition as a new wolf. You'd have to be restrained and on the night of the full moon you couldn't go out and hunt. None of us attack people. We live off animals when we're in wolf form."

"Yeah, I know. And I'm ok with that. I already eat meat." Rick shrugged.

"Give me some time to think it over, ok? I'll make a decision and let you know when I can."

Rick's face dropped. "Yeah, ok."

"Don't rush into this. Take some more time to think it through. Talk to Cooper about it."

"I will." Rick stood up, walked over to the door and opened it. "Thanks, boss."

Right now Eli had enough to deal with and deterring Rick from becoming a wolf was the best thing for the both of them.

Eli closed the front door and climbed the stairs. He assumed Paige would be in the nursery with Tristan. She was. When she saw him in the doorway she smiled. "How was your day?"

"Not as productive as I'd have liked. But I did get a call from Sheriff Mossman from the Bellehurst PD. They're monitoring strangers coming into town and are trying to locate two men that arrived this morning."

Paige's eyes widened. "You think they're connected to Stephanie?"

"I do." Eli crossed the room, lowered himself onto his knees and leaned in to kiss his sleeping son gently on the forehead, then planted a firm kiss on his wife's lips.

"Still no word on Stephanie's whereabouts?" Paige asked.

"Nothing yet. But if she's over Bellehurst way we'll find her. Daniel and his guys are doing a sweep of the woods there, while Cooper and Brent are doing the same close to Archer's house, in case she doubles back."

"You don't think she'd hide at Archer's after what she did there, do you?"

"Like I told Sheriff Mossman, I wouldn't put anything past her. She's a psychopath like my father was and she has his blood coursing through her veins."

A shiver ran through Paige. "She's not the same person I knew. I mean, she was always a bit of a go getter and would often push me to do things I would've preferred not to do, but nothing like she is now."

"That's my father's genetic influence on her and nothing can change that." Eli stood. "I'm going to wash off the day and then we can order some dinner. Save you cooking."

Paige smiled up at him. Thanks, I appreciate the thought."

As Eli headed along the hall to their bedroom, his cell vibrated in his shirt pocket. "Sheriff Eli Blackwood speaking."

"Sheriff, it's Stephen Knox."

"Well, hello. I didn't expect to hear from you so soon."

"I have some news you might want to hear."

Eli frowned. "Go on."

Stephanie's acquiring werewolves from Washington and other states around the country. Two have already traveled to Bellehurst, and more are leaving tomorrow. I wanted you to know I've applied for the job."

"Are you going in alone?"

"Yes, I thought it was best. Once I know where she is I'll be in touch."

"Be careful. You know what she's capable of."

"You can count on it."

Once Tristan had had his bottle of formula and was asleep, Eli ordered some take out from the Jade Dragon and he and Paige sat on the sofa snuggled together in the living room, sipping a mellow Merlot. "This is nice," Eli said. "Feels normal."

"Pity it's only temporary." Paige took a sip of the deep red wine.

"Let's make the most of it while it lasts." Eli pulled her closer and checked his watch. "The food should be here any minute. I'm starved."

"Me too."

A knock echoed into the entry hall and Eli got up to answer the door.

"Max. What are you doing here?"

"I need to talk to you. Can you come outside?"

Eli motioned to Paige that he was stepping out for a moment and she nodded. "What's the matter?"

"I found this in Archer's drawer at the Tribune while I was packing up his stuff." Max reached into the pocket of his jacket, tugged out a small drawstring bag and handed it to Eli.

Eli frowned at the maroon velvet bag. "What's in it?"

"Take a look."

Eli pulled the neck of the bag open and turned it upside down so the object inside would drop into his palm. His eyes widened when he saw what it was.

"How?"

"I don't know. I thought it couldn't come off your finger once you claimed it."

"That's true. I don't remember losing it. How did Archer have it?"

Max shrugged. "Maybe he found it and was going to give it back to you but didn't get the chance."

Eli wanted to believe that more than anything, but he still wondered how his friend got his hands on the moonstone ring.

FORTY ONE

The hazy gray fog lent a distinct foreboding feeling to the street as Eli walked along the sidewalk, heading to the Moon Grove Tribune. He knew Archer wasn't there so why was he making his way to the newspaper office? He stopped short just before the door and peered through the window. The place was in darkness, not even the printing room had a light on. Eli walked into the alcove and jerked the brass handle down, then stepped inside, the bell jingling above his head, and closed the door.

Archer's desk was devoid of anything belonging to him and Eli wondered who would take his place. Archer had taken over from Wendy Ellis after she'd been killed by Ross Redmond the town's former mayor. Now there would be another editor to take Archer Hamilton's place at the Tribune.

As Eli moved closer to the desk, a shadow came out from a door under the stairs and stood in the dark. "Who's there?"

The figure stepped into the office. "It's me, Eli, who else would it be?"

Eli's eyes widened. "But… it can't be… you're…"

"Dead? Yes, unfortunately." Archer came up to him. "I want you to know that I didn't steal your ring. I found it on the floor after you'd left the last time you were here, and I planned to give it to you but Stephanie Harris prevented that."

"I didn't think…"

"Come on, Eli, there was a moment when you thought I'd taken it from you somehow."

"Ok, yes, the thought crossed my mind, but only for a moment."

Archer reached out and rested a reassuring hand on Eli's arm. "I forgive you." He smiled.

"How, how is this possible?"

"Right now, we're in the shadow realm."

Eli had been in the shadow realm with Eldridge Crane and the witch Scarlet Balfour, the High Priestess of the Coven of the Full Moon. He knew what this place was capable of and he took a step away from Archer.

"What is it, Eli?" The editor frowned into the sheriff's honey colored eyes.

"I have to get out of here." Eli hurried back to the front of the office and tugged on the handle. The door wouldn't budge. When he turned around Archer was gone and in his place stood Scarlet.

Eli hurled his tall frame out of bed, his breathing ragged, his pulse pounding in his ears.

Paige sat up and turned on the bedside lamp when she felt him fly out of their bed. "What's wrong?"

Eli paced the room. "I had a dream about Archer in the shadow realm… and Scarlet Balfour was there."

Paige threw back the covers, came around the bed to him, and wrapped him in her comforting embrace. "It was a bad dream, Eli, just a bad dream."

"I'm not so sure about that."

"Why?"

"Because Archer told me he didn't steal the moonstone ring. That he found it at his office and planned to give it back to me, but couldn't."

"Isn't that what his brother said?"

"Well, yes, but…"

"You still feel guilty for not being able to save him. Your mind is playing tricks on you." She rubbed his back. "I don't believe Archer would've stolen the ring. How would he have gotten it off your finger, short of cutting it off?"

"I know, you're right. But, then, why did the ring come off in the first place?"

"Maybe that's something we'll never know the answer to. You have to let it go."

Eli gave a heavy sigh. "You're right."

"Let's go back to bed. We need sleep before our son wakes up at the crack of dawn." She smiled at him, leaned up and kissed his lips gently.

Eli lifted her in his arms and carried her back to their bed, setting her down gently on the sheets, then walked around and climbed in beside her. "I love you Paige Blackwood."

"I love you too, Eli Blackwood."

The pair pulled the covers up, snuggled into each other and fell into a deep sleep.

When Eli woke up the next morning, Paige wasn't beside him. He figured she'd gotten up to feed Tristan then gone downstairs to make breakfast. Eli took a quick shower, dressed in a pair of jeans and T-shirt, and stuck his head into the nursery before heading down the stairs to the kitchen. As he reached the bottom of the staircase, the smoky smell of fried bacon wafted into his nostrils and his stomach growled its approval.

"Hey," he said as he entered the kitchen. "Anything I can do to help?"

"Thanks, but it's almost ready. Have a seat and I'll bring it over in a minute."

"I'll just go out and see if the paper is on the porch." Eli wandered through the dining room to the entry hall and opened the front door. He picked up the newspaper, closed and locked the door and went back to the kitchen. Sitting down, he opened the paper and began reading. It was nice to have a weekend free for once, even though they were in a crisis situation. Steven Mossman had things under control in Bellehurst, and now that Eli knew Stephen Knox was also involved he felt more confident that they would apprehend Stephanie Harris, and all would be right in their world once again. He sighed. Well, at least he could dream a little. Would there ever be a time when Moon Grove was at peace? He hoped so, for his son's sake.

He really wasn't on a complete day off, he was on call, so if anything went down he'd be out the door.

Paige brought their plates over and sat down opposite him. "Another pleasant moment for us." She smiled, picked up her fork, stabbed a piece of bacon and popped it in her mouth.

"Yes. Let's hope it lasts." Eli did the same. "Mm, I love bacon and eggs."

A knock echoed into the entry hall and both his and Paige's gazes moved to the dining room doorway.

"I wonder who that could be," Eli said, standing and walking through the room to the front door. His grandmother was on their doormat. "Morning, Clary, want some breakfast?"

The older woman shook her head. "No. I need to talk to you... right now."

"Come on in. Paige is..."

"Right here," she said. "What's wrong, Clary?"

"I had a vision." Her face looked grim.

"Come in and I'll get you a cup of coffee." Paige eased her arm around Clarissa and walked her into the kitchen. "Have a seat."

Clarissa sat down at the table wringing her hands together. "Scarlet Balfour is back."

Eli's hackles rose. He'd had a dream about her the previous night and now she was here.

"Is she in Moon Grove?"

Clarissa shook her head. "Bellehurst. She's in Bellehurst."

"We need to get in touch with Ruby and the remaining members of their coven. Scarlet might try to utilize their abilities by forcing them to help her." Paige sat the mug of coffee in front of Clarissa.

"I'll do that now." Eli walked back through the dining room and into the living room. Within minutes, he was back. "They're already aware. They felt the dark energy when Scarlet arrived in the town."

"This has to be Stephanie's doing. She's creating a supernatural army to fight us with." Paige sat down beside Eli's grandmother. "She's out of control."

"Can we find Eldridge Crane?" Eli asked. "He's the only one that can handle Scarlet."

"I can send out feelers into the magical ether and see what comes back. If anyone knows where he is they'll let him know we need his help." Clarissa's shaking hands lifted the mug and she took a cautious sip.

"He might not come, even though we're going to need all the help we can get with Scarlet close by. She has a score to settle as well." Eli paced. "I warned him not to come back to Moon Grove, remember?"

"Eldridge will come." Clarissa set her mug down. "He never allows his emotions to stand in the way of injustice."

"I hope you're right about that, Gran, or we're all in imminent danger."

FORTY TWO

Scarlet Balfour tugged her floral carpet bag from the hand of the bus driver and stepped onto the sidewalk. Where was her ride? She had been told someone would be at the depot to pick her up, and as yet, no one had showed. She crossed the street, pushed the café door open, stepped into the warmth of the store and took a seat in a booth. If no one came in to find her she'd locate a bed and breakfast and wait for a call.

A waitress came over to her table. "What can I get for ya?"

"Coffee's fine, thanks."

With a judgmental glance, the waitress turned on her heel and went back behind the counter to retrieve the coffee pot. When she came back to Scarlet's table she upturned the clean cup, sat it in its saucer, and poured the black brew into it. "Anything else?"

"No. Thank you."

The waitress disappeared behind the counter again to serve customers sitting on the stools in front of the red laminate façade.

Scarlet sipped her coffee, her eyes roaming the street through the café window. A woman with long brunette hair crossed the road and entered the store. On spotting Scarlet, she walked over to the booth and sidled into the bench seat opposite. "Hello, I'm Stephanie Harris." She extended her hand. Scarlet didn't shake it.

"You were meant to be here to pick me up."

"Yes, well, sorry about that. I got held up." She gave the witch a thin smile. "I'm here now."

"So you want to exact revenge on Eli Blackwood and Moon Grove. Big task." Scarlet took another sip of her coffee.

"I want to do whatever it takes to be rid of Paige and Eli Blackwood and anyone else that stands in my way."

"You're angry for being turned into a werewolf. But you already know it wasn't Paige's fault so why do you want to take it out on her? Why not just deal with Eli Blackwood?"

"Eli loves Paige and if I can hurt her I hurt him too."

"That's true. But will it bring you the kind of satisfaction you're seeking?"

Stephanie gave the question a moment of thought. "Yes, I believe it will." A smug smile spread across her glossy red lips.

"Very well. Then we need to get prepared for the fight of your life."

"I am more than ready."

"There are certain items I'll require." Scarlet sipped her coffee again.

"Whatever you need. I inherited a small fortune when my parents passed, so money isn't an obstacle." Stephanie motioned for the waitress to come over to their table.

"Coffee, thanks." She returned her gaze to Scarlet Balfour. "What kind of items?"

"I'll need other witches to start with. I've been on my own for a while and haven't been part of a coven."

"Well you're in luck. There's a coven here in Bellehurst that recently lost a couple of their witches. One of which was their main squeeze."

"Oh, is that so?"

"Yes." Stephanie picked up her cup of coffee and took a cautious sip.

"What happened to them?"

"I did. They were trying to capture me and I shifted into wolf form and… well… the rest is history, as they say."

"I see."

"Don't give me that kind of look. I had to protect myself, didn't I?"

"Of course." Scarlet realized she would have to keep a close eye on this one.

FORTY THREE

Eli had headed into the station, leaving Paige and their baby son at his grandmother's. It would be safer for them there than being alone at home. When he entered the station, Ruby was waiting to see him. "Morning all," Eli said, crossing the office and heading for his. "Come in, Ruby."

The witch followed him in and closed the door. "Scarlet Balfour? Now we have two deranged supernatural women to deal with." She paced.

"Have a seat." Eli motioned to one of the two chairs in front of his desk.

"I can't sit still right now. I know what's going to happen, Eli."

"What's going to happen?"

"Scarlet will try to infiltrate our coven and use us against you." She sat, then popped up off the chair and paced again.

"Isn't there anything you can do, as a coven, to prevent her from doing that?" Eli sat down and folded his arms.

Ruby threw her hands up. "I – I'm not sure."

"Then perhaps you should talk to Clary."

Ruby spun around, a smile on her face. "You're right. That's exactly what I need to do." She marched across the room, tugged open the door, and headed for the parking lot.

Eli pulled himself out of his chair and followed her out. "Ruby, wait." Once in the car park outside, he grabbed her arm to pull her up. "Please be careful. You already know what Scarlet can do."

"I will be. Thanks for listening." She climbed into her Volkswagen Beetle and drove out of the parking lot.

Eli stood with hands on hips watching her leave. What if Scarlet gets to the coven before Ruby gets back? He hoped that wouldn't happen. He prayed it wouldn't.

By the time Ruby pulled into the driveway, Clarissa, Paige and her baby son were waiting on the front porch. She climbed out of her rainbow colored car, crossed the lawn and climbed the steps. Hugging Clarissa, then Paige, and snuck a peek at the baby before entering the house.

Once everyone was inside, Clarissa closed the door and cast an extra spell on it for protection. No one would be coming in.

The two younger women had gone into the living room and had sat down on the sofa together.

Clarissa came into the room and remained standing. "We can cast a protection spell on your place, Ruby, so that Scarlet can't enter... at all. Even if someone invited her in she wouldn't be able to."

"But will that prevent her from conjuring a spell to control our minds?"

"With certain items in place, it should." Clarissa turned around and headed for the basement door.

"Where are you going?" Ruby asked.

"To collect what you'll need. I have something that will be perfect for you and your sisters."

Ruby and Paige talked while Clarissa was gone and when she returned with her arms laden with candles, incense, crystals, several talismans, and other items, she dropped everything onto the coffee table. "This will do the trick."

The other witch sifted through the small pile of magical items. "We can place a talisman in each room of the house for added protection."

"Yes, and burn the dragon's blood for enhanced energy as well as protection, and Myrrh to ward off evil." Clarissa picked up a candle from several sitting on the table. "And these red candles will return to the sender whatever they cast at you and give strength during battle."

"I know most of this, Clary, but will it be strong enough against Scarlet. She's a powerful black magic practitioner and she scares me."

The older woman picked up a yellowed page that appeared to be quite old. "This spell will prevent her from using your powers for her own gain." She handed the page to Ruby. "When she comes to your home, and we know she will, you and your sisters must repeat this incantation over and over until Scarlet is gone."

"What if she comes back?"

"Rinse and repeat." Clarissa gave Ruby a thin amused smile. "I've always wanted to say that."

Both Paige and Ruby chuckled. At least it broke the tension in the room.

Ruby wrapped her arms around the older woman in a tight hug. "Thank you so much for helping us."

"How could I not?" Clarissa eased out of Ruby's embrace. "Now get along with you before Scarlet makes an appearance. Set everything up and be ready." She rubbed the witch's arm. "I'll be praying for you."

Something cold slithered in Ruby's stomach. "Me too."

Rosemarie came to Eli's door with a mug of coffee and a plate of cookies. She cleared her throat to get his attention and waited for him to invite her in.

Eli glanced up from the computer screen and smiled. "Come in, Rosy. You don't have to wait at the door."

The receptionist crossed the office and set the mug and plate down in front of him, wringing her hands together, a frown of worry on her face.

"What's the matter, Rosy?"

"I'm concerned for Ruby and her sisters. Scarlet Balfour is a dangerous witch and could do anything she wants to them. Aren't you worried?"

Eli motioned for her to sit down and came around the desk to her, perching himself on the corner. "Rosy, I am worried. I'm worried about all of us. I know how powerful Scarlet is and it concerns me greatly. Right now, Clary is giving Ruby advice on how to handle the situation, if and when it arises. We have no idea what Scarlet will do or what Stephanie has asked her to do."

"Well, then, can I go over there and lend a witch hand? Would that be ok?"

Eli's eyes widened and he gave a sigh. "I would prefer you didn't. I don't want to be worried about you too."

"But I can help them."

"You know Clary is powerful, right?" Rosemarie nodded. "Then whatever she offers Ruby and her coven will benefit them without you putting yourself in harm's way. I couldn't bear it if something happened to you too." He reached across and patted her arm. "You're family."

The receptionist nodded again. "Ok. But only because I don't want to put any added stress on you right now." She gave him a warm smile. "You're my family too."

Cooper came to the door. "Hey, boss, are we heading over to Bellehurst?"

Eli's gaze moved from Rosemarie to him. "Not yet. I'm waiting on a call. Everything is in place, so it shouldn't be much longer." At least he hoped it wouldn't.

"Ok. Let me know when we're heading out then." Cooper turned on his heel and marched back to his desk.

"That young fella is so keen, it's scary." Rosemarie turned her head and glanced out of the office window into the station.

"Yes, I know what you mean."

"Did Rick talk to you?"

"About becoming part of the pack? Yes, he did. But with everything going on it's not a good time to even contemplate it."

"Having an extra wolf could benefit us." She leaned across the desk, took a cookie off the plate and bit into it.

"Maybe. I'll think about it."

Rosemarie stood up. "Well I'd better get back to it."

"Thanks for the coffee and cookies. You're ok with my decision?"

She nodded. "I understand."

"I know you have strong powers, Rosy. I remember what you did with Clary, Ruby, and Eldridge during the battle with Scarlet and her coven. I don't doubt you could help, I just need you here for the time being." He couldn't lose anyone else at this point.

Rosemarie gave him a thin smile, patted his shoulder, and headed back to reception.

Eli let out a heavy sigh and returned to his chair. Was he doing the right thing by holding Rosemarie back?

FORTY FOUR

ater that day, as Eli pulled into his drive and turned off the engine his cell vibrated on the console. He picked it up to check the screen but didn't recognize the number. "Hello, Sheriff Blackwood speaking."

"Sheriff Blackwood."

His hackles rose. He knew that voice. "What do you want?"

"I'm giving you a courtesy call." A devious smile spread across Scarlet's lips. "I've been attained to assist Stephanie Harris with her problem."

"Oh? And what problem would that be?" Eli's gut shrank into a chilled ball.

"She wants to ruin your life. That, in itself, appealed to me after what you did to my coven."

"What happened to your coven is on you, not me."

"That's a lie."

"Keep telling yourself that." She was unraveling.

"It's a new day, Eli Blackwood. And we're coming for you and anyone that stands with you."

"Good. Because I have a weapon of my own," he bluffed.

Scarlet's left eyebrow arched. "Do tell."

"You'll have to wait and find out. Why are you in Bellehurst alone? What happened to the remaining coven members? Did they get tired of your incompetence?"

"I am going to enjoy destroying your life and those you love."

"Like I said…" He rang off, his gut churning beneath his belt. Flinging open the patrol's door, he climbed out and crossed the street to his grandmother's. Thank goodness Scarlet couldn't get inside. The protection spell Clarissa had placed on her home when the High Priestess was in Moon Grove previously had held solid. He climbed the steps onto the front porch. The door opened. "I never get tired of this," he said, leaning down and kissing his grandmother's cheek.

"Tired of what, dear?"

"You knowing I'm here before I reach the porch."

"I was a little off today. You're already at the door."

"Doesn't matter." Eli stepped into the entry hall. "Where's Paige?"

"She just went upstairs to pop Tristan down."

As Clarissa closed the door, Paige came down the stairs and ran into Eli's arms. "I'm glad you're back." She leaned up and pressed her lips to his.

"Me too." His eyes moved to his grandmother. "Any word from Eldridge?"

Clarissa shook her head.

Eli sighed. "Let's hope you're right about him not feeding into his emotions because we desperately need his help. Scarlet called me."

"When?" Paige asked, a look of shock on her face.

"Just before I came over here."

"What did she want?" Clarissa frowned.

"To let me know she'd been hired by Stephanie Harris to destroy my life."

"I thought she wanted to kill me... not you." Paige wrapped her arms around his waist.

"Apparently, she wants to take me down and anyone who stands with me. I don't see that as being Stephanie's plan." Eli eased Paige away from him and, taking her by the hand, headed to the kitchen.

Clarissa busied herself with making tea while he and Paige sat at the table. "I think Scarlet will do whatever she wants regardless of Stephanie. She's just as deranged as Ms. Harris is."

"Yes, and that's what worries me. How did it go with Ruby?"

"They'll be safe as long as they follow my instructions to the letter."

"Good to know. I can't be worrying about everyone at the same time, there's too much going on. Rosemarie wanted to go over there to offer her support."

Paige's eyes widened. "I hope you told her no."

"I did. I can't lose anyone else. Especially not Rosy."

The phone on the wall jingled and Clarissa stopped what she was doing to answer it, her stomach in knots at the thought it could be Scarlet. "Hello?" She frowned. "Yes, yes. You are? All right then." Clarissa hung up the phone and disappeared through the door.

Eli and Paige leaned around the frame wondering what was going on.

Clarissa opened the front door and Eldridge Crane entered the house.

Eli jumped up from his chair, rushed into the hallway, and gripped the warlock's hand in a firm shake. "Thank you for coming."

"It's all right. I wasn't about to let you battle that witch alone." He walked into the kitchen. "Congratulations." His gaze moved to Paige.

"For what?"

"Why the birth of your son, Tristan, of course."

"How did you…?"

Eldridge raised a hand. "We tend to know everything about the people we've been in contact with. And I've kept track of Moon Grove."

"Please, have a seat," Clarissa offered, then went back to preparing the tea.

Eldridge propped his antique walking cane beside his seat after sitting down. "So how have you all been?"

"Up until Stephanie Harris showed up things here were peaceful," Eli told him.

"Yes, but then, that's the problem with supernatural towns. They always draw evil to them in one form or another."

Clarissa came over to the table with a tray, set it down and proceeded to hand around the tea. She returned the tray to its spot on the kitchen counter and picked up a plate of brownies. It was a good day for brownies. "What are we going to do about Scarlet?" she asked, picking up a cake and breaking it in two before taking a bite.

"I think it's time to eradicate the vermin from Bellehurst." Eldridge gazed around at the faces at the table. Tired faces. "Don't you?"

FORTY FIVE

Stephen Knox stepped off the bus at the Bellehurst Bus Depot and ran his Lycan gaze along the main street. He'd been chosen by Stephanie Harris as one of her mercenaries and was pleased with the outcome. When he could, he'd contact the sheriff to let him know he'd arrived and wait for instructions as to what course of action to take. In the meantime, he would play along with whatever the deranged psychopath requested, within reason, and keep track of her movements – and anything else that might prove useful.

When his eyes returned to the blue Greyhound bus, the driver had opened up the baggage compartment so passengers could retrieve their luggage. Stephen picked up his over-sized, brown suede duffel bag, slung it over his shoulder and headed for the corner. He'd been told a car would be there to pick him up and take him to the accommodations arranged for them. As he reached the intersection, a dark green pickup pulled into the curb and the driver wound down the passenger window. "Hey, pal, are you Stephen Knox?"

"Yes, I am."

The guy waved him over. "Throw your stuff in back and climb in."

"Ok." Stephen tossed his heavy bag into the tray and got into the truck.

The driver extended his hand. "I'm Wade."

"Hi. Thanks for picking me up."

"No problem." He pushed his booted foot down on the accelerator and the pickup puttered off along the road.

"Where are we going?"

"We've got a cabin in the woods not far from here. There're some other guys already out there too. We're coming in on a daily basis at the moment."

"Oh, ok. Is the place big enough for everyone because if not I can find somewhere in town?"

"Nah, it's all good. There's plenty of room. Some guys are choosing to set up tents outside anyway, so..." He shrugged.

"Ok. Cool."

Silence.

Stephen didn't want to make the guy suspicious so he didn't ask any more questions. He'd get a feel for the place and the guys out there and work from there."

About five miles out of town, the truck took a right and headed into the thicker part of the woods. The tall pines clustered closer together gave the forest an eerie feel.

"So, you're a wolf too?" the driver asked.

"Uh, yeah. Did you come from Washington?"

"Nah, Los Angeles. I saw the ad in the paper and called the number... and here I am."

"Fair enough."

"What about you? You from Washington I gather?"

"Yeah, I live just outside the capitol."

"What do you do? What's your line of work?"

"I do a few different things. I have a small team and we do PI work, retrievals, that kinda thing. What about you?"

"I'm a tradesman. Plumbing."

"Yeah? Cool."

More silence.

After another thirty minutes Wade said, "We're almost there."

"Good. I'm pretty tired. The bus ride was long."

"Yeah. And not all that comfortable. Kinda hard sleeping sitting up."

"I hear you. How's cell reception out here?"

"Not great. Why? You need to call somebody?"

"Yeah, my girlfriend asked me to give her a call as soon as I got settled in." Stephen had to think quick. He didn't have a girlfriend.

Wade made a whipping motion above the steering wheel and chuckled.

"It's not like that. She worries about me when I'm away."

"Ok. Whatever you say."

They pulled up at a metal gate blocking access to the continuing dirt track with a chain link fence traveling in each direction as far as the eye could see. Wade got out to unlock the padlock and push the gate back, then climbed in, drove the pickup through and climbed out to relock it.

Stephen didn't like the feeling of being trapped.

Eldridge came downstairs and walked through the entry hall to the kitchen. He would stay with Clarissa Baker for the time he was in Moon Grove and was grateful for the humble accommodations. "It would be remiss of me not to thank you for your hospitality," he offered.

Clarissa smiled. "It's the least I can do."

Eli stood up. "Can we talk in the living room for a bit?"

Eldridge's right eyebrow arched. "Of course." His gaze moved from the sheriff to Clarissa. "Would it be rude of me to ask for a cup of coffee?"

"Not at all." Clarissa got to her feet. "I'll bring it in once it's made."

"Thank you, kind lady." He smiled, then turned on his heel and followed Eli into the living room, taking a seat in one of the armchairs, crossing one leg over the other, and clasping his hands in his lap. To look at him, you would think the warlock was in his late thirties, early forties, but by his attire you would think he time traveled here from the 16th century or there about. His dark hair, square jaw, and piercing eyes gave him an ominous appearance as well. "I gather there is something on your mind, Eli Blackwood. Would you like to convey your thoughts?"

Eli sat down on the sofa opposite him. "I'm concerned for Ruby and the remaining coven members. Clary has provided some instructions and other items as protection, but we don't know what Scarlet is capable of now and whether or not her powers have increased."

"I'm sure whatever your grandmother has offered will be of great value. She's an incredibly powerful witch."

"Yes, I know. Were you aware that Stephanie Harris killed the High Priestess and another member of their coven?"

"I was made aware of it, yes." Eldridge unclasped his hands and leaned forward. "That is something she will pay for."

"And she will. I'm in contact with Sheriff Steven Mossman at Bellehurst. He's looking into Stephanie's location as we speak."

"Excellent. The sooner we know where she is the better it will be for us all."

Clarissa came into the living room with a tray and set it down on the coffee table, before picking up one mug and passing it to Eldridge, then picking up the other and passing it to her grandson. She left the plate of brownies sitting in the middle of the tray and went back to Paige in the kitchen. She didn't want to interrupt their conversation.

Eldridge glanced over his shoulder as she left. "Thank you, Ms. Baker. Very much appreciated." He reached across and picked up a brownie, held it up and said, "These are delicious."

"Yes, it's my mom's recipe."

"We need to put plans in motion, Eli Blackwood." His eyes moved back to the cake in his hand. "Once I devour this scrumptious sweet treat."

After talking to Eldridge at length, the time ticking by, Eli left his grandmother's house, crossed the street and entered his. Paige had gone home to feed Tristan and get him ready for bed, and with Stephanie in Bellehurst, the issue of safety wasn't a problem right now.

He climbed the stairs and walked along the hallway to the nursery, poked his head in and found Paige asleep in the rocking chair with Tristan wrapped firmly in her arms. This situation was wearing everyone down. He snuck backwards and made his way down to their bedroom to take a quick shower and change out of his uniform, then he'd order some dinner for a seven o'clock delivery.

Having Eldridge Crane in Moon Grove gave him the confidence he needed to ensure they would finish what Scarlet had started when she was here last, and to locate and capture Stephanie Harris so she could be tried and executed for the crimes she had and would commit. Shrugging out of his shirt, stepping out of his jeans and boxers, and wandering into the bathroom, Eli turned on the shower and felt the exhaustion hit him like a dense dark wave when he stepped under the hot spray of water.

A noise behind him made him swing around and he saw Paige standing in the doorway. "Mind if I join you?" She came into the room, stripped down, and stepped into the shower with her husband.

"Not at all." Eli cupped her face in his hands, raised her chin up and kissed her hard on the mouth. "We're going to get through this, Paige. You have my word."

"I know we are." She wrapped her arms around his neck and pressed her lips to his.

FORTY SIX

The next morning, Eli pulled open the drawer to his nightstand and noticed the small maroon drawstring bag Max had given him a few nights before. It disturbed him because when he'd tried to put the ring back on his finger it wouldn't take. Why had the ring come off at all? And why wouldn't it allow him to accept it again? Questions he hoped his grandmother would be able to find answers to. He dropped the bag into the drawer, closed it and headed back downstairs.

He had made breakfast this morning, and Paige was enjoying some time to eat her meal without having to make it.

Eli came into the kitchen and sat at the table opposite her. "Tristan is sleeping peacefully so no need to worry. How's the eggs?"

"You know I love your scrambled eggs. I was just remembering the first time you made them for me." She smiled. "You'd spent the night on my sofa because of the break ins and offered to make me breakfast."

He nodded. "I remember. Do I still make mean scrambled eggs?"

"You sure do." She scooped more onto her fork and popped it in her mouth. "Mm."

"What's happening with your clients?"

"I'm doing phone consultations with them for the time being, seeing as I don't want to let our son out of my sight with what's going on."

"Agreed. How is that working for you?"

"Pretty good, actually. And they don't seem to mind at all. It's still confidential and no one has to travel for a consult. So it's a win win." She smiled.

"Good. I'm glad." Eli finished his coffee and stood up. "I'd better get moving. Clary's going to come over and spend some time with you later." He sat his dishes and mug in the dishwasher.

"She doesn't have to. I'm sure she has other things to do, and we'll be fine here. The protection spell will keep any supernatural creature out, including Scarlet and Stephanie so…"

Eli kissed the top of her head. "Just be safe. And if you need me call."

"I will. Have a good day."

"You too. Bye." Eli headed out the door. Would it be a good day? He hoped he'd hear from Stephen Knox.

When he pulled into the station's parking lot, Rick and Taylor were also parking their cars. He gave them both a brief wave and headed inside.

The deputies caught up to him and followed him in.

"Any word on the location of Stephanie Harris yet, boss?" Rick asked.

"I'm hoping to hear something today. The Bellehurst PD are patrolling the streets looking for anything out of the ordinary, and the sheriff there said as soon as they have anything he'd let me know. We also have a mole on Stephanie's team. You remember the three that came to Moon Grove to take her back to Washington?" Everyone nodded. "He answered her ad and is now part of her supernatural army." Eli pushed through the swinging gate and headed for his office. "Oh, by the way. Eldridge Crane is back in town. He's here to offer his assistance."

Rosemarie popped up off her office chair. "He is? Oh my."

"With Scarlet Balfour being in Bellehurst, I thought it best to have someone with powers equal to hers to help us fight."

"Yes, and he's proficient in both types of magic – white and dark." Rosemarie walked over to the door leading to the kitchen. "Anyone want some refreshments?"

"That'd be nice, Rosy," Eli said. "Do you need a hand?"

She waved the comment off. "Oh my, of course not. It's certainly not a chore making coffee for you guys."

"Appreciated." Eli stepped into his office and closed the door.

Cooper stood with hands on hips. "Eldridge Crane is in Moon Grove? He helped us defeat Scarlet Balfour before, so it's good he's come back to offer assistance again."

Taylor frowned. "Who is he?"

"He's a warlock… and ancient warlock with powers that are light and dark."

"He sounds scary."

"There are scarier creatures than him out there, Taylor. You don't know the half of it." Cooper crossed the office and sat down at his desk.

"Like what?" Rick asked, folding his arms and leaning back on his chair.

"We had an ancient vampire here a couple years ago. Now what was his name? Oh yeah, Gregor Petrov. He was a mean mother. He drank some of Paige's blood, after mesmerizing her and stealing it, and turned into a hideous monster."

"What the hell?" Rick came around his desk and sat on the corner.

"Yeah, he killed everyone in our pack, except me, and Eli, of course." Cooper's expression change to sadness.

"Hey, Coop, it wasn't your fault."

"I know, but we lost good people. People I considered family."

"That's tough."

Cooper nodded.

Rosemarie came back into the office with a tray loaded with coffee pot, mugs, sugar, milk and muffins. "As usual, help yourself." She plated a couple of muffins for Eli, picked up the mug of coffee and took it in to him.

"I'm going to gain ten pounds eating like this every day," Taylor joked, biting into a blueberry muffin. "But, damn, these are the best."

"Rosy makes 'em," Cooper told the pair.

"Wow. Well they're great."

"I'm sure she'd like to hear that." Cooper took his coffee mug over to his desk.

When Rosemarie came back into the office Taylor told her how awesome her muffins were. It put a smile on the receptionist's face. "Well thank you, darlin'. Aren't you sweet."

The door to the station swung open and Eldridge Crane walked in. "Good morning. Eli about?"

Rosemarie's eyes widened and she pointed to the fish bowl. "Can I get you anything?"

Eldridge crossed the office, pushed through the swinging gate and perused the morning tea. "Alright if I take one of those?" he asked, pointing to the blueberry muffins.

The receptionist's cheeks flushed. "Of course. Help yourself. Do you want coffee to go with it?"

He raised his hand. "I can manage. Thank you." He poured himself a coffee, picked up the mug and muffin and stepped into Eli's office, closing the door behind him.

"So that was Eldridge Crane?" Taylor asked.

"Yep," Rosemarie said.

"Eldridge. What can I do for you?" Eli stood and shook the warlock's hand.

"I see you have some newbies in the office. And not supernatural beings either."

"They're aware though." Eli motioned to the chairs. "Please have a seat."

"Thank you." Eldridge placed the mug of coffee and muffin on Eli's desk and folded his arms. "Any word from your mole?"

"He's not my mole as such, but no not yet. I'm hoping to hear from him today."

"Nothing from Bellehurst PD?"

Eli shook his head. "Nope, nothing."

"I think it's essential to prep your pack and be ready to move. Wouldn't you say?"

"We are prepped. I just need to know where Stephanie Harris is and we're good to go."

"All right then. Looking forward to getting this situation under control so you and your wife can enjoy your son." The warlock picked up the blueberry muffin and took a substantial bite. "These are so good."

"Rosy makes them."

"Well, isn't she a clever little witch." He smiled and popped the rest of the muffin into his mouth.

FORTY SEVEN

Stephen Knox walked into the small kitchen to pour himself a coffee and to see who was still inside. Most of the guys had gone out onto the front porch to talk, smoke, and get some much-needed sun in their bones. He wondered if they were allowed to leave the property to go into town, and figured they probably weren't able to. But it couldn't hurt to ask. He needed to get in touch with Eli, although, at this stage, he didn't have a lot of information to share. No one here knew anything, just like him. They were being kept in the dark.

"Hey, Wade." Stephen wandered over to him.

"Hey, yourself." He stuck his hands into the pockets of his jeans. "Must've been real tired."

"Uh, yeah, I was. Is there any chance of getting a lift into town?"

Wade's right eyebrow arched. "Do you need something?"

"I need to call my girlfriend. She'll be worried. Like you said there's no reception out here, at least none I can find." He glanced at his cell in his hand. "I also need a couple things I forgot to pack."

"Yeah, the reception is pretty bad. I play this online game on my phone and I can't even do that. I was winning but now I'll have fallen behind." Wade's gaze moved to the pickup. "We've been told to keep a low profile. Not to get into any trouble."

"I get that, but does it mean we can't leave?"

Wade shrugged. "Don't know." He walked along the porch and into the cabin, then returned with the keys for the pickup. "Let's find out."

"Great. Thanks."

"Hey, if the spam hits the fan I'm blaming you." Wade chuckled.

"Fair enough. I really appreciate you doing this."

"Yeah, well, you don't want to disappoint your girl. Wouldn't be a good thing."

The pair climbed into the truck.

Eli's phone vibrated on his desk and he snatched it up hoping it was Stephen Knox. "Sheriff Blackwood speaking."

"Sheriff, it's Stephen. I don't have a lot of time. There are eight of us holed up in a cabin about six to seven miles east of Bellehurst. Right now, no one knows what the story is. They haven't been made privy to any information. From what I can gather, Stephanie is staying in town somewhere. Someone mentioned a house, but no one knows where it is."

"Are you ok?"

"Yeah, I'm fine. None of the guys suspect me."

"That's good. So Stephanie hasn't been in contact?"

"Not yet."

Eli frowned. "I wonder what she's planning."

"My thoughts exactly."

"She's acquired the help of a dangerous witch. We've had encounters with her before and none of them good. Be careful. If you need help contact the local PD there. The sheriff is assisting us and he knows what's going on."

"Will do. Hey, I'd better go."

"Be safe. And try to let me know what's happening when you can. We need to keep one step ahead of Stephanie if possible, for the safety of us all."

"As soon as I know anything I'll be in touch."

"Ok. Take care."

"Yeah, you too." Stephen rang off.

Eli frowned at the phone in his hand. He hoped Stephen wouldn't be discovered and something crucial would come to light. Without anything to go on, they would be going in blind, and with Scarlet helping Stephanie that would be a very dangerous move. Unless...

The snap meeting at the church had everyone on edge. Eli stood on the platform with hands on hips gazing at the concerned faces sitting in front of him. The idea had come to him the moment he'd finished speaking to Stephen Knox, and Eli hoped he wouldn't be angry when his plan was implemented. But it was something he had to do to ensure the fight was weighted in their favor.

He clapped his hands to get everyone's attention. "Ok, listen up. Our informant has been in touch and I have a basic idea of where he and the other wolves are located.

We're moving in to capture them and lock them up. It will give us the advantage, at least against the wolves."

Rosemarie raised her hand. "Eli, wouldn't it be more effective if we can locate Stephanie and Scarlet and deal with them? I mean, once they're out of the picture the guys she hired will leave and go back to wherever they came from."

"Good point, Rosy," Eli said. "Finding Stephanie hasn't yielded anything so far, so I think we need to knock out the competition."

Brent stood up, shoved his hands into the pockets of his charcoal hoodie. "Then we still have to deal with the witch and Paige's ex-friend. Scarlet is more powerful than all those wolves together."

"Yes, I'm aware. But I think if we can undermine her plan it might unnerve her and cause her to make a mistake."

Abbey raised her hand. "So Sheriff Mossman's men haven't found out anything?"

"Not yet. They've done a thorough sweep of Bellehurst and have come up empty handed."

Abbey frowned and thought for a moment before speaking again. "What if she went back to the house Paige was held in? If the sheriff's team already checked it out they wouldn't need to again. Maybe she's there for that very reason. It would be a safe house."

Eli folded his arms. *Abbey could be right.* "I'll give the sheriff a call and head over there to take a look. I want you all to be on standby. We're moving in today. This can't wait any longer."

Eldridge Crane stood. "May I make a suggestion?"

"Of course," Eli said.

"I can place a containment spell on the house to lock the woman and the witch inside. Would that not offer a more appropriate means of capture?"

"What if Scarlet can break the spell? We have no idea how powerful she is now."

"This is true. Nonetheless, my powers are far more advanced. I believe it would work successfully."

"And how do we get in to get them out?"

"Anyone can enter…"

"But no one can leave?"

"Not until I bind the witch. And you capture Stephanie. Then I can release the spell."

"Are you sure it'll work?"

Rosemarie popped up off the pew. "Yes, Eli, it'll work. If Eldridge binds Scarlet she won't be able to use her magic."

Eldridge's serious gaze moved to the witch and he gave her a brief smile. She was smart.

Eli gave a heavy sigh. "I still think it would be in our best interest to knock out the wolves first."

"Very well. Do what you must." Eldridge returned to his seat.

"Once they're contained we can go into the house and capture Stephanie and Scarlet. This needs to be a covert operation and stays with everyone in this hall."

As the group dispersed, Paige crossed the floor to the platform carrying their son in her arms. "I wish I could go with you, but…"

"I need to know you and Tristan are safe. That's all I need from you right now." He wrapped an arm around her back and kissed the top of her head, then leaned in and kissed his son's head. "We have to try to preempt

Stephanie's plans, whatever they are, and get control of this situation."

"She's shrewd and devious, and now that she has Scarlet on her side that makes her even more dangerous." Paige bounced the baby gently in her arms.

"Yes, I know." Eli's gaze roamed the church hall. Everyone had left. "I want you to stay with Clary. You're safer there. I don't want you on your own while I'm away."

Paige nodded. "Ok. I understand." She didn't want to put any added stress on her husband.

"Let's go. There's a lot to get done."

On the drive back to the cabin, Stephen tried to subtly extract information from Wade. If he asked too many questions his companion might become suspicious and figure out what he was really doing there. "Have you met Stephanie Harris?"

"Nah, but Calvin has. When he and his buddy arrived in town she picked them up and drove them out here."

"They were the first ones to arrive for this gig?"

Wade shrugged. "Yeah, I guess so."

Stephen folded his arms. "I'd feel better if we were told what we're doing here, wouldn't you?"

"As long as I get paid, I don't really give a rat's ass."

"Yeah, I guess you're right."

Wade gave Stephen a sideward frown. "What's with the twenty questions?"

"Nothing. It's just, well, I usually know what I'm doing in advance. This seems a little off to me, that's all."

"Fair enough." Wade gave it some thought for a moment, then said, "What do you mean by 'a little off'?"

"The ad had no information and now we're here we still have no idea what we're here for. My gut's telling me something's off."

"I'm sure when the time's right we'll be told." Wade pulled the truck up at the gate and climbed out to unlock it.

Stephen already knew why they were there. He'd hoped Wade had known more than he'd initially told him, but it appeared he didn't. Stephanie was keeping tight-lipped about her plans.

FORTY EIGHT

hen Eli stepped into the Bellehurst PD sheriff Mossman came into the office, hand extended. "Good to have you here, Sheriff Blackwood. Come on through." The pair walked down a narrow passage to a door at the end of the corridor and the sheriff opened it, motioning for Eli to go in ahead of him. He closed the door and asked Eli to take a seat then rounded his desk and sat down. "So you think Stephanie Harris and Scarlet Balfour are at the house on Sycamore Drive?"

"Yes, I do. It would be the perfect place to hide considering it was thoroughly checked out the night of the murders."

"If they are there, what's your strategy?"

"I have something else I need to do first. I just want a definite confirmation on the location before we do anything." Eli leaned back on the chair and folded his arms.

"What's your plan then?"

"As you're aware, Stephanie has enlisted the help of several wolves. They've arrived in Bellehurst from all across the country. I plan to round them up and contain them to knock them out of Stephanie's game, then go into the house and apprehend both her and Scarlet."

Steven Mossman gave Eli an incredulous frown. "And you think it'll be that easy?"

"Not by a long shot. But I have a powerful warlock that will assist in containing the pair inside the house, so he can bind Scarlet's powers and I can arrest Stephanie Harris."

The sheriff blew out a noisy breath. "From what you've told me, I can't see it being so simple, regardless of you having a warlock on side."

"I know it won't be, but it's the basis for our plan to take the women down."

Mossman squinted at Eli. "And you don't think they'll have some kind of backup plan?"

"Stephanie hadn't had a lot of time to put her scheme into action. The wolves only finished arriving yesterday and they haven't been informed of why they're here as yet."

The sheriff's right eyebrow arched. "Sounds odd."

"That's how I know she has something else planned. And that's why I have my pack in Moon Grove on standby."

"Ok, then. What can I do to help?" Mossman leaned forward, clasping his hands on the desk blotter.

"I need you and your guys on standby too. Once I've set our plan in motion I'll let you know."

The sheriff stood up. "All right. I'll wait to hear from you."

"I'll be in touch later today."

Mossman opened the door and Eli stepped out into the corridor. He wanted to suss out that house.

Eli parked the patrol in an adjoining street and walked through several open back yards. When he reached the house on Sycamore Drive, he moved around the side of the house next door and checked the back of the building. No one. He walked back to the front of the neighboring house and checked the street view. Again, no sign of movement. Stepping onto the front porch of the home he was using as a shield, he knocked. An older woman, somewhere in her sixties, wearing a bright floral kaftan, with white hair and a huge smile answered the door. "Good afternoon, Sheriff. Can I be of some help?"

Eli tipped his Stetson. "Ma'am. I was wondering if you've seen anyone in the home next door." His gaze moved to the house then back to her.

The woman's mouth and eyes widened. "You mean since those poor young women were murdered?"

"Yes. Has anyone been staying at the property?"

The older woman gave it some serious thought. "I don't think so. It's hard to say because the garage is on this side of the house and there are no windows."

That was true.

"No movement at all?"

"Not that I'm aware of." She raised her hand to her chin in the same way his grandmother did when contemplating something. "No, wait a minute, that's not entirely true."

"Oh, how so?"

"I think I heard the garage door a couple of days ago. It has a distinct sound when it rolls up. Kind of like a squealing grating noise. At least I think it was there."

"Thank you. I appreciate your assistance." Eli turned to walk down the front steps.

"Uh, Sheriff, would you like some tea?" Her smile grew bigger.

"Sorry, I'm working right now. But thanks for your time." Eli tipped his hat again and headed back through the yards to Blossom Grove where he'd parked the Jeep. He pressed the remote and climbed in. He wished he could confirm whether or not Stephanie was staying at the house. He let out a frustrated huff. He'd have to stake the place out after dark to find out if what his mother-in-law had suggested was correct. Starting the engine, he drove back into town to find a place to get a meal. He hadn't eaten since morning tea and it was now in the latter part of the afternoon.

Pulling the patrol nose into the curb in the diagonal parking bay, he turned off the engine and sat for a moment. He hoped his plan of containing the wolves would pan out without a hitch, but there was always room for error where supernatural creatures were concerned. When they went in, he'd have to detain Stephen Knox as well, so his cover wasn't blown, and he was sure the wolf would not appreciate it. Nothing he could do about that. They needed to get the wolves out of harm's way because he was certain Stephanie wouldn't care about casualties of war. He'd seen the ad she'd placed, offering thousands of dollars she knew she would never have to pay.

Tugging the keys from the ignition, Eli climbed out of the Jeep, walked across the sidewalk and entered the cozy café. The sign in the window said Home Cooking and he was hungry enough to eat a horse.

Eli's pack was in place, everyone wearing a communication device in their ear. Once the guys were asleep they would storm the cabin with tranquilizer guns, knock the sleeping men out and transport them to the underground cages. The place had been set up years ago by Remus when he tried to eradicate Eli and his pack from Moon Grove, and it was a secure location. The wolves wouldn't get free.

As the time ticked down, Eli and the others waited until all was quiet in the cabin. "All right let's head in. We want this to be a clean sweep."

Each team moved in, entering the wooden structure from the front and the rear. You could hear a pin drop, the place was so quiet. Stephen had said there were tents outside, but none were out there now. Cooper's gut squirmed as he stepped through the back door, tranquilizer gun raised ready to shoot. Brent moved in behind him, followed by Daniel and Braydon, their hackles up. The place seemed too quiet.

Eli moved in through the front door. Joshua, Ethan, and Rick behind him. He hadn't wanted his deputy on the raid but Rick wouldn't take no for an answer.

The teams swarmed silently through the cabin, easing open the bedroom doors and finding no one in the rooms.

Eli pressed his comm. "Let's head out back."

Everyone followed him out the door into the yard.

"Where are they?" Cooper asked. "And how did they get away?"

"I saw a trap door in the floor at the end of the hallway," Braydon offered. "There has to be a tunnel leading out of the property under it."

"Someone must've tipped them off," Daniel said. "Maybe your mole?"

Eli shook his head. "I don't think so. But I have a feeling I know who did." He'd gotten a concerning vibe from one of Mossman's deputies and thought it was just his imagination. Obviously, he'd been wrong.

After sending his pack members home, Eli headed to the Bellehurst PD. As he got closer his gut tightened. Were his suspicions correct? He pulled into the curb, got out of the Jeep, and walked into the station.

Where were the officers on duty?

Eli's gut tightened even more. Something was wrong.

He pulled his weapon, headed down the corridor to the sheriff's office, gripped the handle and opened the door. Steven Mossman was sitting in his chair gazing out of the window.

Eli approached the desk. "Sheriff? Everything ok?"

No answer.

Eli swallowed hard, his gut churning now, and rounded the desk to find the sheriff covered in blood with his throat ripped out. He knew who had done this. Deputy Joseph Parkes, a rogue werewolf working in the guise of a good cop. And the one who had tipped off the wolves out at the cabin.

FORTY NINE

As Eli sat and watch the house from a couple houses away, he thought about Stephen Knox. The wolves had gone underground and he'd had to go along with them, otherwise it would've looked suspicious. Where were they? As his gaze moved back to the unlit home, he thought about Paige and their son out of harm's way in Moon Grove. At least for now. He loved them both so much and would do whatever it took to keep them safe.

He spotted movement. The garage door rolled up. The neighbor had been right about the squealing noise. It sounded like rusty bed springs.

A white hatchback reversed out of the garage without headlights on and the door slid down again. The car pulled out onto the road and headed away from Eli's direction, the twin circles of the headlights lighting up the road and trees ahead of it now. He'd give them a few seconds then follow at a safe distance.

Checking the dashboard digital clock, he realized it was late. 11PM. He'd been sitting outside the house for a few hours.

He continued to follow the hatchback. Where were they going? Not into Bellehurst.

The car took a left at the next intersection and zipped along the residential street, heading for the main road leading out of the town. Eli kept back but still within enough distance to catch them if they sped up.

Eli got on the radio. "Cooper, come in."

Cooper was on the mic immediately. "Yes, boss?"

"I'm following a white hatchback, it's a rental, and I believe Stephanie Harris is driving."

"Do you need backup? Can I call Sheriff Mossman?"

"The sheriff's dead, Coop."

"What the hell?"

"One of his deputies, I think. I got a bad vibe from him when I met him earlier and I believe he killed his boss and took off. He might know where the other wolves are and went to join them."

"Far out!"

"I wish we could call in the State Police but we can't. I'm going to continue following the car to see where it goes. Can you track my phone?"

"Yep, ok. Be careful, Eli."

"I will."

After traveling out of Bellehurst for an hour, the hatchback pulled off the main road onto a dirt track. Eli pulled onto the shoulder and allowed a minute to pass before turning into the trees. The four wheel drive bumped around on the road as he attempted to catch up to the car. He couldn't see any taillights in the distance, so where had they gone?

After continuing on the track for another mile, Eli turned the Jeep around and headed back the way he had come. *Where did the car go?* His Lycan vision expanded and he searched the surrounding trees as he drove at a slow pace. Nothing. *Wait. What's that?* He pulled up the wagon and climbed out. Another hidden gate like the one at the well site. These locations would be Matthias's hide outs that Stephanie had learned about from Samuel and Heath. There was no other explanation.

Eli knew it would be too dangerous for him to go in alone so he checked Google maps and set the coordinates into his phone. He would come back with reinforcements. This location had to be where the other wolves were, including Stephen Knox. At least he hoped Stephen was with them and hadn't been discovered. He drove back to the main road, turned right and headed to the Bellehurst turnpike. He'd hook onto the freeway and get back to Moon Grove as fast as he could. This time they would go in prepared for battle and finish the job. It had to end tonight.

Scarlet walked along the quiet tree-lined street. It was midnight and she had a task to perform. She needed the magical power of other witches and she knew just where to find it. She stepped through the front gate, walked around to the back of the house, raised her hands, and ordered the door to open. It didn't. She frowned and repeated the process.

Ruby came up to the wood and glass back door and peered out at the High Priestess. "You are not welcome here. Leave."

Scarlet let out a high pitched, demented laugh. "You're no match for me. I will have satisfaction." She raised her hands and repeated the spell. The door remained locked. "Well, it seems you've had help from Clarissa Baker." She paced. "But do not fear, I will find a way."

Ruby went back to the living room where her sisters were waiting. They formed a circle, gripped each other's hands and chanted the protection incantation Clarissa had given her. After ten minutes, Ruby left the circle to check if Scarlet was still in the back yard. She wasn't. Had she left? Or was she planning some other form of magical attack on the house and them? Ruby returned to the circle and took her place. They continued to repeat the incantation over and over.

A sound on the roof caused everyone in the circle to stop chanting.

"What was that?" Erica asked.

Ruby's gaze moved to the ceiling. "Scarlet. She's attempting to get into the house through the roof."

"Can she do that?" Crystal's body trembled. She didn't want to become a dark witch.

"Let's keep the incantation going. I'll be right back." Ruby left the living room and walked down the hallway to the attic door in the ceiling. She pulled the cord and the ladder unfolded. Climbing up, her eyes roamed the dark space. Scarlet wasn't there, which meant she was on the roof outside.

Ruby walked to the circular window at the end of the attic and looked out. As she turned to go back downstairs, Scarlet appeared behind her.

Ruby raised her hand and thrust a bolt of magic at the witch. She disappeared into a hazy cloud. So she astral projected into the attic but she can't get into the house. Good. Ruby climbed back down the ladder, pushed it up into place and closed the ceiling door. On returning to the living room, she found her sisters lying on the floor unconscious. She got on the phone to Clarissa.

"Clary it's Ruby. Scarlet's here at the house and she's done some kind of spell to knock out my sisters."

"Oh dear, that's not good. She can't get inside, can she?"

"I did everything you told me to do and I don't think so. She astral projected into the attic but she's still outside on the roof."

"You need to keep the incantation going, even if it's only you. The others will wake up as long as you don't stop repeating the spell."

Ruby nodded. "Ok. Is there anything else I can do?"

"No. As long as she can't get in she can't attack any of you physically. She's cast a sleeping spell so the incantation isn't as strong, but as long as you keep it going you're all safe."

"I will. Thank you, Clary." She rang off and began the incantation with such vigor it was bound to work. Scarlet would not get into their home. She would make sure of it.

Eli's pack had surrounded the cabin hidden amongst the tall pine trees. They would wait for him to give them the order to move in and take the cabin from all directions. The hatchback was parked outside which meant Stephanie Harris was inside. Was Scarlet? They would soon find out.

Once they shifted into wolf form they would take down the other wolves they knew were hiding there.

Eli gave the order and everyone moved in.

When he reached the front door, Eli raised his size fourteen boot and kicked it in, he and his team storming the cabin, shifting into wolf form, and the wolves within the cabin doing the same. The fight ensued with blood and fur flying across the room.

Where was Stephanie?

Eli roamed the cabin, still in wolf form as the other wolves fought to gain control. She wasn't here, unless she had a hiding place, the same as the other cabin. He stalked the rooms, his muzzle sniffing the air. Where was she? She had to be here. The car was still outside. He stopped and used his Lycan hearing to pick up any heartbeats other than the wolves in the other room. Nothing. Maybe she was part of the conflict.

He bounded back to the living room. The wolves had taken the fight outside, his pack winning. Some of Stephanie's wolves had taken off into the woods, leaving only a couple to finish the fight. Once his wolves had control over the pair, they changed back into human form and held the two wolves captive.

One wolf shifted. Stephen Knox.

"I'm glad you're ok," Eli said, racing across the yard to him.

"Thanks. Glad you got out here."

"Where's Stephanie?"

He glanced down at the wolf on the ground.

Eli's eyes widened. They had her.

"What about Scarlet?" Eli asked.

"Who?"

"She's a witch. Wasn't she here with Stephanie?"

Stephen shook his head. "No. Stephanie came out here alone."

Eli frowned. "Then where is Scarlet Balfour?"

Stephen shrugged. "Don't know. Hey, do you have clothes in your cars?"

Eli realized they were naked. "Uh, yes, we do. Come on."

Daniel and Joshua shackled Stephanie still in wolf form and carried her back to the wagon.

Eli pulled the metal case out of the Jeep, opened it, pulled on the gloves and tossed the Forsythe cloak onto Stephanie as she lay unconscious in back. He wasn't taking any chances.

After everyone dressed and climbed into the vehicles, they headed back to Bellehurst. Eli had an awful feeling about Scarlet Balfour that he couldn't shake.

Ruby's house was quiet when Eli pulled the wagon into the curb not far along the tree-lined street. Was she and her sisters all right? With the spells and other artifacts Clary had given them for protection he hoped so. He told the others to wait in the Jeep while he took a look around. As he approached the house, he saw Scarlet standing on the roof.

Making his way back to the patrol, he climbed in and told his team they were going to apprehend the witch.

All eyes were on Scarlet Balfour as she stood on that roof. What was she doing?

Eli picked up his cell from off the console and keyed in Ruby's number.

She answered on the first ring. "Eli, where are you? We're being attacked by Scarlet. She's cast a sleeping spell on my sisters and I'm the only one chanting the incantation. I'm scared."

"We're outside. I can see Scarlet. We're going to help you, so sit tight."

"Thank you." Ruby dropped her phone into the pocket of her dress and continued to chant with all her might. She would not allow Scarlet to use her or her sisters to fight against Eli or anyone else she cared about.

Ruby heard an odd noise on the roof. What had happened? She raced over to the window and saw Scarlet tumbling onto the lawn. The witch was on her feet in seconds and turned toward the sidewalk, hands raised.

Eli came toward her with the Forsythe cloak. Stephen had said it would work on most supernatural creatures and the sheriff wondered if it might subdue her. He tossed it into the air and as it flew across the yard toward Scarlet she raised her hands, chanted something in Latin, and the cloak disintegrated before their eyes, the small interlocked silver links falling onto the grass like droplets of rain.

"Take cover," Eli yelled.

Everyone behind him dashed for the safety of trees and nearby house walls.

Scarlet thrust her hands out in front of her again, and the tree Cooper was behind split down the middle. He hurled his body behind a parked bronze Land Cruiser on the street. She turned and tossed a bolt of magic at Eli standing behind another tree on the sidewalk. He threw himself behind a parked black BMW wagon as well.

"You cannot defeat me," Scarlet yelled, and cackled like a scary witch from cartoons on the TV.

Another vehicle pulled into the curb not far from the intersection and Eldridge got out. He raised his hands and shot a vivid blue bolt of magic at Scarlet. She swung around, lost her footing and fell in a heap on the front lawn. Climbing to her feet, she lifted herself into the air and back onto the roof, a smug smirk spreading across her face. She was more powerful than she had been when she'd last encountered Eldridge Crane.

The warlock strode across the street and stepped onto the sidewalk, continuing to cast energy at the witch.

Scarlet stumbled backwards and landed on her behind, but jumped to her feet again in the same movement. She shot a bolt of magic back at him and it hit the ground at his feet with a loud crack, white sparks of light spraying across the sidewalk.

"You will not escape me this time, Scarlet Balfour," Eldridge warned.

She cackled again. "You cannot contain me or my powers." Energy crackled in her fingertips and she hurled it across the lawn at the warlock.

Eli kept low and made his way along the line of stationery cars to the connecting street. He stayed within the shadows of the unlit backyards, close to the neighboring houses as he snuck across the damp lawns to the coven's house.

When he reached it, Ruby opened the back door to let him in. "What are you doing, Eli?"

"I want to get into your attic so I can climb out onto the roof."

Ruby's eyes widened. "You're no match for Scarlet. She'll kill you."

"Not if I can sneak up on her."

A knock on the back door startled the pair and they went into the hallway to see who it was.

Cooper, Daniel, and Braydon.

Eli unlocked the door to let them into the house. "What are you doing? You should've headed back to the patrol."

"We want to help."

"Unless you have magical powers there's not a lot you can do," Eli told them.

The energy onslaught continued outside with both witch and warlock hurling shocks of magic at each other.

"Hell, yeah, we can," Daniel said. "Let us up on that roof and see how long she lasts."

"You mean go up there as wolves?"

"Naturally. The three of us can take her out before she has a chance to react. Eldridge Crane is occupying her focus and she can't be fighting all of us at the same time, can she?"

That wasn't as crazy as it sounded.

"All right. Let's get into the attic." Eli turned to Ruby. "Stay down here and keep the incantation going."

Ruby glanced over her shoulder at her sleeping sisters in the living room. Why hadn't they woken up? She wandered into the room and began chanting again.

Eli and the others climbed into the attic, his three pack members stripping down to shift into wolf form once on the roof. He found a step ladder in the corner, opened it and climbed onto it to remove some roof tiles to make enough room for Cooper, Daniel, and Braydon to get out. Once they were outside, they would shift and move in to take Scarlet out for good.

Daniel pushed his tall frame up and out onto a section of roof behind the chimney and waited for the other two to join him. All three turned and eased their way along the apex of the slanted roof to where the witch stood. Her back to them. When they reached her Daniel leaped forward, his muzzle latching onto her left arm, his canines sinking into flesh and bone.

Scarlet gave a shrill scream and tried to dislodge the wolf from her forearm without success.

Braydon snapped at her right arm before she could hurl a bolt of magic at him and latched on.

She let out another high-pitched scream, tears spilling down her face. "You will pay for this," she said through sobs of pain.

Cooper bounded up and as his companions released her, he knocked her off the roof.

Scarlet landed on the concrete front path, her neck twisted at an odd angle, her eyes staring at nothing.

Ruby threw open the front door and rushed outside. As she did, her sisters came to, one at a time, and joined her on the lawn.

"She's dead," Beatrice gasped, her eyes wide.

Eli came out into the yard. "Looks like it worked."

Eldridge opened the gate and stepped into the garden. "Do not let her appearance deceive you. She is not completely dead. She is in the shadow realm but can come back if she finds a way to do so. The only way to be truly rid of her is to burn the body so she will be trapped there forever."

Eli stood with hands on hips. "Then that's what we'll do." His eyes roamed the roof. His guys were back inside the house. He left the group standing over the body and returned to the living room. "There you are. We need to load Scarlet's body into the patrol with Stephanie and take them back to Moon Grove. We can get rid of them both there."

"What's going to happen about the cop that killed the sheriff?" Cooper asked.

"That's up to the authorities here in Bellehurst. I've given them my opinion about what I think happened. The un-supernatural version. They'll investigate and do whatever is necessary to find and arrest him."

Cooper and Daniel were about to lift the witch's body off the path and load it into the Jeep when it burst into flames and disintegrated into ash.

"What happened?" Cooper asked.

"That, my fine young fellow, is a good question." Eldridge stood and stared at the smudge of black soot staining the path. *What indeed.*

FIFTY

Once they were back in Moon Grove, Eli parked the Jeep around the back of the station house and he and the others climbed out of the vehicle. Tugging a wad of keys from the pocket of his jacket, he unlocked the rear staved gate, then the solid metal door, and opened the cell. Stephanie had been injected with a tranquilizer to keep her sedated so she couldn't change back into wolf form now she was human again. They would call a judicial hearing at the church for the following morning so a consensus could be formed as to what punishment should be implemented. Eli knew it would be a death sentence after everything she'd done.

Braydon and Daniel carried her into the cell and set her down on the cot, covering her naked body with a blanket.

"Why don't we just execute her?" Daniel asked. "She murdered people and would've murdered Paige too if we hadn't been able to capture her."

Eli gave a heavy sigh. "I hear what you're saying, and it's true, but I want to keep with Lycan tradition and laws. What kind of Alpha would I be if I put wolves to death without a fair trial?"

Daniel nodded. "You're fairer than I would be with her. She doesn't deserve it."

"Maybe so, but while I'm Alpha I'll go by the book. Any objections?"

He shrugged.

"Ok, good."

The pair came out of the cell and Eli locked the door. "Can you stay to keep an eye on her? I'd like to go home to see my wife and son."

"Absolutely," Daniel said. "Do what you gotta do." He glanced at Braydon. "We'll both stay."

"Cooper, you'll need to be here as well."

"No problem."

"When I get home I'll order some food for you guys. What would you like?" Eli pulled his cell from his shirt pocket and opened up notes.

"Burgers?" Cooper's gaze moved to Daniel and Braydon.

"Hell, yeah, I love a good burger," Braydon said. "As long as we can get them from Dot's Diner. They're open all night and their burgers are the best in Moon Grove. At least, I think so."

"Dot's it is." Eli pocketed his phone and headed for the door then turned around. "Want fries with that? And drinks?"

"Fries, yeah, and a couple chocolate shakes." Cooper's stomach growled. He was hungry. "Oh, and can we make it two burgers each?"

Eli's right eyebrow arched. "That hungry, huh?"

"You bet."

"Ok." Eli continued out the back door. "Lock up and don't let anyone in unless it's me."

"Will do." Cooper followed Eli to the door and pulled is shut, setting all the bolts and locks in place.

"How did this happen?" Eli asked, standing with hands on hips staring into the bloody cell.

"I – I don't know, boss," Cooper stammered. "We, me and Daniel, went down the road to grab some breakfast things before everyone else showed up and when we got back this is what we found." He gave Eli a sheepish look.

"So we can assume Scarlet is still active and came here to free Stephanie." Eli shook his head to himself. "Let's get this cleaned up..." His serious gaze moved to Daniel. "I'm sorry for your loss, Dan. We need to find those two and finish what we started."

Daniel scowled. "If we'd done the deed last night Braydon wouldn't be dead."

Eli walked up to him. "Do you think I made the wrong decision?"

"Yeah, maybe. When Eldridge said it wasn't a good sign that the witch had vanished we should've been prepared."

"We couldn't have known she'd come here to bust Stephanie out of jail. How could we?"

Daniel folded his arms. "I get that, but with both women being so dangerous it was in our best interest to end them, rather than wait until today to make a lawful pronouncement of their death penalties. Lycan law or no Lycan law."

"You're entitled to your opinion, Dan. But like I said last night, I do things by the book."

"And that's what got my friend killed." Daniel stormed through the station house out to the parking lot, climbed into his car, spinning the wheels on the gravel as he sped out onto the road.

"He'll come around, boss. Once he's had time to think it over." Cooper stood eyeing the mess in the cell, thinking he'd be the one to clean it up.

"I'll call in our cleaner and get this sorted. Looks like we'll be having two memorial services Wednesday." Eli turned on his heel and headed back to his office. He wasn't prepared to let anyone else die.

Later that morning, Eli drove over to the mansion to speak to Alistair. Perhaps the council could put feelers out to help find Stephanie's and Scarlet's location. Daniel had been right to a certain extent, if he'd followed his gut, which had been to execute Stephanie without a trial, Braydon would still be alive. Maybe it was time to break a few rules.

He pulled the Jeep up at the bottom of the double circular staircases, turned off the engine and got out. Alistair would normally be sleeping at this time of day, but Eli had called in advance and woken him up. He needed the vampire's help, which he knew would cost him at some point in the future. Right now he didn't care that he would owe a favor for a favor. They had to eliminate Stephanie and Scarlet ASAP. No more near misses.

When he reached the top of the concrete stairs, one of the black double doors opened slightly, allowing enough room for Eli to step inside. The door slammed abruptly behind him and Alistair came around to him. "This situation is out of control. You've lost lives and it could have been avoided."

"I know. I was trying to do the right thing. The just thing."

Alistair's left eyebrow arched. "And look where that's gotten you."

"You don't have to rub it in, you know."

"Maybe I do. Maybe it's time to play by your own rules and not the Lycan way."

Eli had already thought of that. "So can I rely on your assistance?"

Alistair gave him an odd smile. "Of course you have my help. I've already spread the word so I should hear something back at any time."

"Thank you. I appreciate it."

"We are on the same side, you and I."

Were they? Eli wasn't so sure. Vampires always had their own agendas and Alistair was no exception.

"I will be in touch when I have some information for you." Alistair gestured at the closed doors. "You can see yourself out. I should be in repose."

Eli eyed the vampire for a moment without another word then walked over to the door. "Thanks again."

"No problem."

Back in the patrol, Eli called his grandmother to find out if she'd had any luck locating the pair. She hadn't, but would continue to try. She knew how important it was.

Traveling back to Moon Grove, Eli wondered if their town would ever be at peace. It seemed to be a magnet for supernatural conflict. Something they could all do without. By the time he reached the station, it was mid-afternoon.

He thought about calling it a day and heading home to spend time with his wife and baby son, but thought it best to wait a while in case Alistair contacted him and they'd have to make a trip out of town. When he sat down at his desk, he tugged his cell from his shirt pocket and pressed speed dial for Paige. No answer. Maybe she'd left her phone downstairs and was in the nursery with Tristan. He would give it a while then try again.

Paige stood in the living room, her eyes on the woman holding her son. How had Stephanie gotten into their home? Clary's protection spell should have prevented it. "Give me my son," she said, trying to conceal the quiver in her voice.

Stephanie gazed down at the sleeping baby, a smile spreading across her face. "He's a cute little guy, isn't he?"

"He has nothing to do with this. It's between you and me." Paige took a step forward.

"I'd advise you not to come any closer."

Paige's heart thumped in her chest. Would Stephanie hurt their son? Was that her plan now? "What do you want? Why are you here?"

"Word has it that Eli's moonstone ring has rejected him. I wonder why that would happen. Perhaps he's going to die." Her smile grew wider at the thought.

"Don't say that!" Paige's mind was traveling a mile a minute as she ran through different scenarios in her head. How could she get rid of Stephanie? She remembered Eli had placed pistols loaded with silver cartridges in every room in their home, telling her they couldn't be too careful. She'd hated the idea at first, but now welcomed it... if only she could get to the gun in the living room sideboard.

"By Lycan law, the ring melds with its new Alpha and doesn't come off until that Alpha is dead or going to die. Look it up for yourself." Stephanie rocked the rousing baby. "Shh, shh, shh."

"Give me my son," Paige asked forcefully, holding out her arms.

"Now why would I do that? He's perfectly comfortable where he is."

"Are you here to kill us both so Eli will suffer? Is that it?" Paige moved to her right. A little closer to the sideboard.

"Stop where you are." Stephanie took a step in Paige's direction.

"You need to tell me why you're here."

"I thought we might sit and wait for Eli to get home. Then I can kill you all together."

Tristan began to cry. He was hungry.

"He needs his formula. Give him to me."

Stephanie's firm gaze moved from the crying baby to her ex-friend. "We'll go into the kitchen together while you get it ready. How does that sound?"

"Ok." Paige crossed the entry hall to the dining room and headed for the kitchen. Stephanie right behind her.

She continued to rock the baby while Paige prepared a bottle for him. "How did you become a werewolf?" she asked.

"It was in my genes. It just had to be awakened."

"Oh, how?"

"That's something we don't need to discuss right now."

"I'd like to know."

"Well I'm not telling you." Paige shook the baby bottle to mix the ingredients. "Now give me my son."

"I'll do it." Stephanie held out her hand for the bottle.

Paige didn't give it to her.

Stephanie gestured with her hand in a backward wave motion. "Hand me the formula."

"No." She was stalling. She knew the pistol Eli had put in the end drawer was so close.

"You wouldn't want me to wring his neck while you watch, would you?"

"Why would you hurt an innocent child?" Paige stepped backwards. One step closer to the drawer.

Tristan's cry was much louder now.

"Give me the damn bottle."

"When you put Tristan in his bassinet." They had been in the kitchen together while Paige prepared dinner.

"What's the point of that if he needs feeding?" Stephanie eyed Paige with suspicion. "What are you up to?"

"Nothing. He'll be more comfortable there and will fall asleep after his feed."

Stephanie thought about it for a moment, then placed the crying baby in his bassinet. Sounded plausible.

Paige threw the bottle across the room, stepped backwards, pulled the drawer open and snatched up the pistol, aiming it at her ex-friend. "Put the bottle on the table and step back."

Stephanie gave Paige a smug smile. "You think I came here alone?"

Paige's eyes flitted around the room and through the doorway into the dining room. "I don't see anyone else."

Stephanie chuckled. "Who do you think broke me out of jail?"

Scarlet.

FIFTY ONE

Eli was about to pick up his cell and try Paige again when it vibrated on his desk. He checked the caller ID. His grandmother. "Hey, Clary, what's up?"

"Something's wrong."

His hackles rose and his gut shrank. "What do you mean?"

"I can feel Scarlet Balfour's presence."

"At your place?"

She shook her head even though Eli couldn't see it. "No. At yours."

Eli flew from his chair, phone pressed to his ear. "I'm on my way. Get Eldridge Crane over there *now*!" He pocketed the phone, stalked through the station to the front door, jerked it open and raced outside.

He scrambled into the patrol, pulled out onto the gravel drive and sped out of the parking lot, stones spraying in all directions as he spun the heavy treaded wheels. His heart pounded in his chest and whooshed in his ears as he flipped on the siren, red and blue strobe lights flashing, and headed for home. *Please let Paige and Tristan be all right,* he prayed as the Jeep hurtled like a rocket along the main street.

It would take him ten minutes to get there the way he was driving (normally it would take about twenty). His breathing quickened as his hands gripped the steering wheel, his knuckles white, and his wolf trying to emerge. *No, stay there.* He had to remain in human form. At least for now.

He swung the Jeep around the corner of their street, pressing his foot down further on the pedal, and screeched the patrol to a stop at the entrance to their driveway. Clarissa was across the road and Eli flew out of the vehicle over to her. "Where's Scarlet?"

"She can't get inside, but Stephanie's in there with Paige and the baby. Scarlet must've somehow created a narrow fissure in my protection spell to allow her to step through. I'm so sorry, Eli."

Two other police units blocked the middle of the street, lights flashing. Cooper, Rick, and Taylor climbed out and rushed up to Eli and his grandmother.

"Is Scarlet in there with Paige and the baby?" Taylor asked.

Eli shook his head. "No, she can't get inside, but she's here somewhere. Stephanie's in there with them."

Cooper stepped up beside his boss. "What can we do to help?"

"Do a cautious sweep of the back yard. My grandmother's protection spell is keeping Scarlet out, but she has to be somewhere nearby."

"Ok." He and Rick pulled their weapons and crossed the road.

Taylor stood with Clarissa and Eli. "I'm so sorry this is happening."

"Me too." Eli's gaze moved to his grandmother. "Where's Eldridge?"

"He was gone early this morning. You hung up before I had a chance to tell you."

Cooper and Rick came back across the road. "All clear, boss. If the witch is here then she's hiding somewhere."

"She's here," Clarissa told them. "I can feel her dark magic. It's so strong."

Eli walked over to the patrol Cooper had arrived in, opened the door and tugged the mic from its clip, switching to the loud speaker function. "Stephanie Harris, give yourself up."

Eli's cell jingled and he snatched it from his shirt pocket. Paige. His stomach gave a nervous flip flop. Was this a negotiation? He didn't think so. "Paige?"

"Yes. I have Stephanie at gunpoint. Can you come in and take her out of here?"

Eli's gaze moved around his team. "She has Stephanie at gunpoint. I'm going in." He crossed the street, rushed up the path onto the porch, and entered the house.

When he came to the kitchen doorway, his eyes surveyed the room. Tristan was crying in his bassinet too close to Stephanie Harris.

"Eli," Paige said, keeping the gun aimed at her intruder.

He walked across the kitchen, gripped the edge of the bassinet and wheeled his son into the dining room, then stepped back into the doorway. "It looks like you have everything under control."

Paige gave him a thin smile. "I'll feel better once you take her out of our home."

"Which is what I'm about to do." Eli snapped the handcuffs off his belt, walked up behind Stephanie, tugged her arms behind her and fastened the restraints to her wrists. He got onto his shoulder mic. "Cooper, come in."

"Yeah, boss?"

"Please take our intruder and secure her in your vehicle."

"On my way."

Eli's gaze moved to his wife. "You're ok?"

"Yes." She nodded.

Cooper entered the house and came into the kitchen. "I'm here."

"Good." He pushed Stephanie toward his deputy. "Get her out of here."

As she was being led out, she glanced over her shoulder and grinned. "As I told Paige, I'm not alone."

Eli's already squirming gut rolled. He knew the witch was somewhere, but where? "I'm going to talk to Clary. Be right back."

When Eli came outside, the patrols were gone. Stephanie was on her way back to the cells. He crossed the street to where his grandmother still stood. "Do you have any idea where Scarlet is? Is she still in the vicinity?"

"No. She's not. And that worries me."

"Me too." Eli snatched the mic off his shoulder and pressed the button. "Cooper, come in."

"Yeah, boss?"

"Can you put a comm in your ear? I need to speak to you privately."

"Ok. Hold on."

Rick was riding with him and opened the glove compartment to pass Cooper an ear bud and pushed one in his own ear as well.

"Ready. Go ahead."

"Scarlet's not here anymore. She must be following you back to town. Be careful."

"Will do. Thanks for the heads up, boss."

"Stay safe. We have no idea where she'll be."

"Yeah, ok."

Rick gave Cooper a serious frown. "Do you think...?"

Cooper shook his head.

Rick nodded.

They couldn't talk in front of their prisoner.

Cooper's gut tightened and his eyes moved to the rearview mirror. No car traveling behind them. Where could the witch be?

Clarissa crossed the road with Eli and entered the house. Paige was sitting at the kitchen table feeding their son the bottle she'd prepared for him. The older woman pulled out a chair and sat down beside Paige, while Eli stood.

"Did you figure out what happened to Scarlet?" Paige asked.

"No, only that she's no longer here." Clarissa raised her hand to her chin. Something wasn't right about this whole situation. "You said when Scarlet died last night her body erupted into flames and disintegrated into ash, correct?"

"Yes, that's exactly what happened. Eldridge didn't think it was a good sign. He'd just finished telling me to burn the body so Scarlet couldn't come back from the shadow realm."

A knock echoed into the entry hall and Eli got up to answer it. When he came back to the kitchen the warlock was with him.

"My apologies for my tardiness. I had some research to look into. I thought I would make it back in time but I got caught up."

"What kind of research?" Eli folded his arms.

"I've discovered that a witch can attach themselves to a living person if they have passed on, as can any ghost really, and I believe that is what Scarlet has done – attached herself to Stephanie."

"So she was in our house while Stephanie was threatening to kill us?" Paige's eyes widened.

"Unfortunately, yes."

"Which means right now my deputies are in danger."

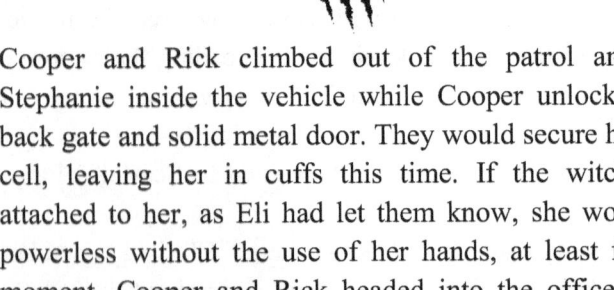

Cooper and Rick climbed out of the patrol and left Stephanie inside the vehicle while Cooper unlocked the back gate and solid metal door. They would secure her in a cell, leaving her in cuffs this time. If the witch was attached to her, as Eli had let them know, she would be powerless without the use of her hands, at least for the moment. Cooper and Rick headed into the office to let Rosemarie know they were back and that they would be monitoring Stephanie until Eli returned. Taylor had gone to do a sweep of the town on her own to keep a visible police presence. As she cruised along the main street, she had a cold shiver crawl up her spine. The town was quiet once again. Did the supernatural residents know something they didn't?

She snatched up the handset on the radio. "Rose? Rose are you there?"

Static.

"Hey, Rose, can you hear me?"

More static.

How odd, she thought.

If the town's residents were in hiding what did that mean?

Taylor turned the police patrol around and headed back to the station. Nothing to report, but she had a definite bad feeling in the pit of her stomach.

FIFTY TWO

Eli stood with arms folded leaning against the wall opposite Stephanie's cell, his eyes fixed on her. She was smiling at him. It was the kind of smile someone had on their face when they knew something you didn't. She didn't know Eli knew about Scarlet and her possible attachment to her, so they were one step ahead. Right at that moment, the witch was trapped because without the use of her hands to cast spells she had been rendered powerless. At least, that's what Eli hoped.

"Where's Scarlet?" he asked.

"How should I know?" She shrugged.

"She's working for you. Don't you keep track of those you employ?"

"Scarlet's different."

"How so?"

"She works to her own set of rules."

Eli pushed himself off the wall and stood peering through the cell bars. "Yes, I'm aware." He waited a beat, then said, "We're not going to try you. Your sentence has been decided."

Her grin widened.

"What's with the grin?"

"Oh, you'll find out."

Eli frowned into Stephanie's eyes. There was definitely something different about her, which made him suspect what Eldridge had learned was true. "Not a lot you can do from there."

"Have you noticed how quiet Moon Grove is?"

He wasn't playing into her demented game. "Not really, no. The town is what it is." He turned to walk away.

"The supernaturals know. They understand what's coming."

Eli turned around. "And what would that be?"

"As I said, you'll find out."

Eli called his deputies and Rosemarie into his office. He needed to fill everyone in on what Eldridge had said and what he, himself, suspected. After giving them a brief on the situation he waited for questions. None came.

He perched himself on the corner of his desk, folded his arms, and ran his gaze around the faces in the room. "You're all up to speed. Nothing you want to know?"

Rosemarie raised her hand. "Can I suss out our prisoner? I may be able to pick up on what Scarlet has planned."

Eli's right eyebrow arched. "You have that ability?"

"Yes, among other things."

"You're more than welcome to try. Just don't get too close, and don't let her get into your head."

"Oh, I won't."

Eli's gaze roamed the other faces. "Any questions?"

"I have one," Cooper said. "If we keep her hands secured will that stop Scarlet from using her magic? Do we know that for sure?"

"No, we don't know anything for sure. But right now it's better than the alternative."

Cooper nodded.

"Are we done?" Eli asked.

Everyone said yes.

"Ok, let's get back to it." He rounded his desk and sat down.

Rosemarie lingered.

"Yes, Rosy?"

"Can I go see her now?"

Eli stood up. "I'll come with you."

"There's really no need. I'll be fine."

"I insist." He walked over to the open doorway and motioned for the receptionist to step out ahead of him.

"All right then."

When the pair reached the door to the corridor out to the cell block Eli pulled her up. "I don't want you putting yourself at risk, Rosy. If anything feels off, anything at all, I want you to stop whatever you're going to try and leave."

"You have my word, Eli."

Rosemarie took a tentative step into the cell block, Eli right behind her. The receptionist swallowed the tingling nerves lodged in her throat and walked along to the cell Stephanie Harris occupied. She stood observing without saying a word, until Stephanie spoke.

"Why are you here?"

"I came to see if I can help."

"Help? Help who. Yourselves?"

"You have a traveler attached to you."

Stephanie gave her the same grin she'd given Eli. "So you know. Oh well, it won't change anything."

"What do you mean?"

"As I told him." She motioned at Eli with her head. "You're all going to find out."

"You came to Moon Grove to exact revenge for what happened to you. That involved Eli and Paige, not the whole town. Not innocents."

"Well, unfortunately for you all, those plans have changed."

"Because of Scarlet?"

"I run this show. Not her." Stephanie stood up, a scowl of irritation on her face.

Rosemarie stepped away from the bars. "I don't believe that. I think she's controlling the situation. She wants revenge too."

"Good, then we're both on the same page." Stephanie chuckled.

"Come on, Rosy, no point in talking to her."

Rosemarie's gaze moved from Stephanie to Eli. "I suppose you're right."

The pair turned around and left.

Once in Eli's office, Rosemarie told him what she'd learned.

"Scarlet is attached to her. Eldridge was correct."

"Then if we execute Stephanie for her crimes won't that rid us of Scarlet as well?"

Rosemarie frowned and gave it some thought. "That's something you'll need to ask Eldridge. She's a misplaced spirit and will look for a new host, I think." The receptionist walked to the door. "Be careful Eli. Don't be alone with Stephanie at any time. Scarlet might want to jump ship."

"You think that could be her plan?"

"I don't know for sure. But she's planning something."

Eldridge was sitting at the kitchen table drinking coffee when Eli walked in. He and Clarissa had been researching both Scarlet's attachment to Stephanie Harris and Eli's moonstone ring problem.

"Good morning, Eli," the warlock said. "Take a seat." He motioned to the chair beside him.

Eli sat down and Clarissa brought him a mug of coffee, then took her seat opposite the pair.

"Anything?" Eli asked.

"As far as Scarlet goes, not much." Eldridge turned the page of the ancient tome with reverence.

"Rosemarie had a chat with Stephanie and told me not to be alone with her because Scarlet might 'jump ship'." He took a cautious sip of his hot coffee. "Could that happen?"

"Yes, indeed. She's a traveler now, which means she can move from host to host."

"If we execute Stephanie would Scarlet…?"

"You have to remember that, right now, Scarlet is a spirit. She's not of this realm."

"Stephanie said something was coming. That the townsfolk knew it and that's why the streets are so quiet. Kind of like the last time the Coven of the Full Moon was here."

"This is a serious situation, Eli. One we must tread through with caution for fear of innocent members of the community being killed."

Eli leaned back on the chair and folded his arms. "So she's planning something big."

"It would appear so."

"We need to be prepared for whatever's coming." Eli's gaze moved to his grandmother. "Any luck on finding out why the ring came off?"

"Not yet. Most of the reference material confirms that the ring cannot be removed until its Alpha passes on."

Eli's gut churned. Was he going to die? "Gran?"

Clarissa scowled at her grandson. "You know I hate being called that." She noticed the sorrowful expression on his face. "What is it, dear?"

"Am I going to die?"

"Why would you ask that?"

He held up his hand. "Because of the ring. If it's not meant to come off…"

"Of course you're not going to die." At least she hoped not.

"Then explain why it came off. There has to be a reason for it."

"I'm looking into it, Eli. As soon as I find something I'll tell you. I will find answers for you. I promise."

Eldridge had remained silent during their conversation. But now he had something to add. "I believe Scarlet caused the ring to come off. She wants you to fight unaided. I don't think it has anything to do with you dying, Eli."

Relief washed over him. "You're sure?"

"One can only be as sure as they can be. Nothing is certain. But I do believe that is the reason for the ring's removal."

"I've never known how the ring works. It's shown me glimpses but nothing substantial enough for me to use it."

"Perhaps you are not the Alpha it is meant for. You may be only its guardian."

Eli frowned into the warlock's eyes. "What do you mean?"

"It may be that the ring needs another Alpha. Like Paige, perhaps." He thought for a moment. "Or even your son."

"My son? He's a baby."

"Yes. Now. But one day he'll be the Alpha of the Moon Grove pack."

Eli's frown deepened and he looked at his grandmother. "Is that possible?"

"Let me continue to seek the answer and I'll let you know."

"Because if it is the ring is useless to us now."

FIFTY THREE

The next couple of days remained quiet. Because they had Stephanie contained in the cells, Scarlet was void of her magic. How long that would last was anyone's guess, but after the memorial was done, the she wolf would be executed for her crimes under Lycan law. Eli had received a text message from Stephen Knox. He'd taken off back to Washington. Strange that he hadn't come to say goodbye, but, then, it wasn't as though they were friends. He'd come to do a job that hadn't panned out and moved on. Eli had been grateful for his assistance and the information he'd provided.

In just over an hour, they would lay Archer Hamilton and Braydon Jones to rest in the Moon Grove cemetery. Eli was still finding it difficult to get his head around. He'd lost two members of his current pack, Archer being an honorary member, and it hurt like hell. His mind wandered back to the night Gregor had murdered Bobby, Ryan, Rebecca, and Paul. A single tear slid down his left cheek and he swiped it away. The ache in his heart would never leave him.

Rosemarie came into his office with a mug of coffee and a blueberry muffin on a plate and set them down in front of him. She was dressed from head to foot in black, the fascinator veil covering her face. "It's a sad day, Eli." She sniffed back the urge to cry.

"Yes, it is." Eli was in a black suit as a sign of respect for the lives lost.

"Paige called to say she'll be here in a half hour." Rosemarie sat on a chair in front of Eli's desk. "What do you think is going to happen here?"

"I wish I knew, Rosy. It's been too quiet in town these past couple of days so something's brewing."

"That's what scares me."

Cooper, Ryan, and Taylor appeared in the open doorway all dressed in black as well. "We're heading up to the church."

"Ok. See you there." Eli sipped his coffee, his gaze moving from the three back to Rosemarie. "Haven't had any glimpses of Scarlet's plans?"

She shook her head. "I wish I did."

"If you do happen to…"

"You'll be the first to know." She gave him a thin sad smile and stood up. "Well, I might as well head on up too. I'll see you there."

"Yes."

Eli stood on the platform in front of everyone in attendance and waited for the final few people to take a seat. It was a truly sad day. He'd known Archer and Braydon for only a short time, but had formed a close bond with them both. As their Alpha, it was his responsibility to protect his pack and he felt he'd let them down. Daniel had been right in a way, but Eli still felt the decisions he'd made at the time had been the right ones.

He raised a hand to quiet the mourners. "Thank you all for coming here today to farewell Archer and Braydon. They lost their lives doing what was necessary to keep our town safe and they will always be remembered as heroes." Tears stung the backs of Eli's eyes and he blinked them away. "When I first met Archer Hamilton, I was adverse to vampires. He had come here on a mission, and when I found out what that was I wanted to end him. But over time he proved to be loyal, trustworthy, and honorable, and I couldn't have asked for a more caring friend." His gaze roamed the wan sad faces sitting in the pews before him and landed on Archer's brother, Max. "Does anyone have anything they would like to share?"

Max stood. "My brother had integrity and was loyal to a fault. He would've given up his own existence to save someone he loved, as we've seen. I will miss him for all eternity." He swiped a blood-stained tear from his right cheek and sat down again.

Daniel stood up and Eli wondered what he would say. "Braydon and I go way back. We were teens together, initiated together. He was like a brother to me and I will miss him." He sat down, his stern gaze moving to Eli.

Eli breathed a relieved sigh. He knew Daniel was still not happy with the decision he'd made about going by the book with Stephanie Harris's trial. Now he wished he hadn't. "Anyone else?"

Paige passed Tristan to her mother and stood up. "I met Archer at a time when I was unsure about who I was and what I wanted. He helped me to figure that out and became a true friend." She sat down, her tear-filled eyes moving to Eli.

"I'd like to ask you to make your way outside and over to the cemetery."

A gentle hymn played over the PA system as everyone sidled out of the pews, making their way outside.

Paige came over to Eli, wrapped her arms around him and they held each other tight for a moment. "This is more difficult than I thought it would be," she said.

Eli nodded, the painful lump in his throat preventing him from speaking.

Abbey crossed the carpet and handed Tristan back to Paige. "I'll see you two outside."

After offering a Lycan prayer, everyone in attendance threw a red rose into the graves on top of the caskets and headed back to town.

Eli remained until the graves had been filled in. The headstones would be set in place in the next few days.

As he turned to leave, the hazy transparent figure of Scarlet appeared before him.

"What do you want? Haven't you done enough?" Eli's furious gaze met hers.

"I'm only getting started, Eli Blackwood. I want you gone."

"Well that's not going to happen." Eli stalked up to her and walked through her.

She vanished.

He climbed into the Jeep and headed back to the station. Tonight they would take Stephanie Harris out into the woods and execute her, her body would be burned and the ashes collected, placed in a plain wooden box, taken to the cliff top and scattered into the wind.

FIFTY FOUR

Paige could see that Eli was perturbed about something as she walked into the living room after putting Tristan down in the nursery. She crossed the room and sat down beside him on the sofa, leaned in and rested her head on his shoulder. "What's the matter?"

Eli glanced down at her and kissed the top of her head. "It's always difficult taking someone's life, even if that person deserved the punishment."

"I know, but you had to do it for the sake of Moon Grove... and us." She raised her head up and kissed his cheek. "You're a great Alpha, Eli. You do everything you can to protect the people you love and this town."

"I try." He waited a beat, then said, "I wonder where Scarlet is now."

"Hopefully back in the shadow realm where she belongs." Paige's body gave an involuntary shiver and Eli held her closer.

"If she is, she won't remain there for long. She has plans for me."

"First it's Stephanie coming here for me and now, because she enlisted Scarlet's help, she's come for you.

When is our town ever going to be at peace?" Paige gave a heavy sigh. "I want our home to be a place of calm for Tristan."

"Sweetheart, he's going to grow up to be an Alpha. He needs to know what's out there."

"Yes, he does, but not until he's old enough to understand it."

She was right.

He kissed the top of her head again. "I'm kinda beat. It's been an emotional day."

Paige eased herself out of his embrace and held out her hand. "Then let's go get some sleep. Tomorrow's another day."

Yes, it was, and Eli wondered what turmoil would land on their doorstep.

While having breakfast, a knock echoed into the entry hall and Eli got up to answer the door. Eldridge Crane pushed past him and stepped inside, the expression on his face one of dire concern. "Scarlet is back. I've felt her presence."

Eli frowned into the warlock's eyes. "Do you know where?"

"Have you heard from your female deputy in the past eight to ten hours?"

"No, why?"

"I had a dream last night... Clary did too. We think Scarlet has your Miss Taylor."

"When you say that you mean she's attached herself to her, am I right?"

"Yes."

Eli shook his head and walked back to the kitchen. "You heard?" he asked Paige.

She nodded. "Yes. You have to find her, Eli. She has nothing to do with this."

"We will." He returned his gaze to the warlock. "I'll need your help."

"Yes, of course. There's no doubt about that."

Eli tugged his jacket from off the coat rack, pushed his Stetson onto his head and rushed out the front door, Eldridge close behind.

Paige came to the open doorway and stepped out onto the porch. "Please be careful," she called.

"I will." Eli climbed into the Jeep, Eldridge too, and they were gone.

When Paige glanced across the street she saw Clarissa standing at her front door. She waved and the older woman waved back. Paige walked down their front path to the sidewalk. "Want to join me for coffee?" Paige asked.

"I'll be right over." Clarissa went inside and closed the door.

Paige entered the house and headed back into the kitchen to stack the breakfast dishes in the dishwasher.

The front door opened and Clarissa came through the dining room to the kitchen. "I made a fresh batch of brownies this morning. I couldn't sleep after the dream so I put the energy to good use." She sat the plate down in the center of the table and took a seat.

Paige brought the coffee pot over and poured the black brew into a clean mug for Clarissa, then some into her cooling mug and sat down opposite her. "I hope they find Taylor soon."

"Me too. Scarlet needs banishing back to the shadow realm as quickly as possible."

"Can you do that? I mean so she can't come back?"

The older woman nodded as she took a bite of a brownie. "Yes, dear. Once she isn't attached to Taylor we can send her back immediately. But it has to be done the instant she's let go of her host."

"And how can Eldridge make her let go of Taylor?"

"He'll have to kill her."

"Wait. What?"

"Briefly. Just so that Scarlet releases Taylor then he'll bring her back."

Paige's forehead wrinkled into a concerned frown. "But what if it doesn't work?"

"It will, dear."

"You're sure about that?"

"Eldridge is an accomplished ancient warlock. He can do things the rest of us can't."

Paige blew out a noisy breath. "I hope you're right."

"Scarlet obviously wasn't expecting Eldridge or I to have a premonition about her. So she doesn't know Eli knows what she's done. It should offer a certain assurance that they can do what needs to be done by taking her by surprise."

"I hope Taylor will be ok." Paige sipped her coffee.

"Trust me, Eldridge knows what he's doing."

Eli had called for backup. Although Eldridge surpassed Scarlet in the magic department, he thought it best to have some extra help. No one knew what would happen and he wanted to ensure they sent the witch back to the shadow realm for good this time.

Cooper and Rick had arrived outside Taylor's house at the same time he and Eldridge did, pulled into the curb behind the Jeep, and both deputies joined Eli in his patrol.

"How are we going to get that witch off Taylor?" Rick asked, his cheeks flushed with anger and concern.

"I will have to stop her heartbeat for a brief period so that Scarlet will release her."

"Wait a minute. You're going to kill Taylor to get rid of the witch?" Rick leaned between the front seats, his serious gaze locked onto the warlock.

"That is correct. I know what I am doing. There is no need for concern."

Rick's eyes moved to Eli. "And you're ok with this?"

"We have to get Taylor free of Scarlet's clutches and this is the only way to do it."

"What if something goes wrong? Or what if Scarlet doesn't release her? What then?" Cooper asked. "Do you have a plan B?"

Eldridge gave the deputy a disgruntled frown. "There will be no need for a plan B."

Cooper leaned against the back seat and folded his arms. "I've heard that before."

Eli swiveled in the driver's seat. "Hey, Coop, have a little faith. If not in Eldridge, then in me. Do you think I'd let anything happen to Taylor?"

Cooper huffed out a sigh. "I guess not."

"Thank you." He turned to Eldridge. "Can you get us into the house?"

"Of course." The warlock climbed out of the patrol and walked up to the front door. He raised his hand, waved it at the lock and the door popped open.

Eli eased it back, his eyes roaming the living room. He motioned with his head and the others followed him inside. As the four moved silently across the room to the hallway, Taylor came out of her bedroom. "Hey, Eli." She frowned. "Uh, what are you all doing here?" She walked along the hall to where the group had stopped.

Eli stepped up to her and stared into her eyes. Stephanie had had a different appearance about her when Scarlet was attached to her, something he couldn't see in his deputy. "Are you feeling ok?"

Her frown deepened. "Sure. Why?"

Eldridge pushed between the deputies to examine her. He gripped her chin, raised her face up and looked deep into her eyes. "She is herself."

Taylor jerked her jaw out of the warlock's grasp. "What's that supposed to mean?"

Eli's frowning gaze moved to Eldridge. "If she's not here then where is she?" Something slithered in his gut. He had a bad feeling about this.

Paige frowned at Clarissa from across the table. The older woman looked different. Perhaps it was because she'd had a lack of sleep. "Are you all right, Clary?"

Clarissa's eyes met hers. "Of course, dear, why do you ask?"

Paige shrugged. "You look…"

"What?"

"I'm not sure. Maybe it's because you didn't get a lot of sleep last night."

"That would be the reason." She sighed, picked up her coffee mug and took a long sip. "I could use a nana nap."

"If you want to go home and rest don't stay on my account. I can check in on you later."

"It's all right, dear, I'm fine."

Paige frowned at her. "If you're sure?"

"I am." She finished the last piece of her brownie.

"Ok then, I'm going to sneak up and check on Tristan. I'll be right back."

"You go ahead. I'll be fine."

As Eli drove toward Clarissa's house to drop off Eldridge, he wondered how both the warlock and his grandmother had had the exact same dream. *That kind of thing doesn't usually happen, does it?* He turned to look at his passenger. "Don't you think it's strange that you and Clary had the same dream?"

"Funny you should mention that because I was thinking the same thing myself."

"Where do you think Scarlet is right now?"

"I wish I could provide you with an appropriate answer, Eli, but I honestly do not know."

"Why would the dream infer that Taylor had been the targeted host for Scarlet?"

"Again, good question, but I have no idea."

Eli straightened in his seat. "Eldridge."

"Yes?"

"What if Scarlet sent us on a witch hunt while she established a connection with someone else?"

The warlock gave the question some thought. "Like who?"

"The only person that could get her into our house without Scarlet having to create a fracture in the protection spell." He turned on the siren and strobe lights and pushed his foot to the floor.

Screeching to a stop on the road outside their home, Eli threw open the door of the Jeep, leaped from the vehicle and raced up the path to the porch. He fumbled with his keys, pushed the one for the front door into the lock and shoved it back, rushing into the kitchen. No one.

"Paige?" he called, his breathy voice frantic. He took the stairs two at a time, hurried along the hallway to the nursery. No one there either. He checked their bedroom, then the other couple rooms, and headed back down the staircase.

Eldridge stepped across the threshold and stopped, his eyes roaming the living room.

"They're not here," Eli told him.

"Let's check Clary's. You could be wrong about this, you know."

Eli strode down the path to the sidewalk and crossed the street, Eldridge doing his best to keep up. "I don't think I am."

"But how would she attach herself to Clary?"

"I'm not sure, but maybe my grandmother went outside at some point last night or early this morning and that's when it happened."

"When I spoke to Clary this morning I didn't notice anything different about her." Eldridge allowed the morning's conversation to return to his mind.

"Then it happened sometime between then and now. Scarlet has Paige and Tristan, Eldridge. We have to find them."

He burst into his grandmother's house, searching the living room and kitchen. Not here either. He climbed the stairs, checked each upstair room. No one. Eli's heart thumped against his ribcage. What would Scarlet do to them? He couldn't wait around to find out. He scrambled down the staircase and out the front door. "We have to find them."

Eldridge followed him back across the road to the Jeep. "You need to calm down, Eli."

Eli swung around, fury on his face. "How can I calm down? She's going to kill them. Finish what Stephanie came here to do."

Eldridge gripped Eli by both arms. "Listen to me. You need to keep a cool head. If you don't..."

Eli jerked out of the warlock's grasp. "All right. I know." He attempted to slow his ragged breathing and heart rate.

"Let's go inside. Give me something of Paige's and I'll do a location spell."

"Scarlet would've cloaked them. You'll never find them that way."

"Anything is worth a try." He motioned to the front door. "Shall we?"

Eli's mind was working overtime. Nothing would adhere. The warlock was right, he had to slow down.

The pair walked into the living room, Eldridge sitting in the center of the sofa while Eli raced upstairs to get something belonging to his wife.

Rushing back into the room, he handed the warlock a bracelet. "Will this do?"

"It should, yes. Now sit." Eldridge had already found a map of Moon Grove and the surrounding countryside and spread it out on the coffee table. He sat Paige's bracelet in the center and chanted the incantation.

FIFTY FIVE

As Eli swung the Jeep around the corner and took the sharp incline too quickly, the patrol lurched to the side and almost left the road. Eldridge used magic to steady the vehicle and Eli thrust it over the rise into the car park of the church, screeching to a halt at the open double wood doors. Throwing the Jeep's door open, he flew from the wagon, raced into the building and down the nave.

Clarissa was holding Paige in front of her, a jeweled dagger pressed against her throat, blood trickling from the wound inflicted.

Where was Tristan?

Paige's tear-filled eyes met his, her breath ragged, and she mouthed the word, *don't.*

Eli eased his tall frame down the nave until he reached the first row of pews. "Clary, what are you doing?" He knew it wasn't his grandmother, not completely. Scarlet had taken control of her body.

"Nothing, dear." She gave him a devious grin that distorted Clarissa's soft features.

"Where's Tristan?"

"He's safe. For the moment."

Eli allowed his Lycan hearing to take in the sounds around him. No crying, no additional heartbeat. Their son wasn't here. "Clary, you don't want to hurt Paige, do you?" He took a step closer to the pair of women.

"I'm not going to hurt her, Eli. I'm going to kill her." She ran the blade across Paige's throat and flew up into the air. Paige slumped to the floor.

Eli rushed to his wife and turned her over, blood spilling everywhere and soaking into her light pink T-shirt. He ripped his button down shirt open, buttons spraying across the floor, tugged out of it and wrapped it around Paige's neck in an effort to staunch the blood flow. Jumping to his feet, he turned around and gazed up at the wooden rafters above him. Clarissa was hovering in mid-air, a demented laugh escaping her lips.

Eldridge came in through a side door where Scarlet couldn't see him and crept up as close as he could.

Eli spotted him but kept his gaze on his grandmother so Scarlet wouldn't know the warlock was there. "Scarlet, you need to let my grandmother go."

"Why would I do that when I have harnessed her power on top of my own?"

Eldridge sidled along the white wood walls getting closer. He raised his hands and shouted an incantation. Clarissa plummeted to the floor, her body splayed like a rag doll on the red carpet.

Eli raced across the platform to his grandmother and pressed a finger into her carotid artery. No pulse. He whipped his head up. "Eldridge!"

The warlock rushed up onto the platform and repeated an incantation over Clarissa's body. She still wasn't breathing.

"Eldridge, do something!"

"I am trying." He continued to chant.

Eli raced back to his wife. She was unconscious but still breathing. *Thank God.*

"Can you help Paige?"

Eldridge made his way across the floor, got down on his knees and removed the shirt from around Paige's throat. "Oh my." He pushed his hand against her neck and gave another incantation. Paige coughed and took in a deep breath but was still unconscious.

Eli crossed the hall to his grandmother. "She's gone, isn't she?"

"I'm afraid so. She was gone before she hit the floor."

Eli jumped to his feet. "Where is Scarlet?"

"I sent her back to the shadow realm. I will work on a spell to trap her there once we get your wife to a hospital."

"Where's our son?"

"Paige is the only one who can tell you that. We need to get her over to Bellehurst post haste. She's lost a lot of blood." Eldridge lifted her into his arms. "Let us go. Now."

Eli's gaze returned to his dead grandmother. He would lock the building and come back for her later. He hated leaving her here, but there was nothing more he could do for her. He had to save Paige.

Eli paced the waiting room of the Bellehurst hospital anxious for news about Paige. She was the only one who knew where their son was and until she came to, their baby boy was lying alone somewhere.

Eldridge came into the room with two Styrofoam cups of vending machine coffee and handed one to Eli. "Here, this might offer a small amount of fortitude."

"Thanks." Eli took a cautious sip of the steaming black brew, as did the warlock. They had been waiting for the last hour and a half for word of Paige and no one had come in to talk to them. "What could be taking so long?"

"You should know by now that the public hospital sector wheels grind slowly." Eldridge took a seat on one of the connecting chairs pressed against the wall.

Eli continued to pace.

Cooper, Rosemarie, Taylor, and Rick appeared in the entrance.

"What happened? Is Paige going to be ok?" Cooper asked.

"We haven't heard anything yet," Eli told him.

Cooper's gaze wandered the room. No baby. "Where's your son?"

"Only Paige knows the answer to that and until she wakes up he's out there… somewhere."

"Oh my God!" Taylor brought her hand up to her mouth. "He's so little."

"Can we do anything?" Rick asked, his face grim.

"Unless you know how to find my son then, no, not at the moment."

A doctor carrying a medical chart entered the room. "Sheriff Blackwood." She extended her hand. Eli shook it. "Your wife is doing well. We've had to give her blood and the wound on her neck has been sutured. I'd like to keep her in overnight just to make sure there are no complications or infection."

Eli nodded. "Ok. Can I see her? Is she awake?"

"She was awake for a short time but we've given her a sedative to help her be more comfortable. If you follow me I'll take you to her."

Eli's gaze roamed the worried faces around him.

"Go," Cooper said. "We'll be here when you get back."

Once Eli was out of the room, Cooper turned to the others. "We need to find Eli's son."

Eldridge stood up and crossed the waiting area. "And how do you propose to do that?"

"What about a location spell?" Rosemarie offered.

"We need something belonging to the baby," the warlock said.

"Ok, I'll go over to Eli's and pick up a toy or…" Rick told him.

"An item of clothing would be better."

"I'm coming with you," Taylor said.

The pair headed out the door while Rosemarie, Cooper, and Eldridge waited. It would soon be dark and the temperature would drop considerably.

When Rick and Taylor arrived at Eli and Paige's house, Rick pulled the lock picking set from his wallet and slid out two lock pickers. Slipping them into the lock, he jiggled the metal pickers around until he heard a click and pushed open the door. He turned to Taylor, a broad smile on his face. "See, told you I could do it."

Taylor folded her arms. "Ok, yeah, you did." She stepped into the entry hall. "Come on, we don't have time for this."

Rick gave a sigh and followed her in.

"The nursery's upstairs." Taylor climbed the staircase while Rick waited at the bottom.

"Hurry up, will ya. We need to get back to the hospital ASAP."

"Ok, ok, give me a minute," Taylor called from above. She pushed open each door, not sure which one was the nursery. When she found it, she stepped into the room, looking for a laundry basket. Spotting a covered basket in the corner of the room, she walked over, opened it and tugged out a tiny white onesie. *This should do.* She folded it and pushed it into the pocket of her police issue jacket, then went back to the top of the stairs. "I've got something."

Rick glanced up at her. "Ok, let's go."

Taylor and Rick stepped out onto the front porch and Rick secured the door. As they were about to head back to the patrol, Taylor stopped. "Listen."

Rick frowned. "To what?"

"Shh. Just wait a minute." She raised her hand and cocked her head. "Don't you hear that?"

Rick strained his ears to listen. "Hear what?"

Taylor marched across the lawn, pushed open the side gate and proceeded around to the back of the house. "That."

"Now I hear it." Rick's gaze moved this way and that. "Where's it coming from?"

"I'm not sure." Taylor moved around the yard.

"If I was a werewolf I'd be able to pick up on that," Rick told her.

"Shh!"

Taylor walked across the back yard to a neighboring fence. "It's coming from over there." She pointed into the next-door neighbor's yard.

Rick hoisted himself up onto the wooden partition and dropped down on the other side. Taylor followed.

"There." She pointed to a garden shed.

The back porch light flashed on and an older woman wearing a blue robe opened the screen door. "What are you doing in my yard?"

Taylor walked across to her. "Police business, Ma'am. Please go back inside."

"Oh? What kind of...?" She stopped short when she heard a baby crying.

FIFTY SIX

Rick came into the waiting room all smiles and everyone there wondered what was going on. "Where's Eli?" he asked.

"Still with Paige," Rosemarie told him. "Why?"

"Has she woken up yet?"

"Not that we know of. What's going on?" Rosemarie frowned.

Taylor came into the room holding Tristan in her arms.

"Oh, my Lord! You found him." Tears welled in the receptionist's eyes.

Eldridge stood up. "Where was he?"

"In a neighbor's garden shed."

"Well that just makes me so mad," Rosemarie fumed, her cheeks flushing pink with anger.

Eli stepped into the waiting room, spotted Taylor holding his son, and rushed over to her, taking him from her arms. "How?"

"We went to your house to get something belonging to him for a location spell and I heard him crying," Taylor said.

"Thank you. Thank you so much." Eli cradled his tiny son close and kissed his forehead.

"How's Paige?" Rick asked.

"She's resting. She couldn't talk to me because of the wound and she didn't know where Scarlet had hidden Tristan."

"She'll be ok, though, right?"

"Yes, she's going to make a full recovery the doctor says." Eli kissed his son again. "I can't believe you found him." Tears stung the backs of his eyes and he blinked them away. "I'll take him in to Paige. She'll be so happy to see him."

Cooper crossed the waiting room and slapped Taylor on the back. "Good work."

Taylor gave him a surreptitious glance and her cheeks flushed. "Thanks, Coop. I appreciate it."

Rosemarie turned to Eldridge. "You're going to make sure Scarlet can't come back, aren't you?"

"Indeed I am. She will never do this to anyone again. Too many innocent lives have been lost. And some not so innocent, but they did not deserve to die."

Rosemarie nodded. "No, they didn't." She waited a moment, then said, "Thank you for coming to help us."

"You didn't need me. You are all quite capable of taking care of your town and yourselves."

"What will you do now?" the receptionist wanted to know.

"I may decide to stay in Moon Grove for a time. I don't have anywhere else to be right now."

Rosemarie smiled. "That would be good. Maybe we can have a chat about expanding my abilities some time?"

"If I do decide to stay, I would be most pleased to assist you." He gave her a warm smile.

"Thank you."

Eli came back into the waiting room alone. "Tristan is staying here with Paige overnight. Let's all head home and get some rest."

Everyone nodded and agreed, said their goodnights and left the hospital, all except Eldridge and Eli. They had a job to do.

Eli stopped the Jeep outside the double church doors, turned off the engine and sat for a moment. Eldridge eyed him sideways, knowing how he must be feeling. He'd lost his grandmother, and the town had lost a very powerful witch. The warlock rested a comforting hand on Eli's arm. "I am truly sorry for the loss of your grandmother. She was a fine human being and a superb witch."

"Yes, she was." It felt odd talking about her in past tense. Eli climbed out of the patrol, Eldridge doing the same, and they walked over to the locked doors.

"Would you rather I take care of this for you?" the warlock offered.

Eli shook his head. "She is... was my grandmother. I need to do this."

Eldridge nodded. "Very well. Let's go inside."

Eli unlocked the doors, pushed one back and the pair stepped into the dark church hall. Flicking on the lights,

Eli's gaze moved to the platform where his grandmother had fallen. She wasn't there.

Rushing down the nave, Eli leaped onto the platform and searched the area around and behind it. He turned to Eldridge. "Where did she go?"

"I am uncertain." He stepped up onto the platform, his eyes roaming the church hall.

"Maybe she wasn't…"

"You know that is not true. She was dead."

"Then where is she?"

A squirming sensation crawled through the warlock's gut. This was not good. Not good at all.

"You don't think Scarlet has reclaimed her body, do you?"

"I would hope not. But anything is possible. I haven't had time to work on the spell to bind her to the shadow realm."

"We need to get back to the hospital."

The pair raced up the nave out to the parking lot, climbed into the Jeep and Eli spun the wheels as he sped away from the church.

On the way back to the hospital, Eli had radioed Cooper asking him to meet them there. When he screeched the Jeep to a stop in the police parking bay in the car park, Cooper was waiting for him at the entrance to reception. "What's happened, boss?" he asked.

"Scarlet's on the loose. We need to make sure she doesn't get to Paige and Tristan." Eli strode into the foyer and along the corridor to Paige's room, Cooper and

Eldridge behind him. He pushed open the door. Paige was asleep, Tristan in a cot by the bed. He stepped out and let the door close. "Coop, I want you to guard the door. Check everyone before they go in. No exceptions. Understood?"

"You bet. No one will get past me that doesn't need to be here."

Eli gripped his deputy's arm. "Thanks, Coop." He turned to Eldridge. "Where do you think she might be?"

"We could try Clary's."

Eli nodded and marched back along the corridor. The warlock followed.

When they reached the street, Eli parked the Jeep a couple houses away, climbed out and came around the wagon to Eldridge. "Do you think she's inside?"

"It's possible. She might be looking for Clary's grimoire."

"That would make sense. She wants to be as powerful as Clary was and the only way to do that would be to have her book of spells."

"I believe she'll be looking for an incantation to restore herself to the human world." Eldridge followed Eli up the steps onto the porch.

"Then we need to find her and trap her in the shadow realm before she can." Eli unlocked the front door as quietly as he could and eased it back. Turning to the warlock he whispered, "My grandmother kept all of her witch stuff in the basement."

"Yes, I am aware."

"When we get down there you need to contain her."

"I am still somewhat bamboozled by the fact that she has used Clary for her host when clearly she was gone."

"It looks like the theory of her attaching to a live host isn't correct."

"Mm, it would appear so. And it is something that has not been accomplished before by a witch with any level of magic." Scarlet was more powerful than he had anticipated.

"Let's go." Eli crossed the entry hall to the door underneath the stairs and eased it back. The basement was in darkness. He turned to Eldridge. "Maybe she's not here."

"Only one way to find out." The warlock pushed past Eli and took to the stairs.

Eli pulled his gun and followed him down.

"She is not here." Eldridge turned to look at him.

He gave a heavy sigh. "Then where?"

"Is that cabin the coven stayed in still out there in the woods?"

"Yes. You think she might be there?" Eli opened the secret compartment in the wall, a panic room of sorts, but a safe place to hide her spells, and checked to make sure nothing was missing. His eyes searched the rows of books on the shelf until he came to a gap between them. "One is gone."

Eldridge stepped into the confined space. "Do you have any idea which one?"

Eli shook his head.

"Then we must hurry."

The pair flew up the stairs and out of the house.

FIFTY SEVEN

Eli stopped the Jeep about half a mile up the road. They would make their way to the luxury cabin on foot to avoid alerting Scarlet to their presence. As the pair got closer, Eli spotted his grandmother's 1956 blue and white Chevrolet parked near the front steps. "She's here."

Eldridge came up alongside him. "Yes. My assumption was correct."

"What now?"

"She has one of your grandmother's grimoires and we don't know what it contains. I'm sure she has placed a protection spell on the property, which means neither of us can go in."

Eli's gaze moved to the cabin then back to the warlock. "Ok, then what do we do to capture her... or banish her to the shadow realm?"

"We need to lure her out of the house."

"And how are we supposed to do that?"

"I'll offer her an alliance. She'll come out onto the porch to talk to me, knowing I cannot go in. Once she is beyond the boundary of the spell, which is the walls of the cabin, I will bind her and send her back."

"Will Clary's body remain here if you do?"

Eldridge gave him a pained look. "No, it will not."

Tears stung the backs of Eli's eyes and he blinked them away.

"I am sorry, Eli, but it is the only way to be rid of Scarlet Balfour."

Eli gave a heavy sigh and nodded. "Ok. If that's what has to be done, so be it." He hated the thought of never seeing his grandmother again. Scarlet would pay for what she had done.

Eldridge tugged a wax figure from the pocket of his black overcoat. "I have fashioned an effigy of Scarlet so the binding spell will adhere."

Eli's eyes widened. It resembled his grandmother. "Why does it look like Clary?"

"Because she is in the guise of Clary and it has to look like the form she has taken."

Eli nodded. "Ok. When do you want to go in?"

"No time like the present." Eldridge gripped Eli's arm, gave him a thin smile, then headed down the gravel drive to the front of the cabin and stopped at the bottom of the wooden stairs. "Scarlet Balfour."

No movement.

"Scarlet, I want to offer you my alliance. Let us talk peacefully together."

The door opened and the witch in Clary's body stepped onto the porch. "Why would you want to help me?"

"You vanquished one of the most powerful witches in the country. Clary Baker. Why would I *not* want to align with you?"

"I will consider it at another time." She turned to walk back into the house.

"Wait. I am in need of your assistance."

Scarlet's left eyebrow arched. "Oh, how so?"

"I am considering residing in Moon Grove. I want to be rid of Eli Blackwood and his pack. You can help me with that purpose."

A smug smile spread across the witch's face and she laughed. "Yes, I can." Scarlet thought it ironic that her host was Eli's grandmother and that she would eliminate him in her form.

"Will you come out and speak with me further?"

"You may come up." She motioned for Eldridge to climb the stairs.

As long as they were outside the perimeter of the cabin itself he could still perform the binding spell.

"Very well."

Eli watched as Eldridge ascended the wooden treads, wondering if the warlock's plan would work, and what he would do if it didn't.

When the warlock reached the top of the stairs, he raised the wax figure in his hand and called out, "With this figure I forever bind your powers till the end of time. To the shadow realm you will depart and remain there alone in the dark."

A magical rope entwined itself around the witch and bound her in place.

Eldridge opened a portal, its electrical yellow current swirling in a large circle, and shoved Scarlet into it, closing it again immediately. He turned toward the legion of tall pines. "It is done."

Eli emerged from the trees. "Are you sure she can't get back?"

"She is bound to the shadow realm. She cannot escape."

"Thank you, Eldridge. I heard what you told her."

The warlock waved the comment away. "I had to play up to her over-inflated ego. I have no penchant to cause anyone any harm."

"But you want to stay here?"

Eldridge nodded. "For a time, yes."

"Let's get back to the hospital. It'll be daylight soon." Eli trudged along the gravel drive, heading to the Jeep.

"Eli?"

The sheriff swung around.

"Can I stay here at the cabin?"

"I'll have to check with Alistair, but I don't see why not."

Eldridge caught up to him and they walked back to the patrol.

Eli dropped Eldridge Crane off outside his grandmother's house then headed to the hospital to pick up his wife and son. It had been an intense few days with Stephanie and Scarlet doing all they could to destroy the life he had built for himself and his family.

The world was a place of danger, no matter where you lived, and he wanted to continue to do all he could to protect his town and his family. He would no longer play by the rules when it came to their safety. It was time to make a radical change.

Now that Scarlet had been banished to the shadow realm, a major supernatural attack had been averted, for now at least, the moonstone ring was back on his finger and would stay there until his time as Alpha was done, when it would be handed on to his son, Tristan, he hoped that, for a little while, life would settle down in Moon Grove and that he and Paige could enjoy watching their son grow up.

He pulled into the hospital's police parking bay, turned off the engine, and sat for a moment. Today was a new start with no supernatural threats on their town, and he planned to make the most of it with his wife and baby son.

As he stepped out of the patrol, Max came out of the hospital's sliding glass doors. Eli crossed the parking lot to him. "Hey, Max."

"Hi. I came to see Paige and your baby son, I hope that's ok."

"Of course it is." Eli ran is gaze over Max's pale vampire face. Even though he and Archer had been brothers, literally, they were very different in appearance. "How are you doing?"

"As well as can be expected. I miss him."

Eli nodded. "Yes, me too. So what are you going to do now? Head back home?"

"Yeah, I'm leaving tonight."

"I hope you'll keep in touch."

Max gave him a thin smile. "Will do my best but you know how it is."

"Yes. Life has a way of keeping us busy... and sometimes not for the better. Take care of yourself, Max."

"I will. You too." Max walked across the parking lot to his brother's obsidian Mercedes convertible, climbed into it, and drove out of the car park.

Eli gave a heavy sigh, turned and headed for Paige's room. He would collect his wife and baby son, go home and spend some quality time with them. He would miss his grandmother so very much. She had played a huge part in who he had become and he would always be grateful.

As the door whooshed open and Eli stepped into the hospital foyer he heard someone call his name. Turning around, he saw his grandmother standing in the center of the parking lot smiling at him. Eli strode over to where she stood. "How is this possible?"

"I want you to know you made the right decision, dear. Scarlet Balfour needed to be banished from this realm for good, and me being sent into the shadow realm with her was the only way. I am moving on, now that she is trapped there." She glanced upward and smiled. "Never doubt yourself, Eli. You are a true Alpha. I will always love you, my boy. Take care of your beautiful wife and baby son and live a full life. Don't allow the moments of conflict to tarnish your joy. Do it for me."

"I love you, Gran." A tear slid down his left cheek and he swiped it away as his grandmother disappeared before his eyes.

Heading into the hospital foyer, he hurried along the corridor to his wife's room and opened the door. She was dressed and ready to go home. Tristan lay sleeping in the cot next to her. Although she couldn't talk for the moment, the look on her face told him everything he needed to know. He was loved and loved her in return. Today was a fresh start. Today marked the new Alpha he would become. No more playing by rules that put lives in danger. From now on, he would do whatever it took to keep Moon Grove safe... to make it a Wolf Haven... and a place where all supernaturals could feel sheltered from the evils that lurked outside their town.

THE FINAL BOOK IN THE MOON GROVE SERIES

WOLF HAVEN

COMING IN 2022

IF YOU ENJOYED THIS BOOK
Leave a review
https://amzn.to/30GMMfa